In My
MOTHER'S
HOUSE

ALSO BY MARGARET McMULLAN

When Warhol Was Still Alive

In My MOTHER'S HOUSE

Margaret McMullan

THOMAS DUNNE BOOKS
ST. MARTIN'S PRESS ❦ NEW YORK

THOMAS DUNNE BOOKS.

An imprint of St. Martin's Press.

www.stmartins.com

Design by Nick Wunder

A version of "Duet" originally appeared in *New England Living.*

Library of Congress Cataloging-in-Publication Data

McMullan, Margaret.
    In my mother's house / by Margaret McMullan.— 1st ed.
    p. cm.
    ISBN 0-312-31824-3
    1. World War, 1939–1945—Fiction. 2. Mothers and daughters—Fiction. 3. Austrian Americans—Fiction. 4. Vienna (Austria)—Fiction. 5. Women immigrants—Fiction. I. Title.
    PS3563.C3873I6 2003
    813'.54—dc21

2003009122

First Edition: November 2003

10 9 8 7 6 5 4 3 2 1

For my husband

In My
MOTHER'S
HOUSE

PROLOGUE

HAVE YOU EVER HEARD ANYONE PLAY A VIOLA D'AMORE? If you play it right—if you can play it the way Uncle Rudi sometimes could—you can feel the sounds echo in the back of your throat. I don't think I ever really told you about my uncle Rudi. He could make extraordinary music. You play the row of strings on top just as you would a violin, but the second row of strings underneath catches and resonates the sounds. The strings underneath are called sympathetic strings and they are tuned in unison with the playing strings. The viola d'amore used to be in great demand in the seventeenth and eighteenth centuries, but now hardly anybody has ever heard of it. It makes a sweet, tender sound, and at night, that sound feels as old as loss. I have heard this little wooden thing fill up a whole hall. It is a beautiful instrument, even in disrepair, and I am glad you have given it to me while I can still see.

Before you, before your father, I had another life. Sometimes I feel as though I were another person altogether. You are right. You have a right to know about the viola d'amore, about my other world, because now I know that what had to do with me *does* have something to do with you.

In his *Spiritual Exercises*, St. Ignatius wants you to go through all

the memories that helped shape you. His questions are a lot like yours—
he pesters you about your past. I have told you there wasn't much to the
life I left behind in Vienna. Still, you pressed me. You wanted the stories.
You wanted my memories. I often thought that if I told you everything,
I would somehow lose it all over again, and these scraps of memories are
really all I have left of a place that is now gone. They are my inheritance
and they are my own.

You know by now that I am going blind, and as my eyesight dimin-
ishes, I find my memory disappearing as well. I have heard it said that
you need only close your eyes in order to remember, but I have always
found it far more helpful to see. When I look at you, I can recall the yellow house where we once lived much more readily than if I shut my eyes
and tried. That yellow house is a vision and a memory I do not look forward to losing.

My story of loss may be no good to hear about. I know a woman
with a better story than mine. She stayed and hid people from the Nazis
in her apartment. She saved lives. You would probably prefer her as a
mother. Me? What have I ever accomplished? I can't say that I witnessed
anything important, and I can't say that I forgive. You don't start by
finding God in the ugly unless you're Anne Frank. I did not lose everything and everybody all at once, but bit by bit and one by one, as though
I were being conditioned to live alone.

I am the only one left. It is freeing in a way. And if someone ever
asks you what your mother's maiden name is, leave out the Engel. They
all say the same thing anyway: "Engel. Isn't that Jewish?"

I want to be careful here. You are not Jewish. I am not Jewish, and,
in his heart, your grandfather was not Jewish. To me, this is not denial.
This is fact. You will see. You be the judge.

Your great-great-grandfather Joseph wrote his memoirs. I know
because I saw them once on my father's desk in Vienna, and periodically,
my father would tell me what was in them—how Joseph had gotten

wealthy in less than forty years; taken his gardener from Pécs, Hungary, to Vienna, Austria; and camped out in the empty shell of the Hofzeile, claiming it for his own, which was at the time the Hungarian way of obtaining property. Joseph wrote it all down in Hungarian, beginning with his birth. He ended his story with the granting of our family's nobility in 1886, followed by the words: "I love life, don't fear death."

My father wrote the story of his life in German. But it wasn't really his life in that book. He told little about who he was or who we were. He wrote lists—how often he spoke with Sigmund Freud, how many times he met with Ezra Pound. I write my memories in English. We each claim a different language.

In Vienna, they called me Genevieve. You should hear the way they say it there—as though my name were a song. Here, in the United States, I am Jenny. This is not the story of my life. This is the story of my soul. This is who I came to be—your mother—the last of the Engel de Bazsis.

PART I
Duet

GENEVIEVE

THERE WAS A TIME WHEN WE LIVED TOGETHER ALL
under one roof. That was when we lived in Döbling, Vienna, at
Hofzeile 12. The *Hofzeile* was a little palace.

You asked me once how big was it really. Well, fifty people could
waltz in one room—that's how big. We had lots of chamber music concerts in the Great Hall. When Uncle Rudi visited, he gave recitals. He
could whistle through his teeth. This showed he was musical, he told
me. He promised that when I grew older and played the piano well
enough, I could accompany him.

I had a brown baby grand in my sitting room, and the walls of my
rooms were covered with blue birds which my mother had hand-painted
herself. Each bird had a sprig of something that looked like parsley in
its beak—I think my mother had an olive branch in mind. The birds had
been green but someone at a dinner party told my mother that to sleep
in a green room was bad for a child's health.

It took her weeks to paint the green birds blue. She used several
small brushes because she said she wanted to make sure the feathers
came out right. She wanted to make sure it looked like they could fly.

I stayed in Grossmama's rooms while they dried.

My parents gave wonderful parties with people who never seemed to have enough time to say all that they wanted to say. Sometimes Uncle Rudi would be there and I would sit at the top of the staircase after they had dinner and listen to him play for the guests down below. He never played anything too sentimental. He kept it upbeat, but thoughtful.

It was at one of these parties that my mother met a gentleman, and the following term, she put me into his school—the Neuland School. A progressive school. At the Neuland School we called our teachers by their first names, which I found very upsetting.

The home economics class cooked for the school and at eleven o'clock every day you could smell them burning lunch. It was always noodles with poppy seeds.

Once, at the end of the day, I ran back to school to pick up a book I had forgotten, and I saw my teacher on her hands and knees scrubbing the floor. Her name was Catherine and a bit of her hair had fallen down over her forehead at that particular moment, and when she moved it with her wrist, she straightened up her back, and still on her knees, she saw me and smiled. This was the woman who just that afternoon told us about yeast and barley. She taught us which ocean lay between us and the United States. She was trying to act as though she didn't mind scrubbing the floors but I was convinced that she was miserable. I thought this sort of work beneath her. After all, my father was a history professor. Certainly he would find scrubbing your own classroom floor demeaning.

When I got home that afternoon, I found my father seated at his desk with a slice of cake and a cup of coffee. I knocked lightly on the door of his offices and he took off his glasses and stared at me glassy-eyed. I do not know what he was working on. Some monograph on somebody not so well known. I was like how you are with your father— I never concerned myself with his work because it had nothing to do with me. Years and years later I discovered what a marvelous historian he was. He did best when he wrote and talked about other people's lives and theories. Historical moments to him were those in which it was possible to discuss not only the past but also germs of the future. His colleague, Sigmund Freud, had asked him to collaborate on a book of jokes organized by country, but my father declined. Freud was a Jewish bourgeois out of favor at the University of Vienna, and my father, like Freud, wanted to become a full professor.

After a minute or two, my father seemed to recognize me standing in the doorway. I remember he spoke to me in French, so he must have been working on his monograph on Chateaubriand. My mother was from Lyons, France, and often spoke of the town where the poet and statesman was born. Even though my father was a historian, he wrote a great deal about French writers—Romantic writers like Chateaubriand. And he dedicated each of these monographs to my mother. Your grand-mother.

Stacks of books and sheets of paper were scattered on the floor around his desk that day. There were more pieces of paper he had stuck together with pins and tacked up on the wall. There were dates and paragraphs scribbled next to a line that ran the length of the paper. He claimed that when he set out to work, he wanted to be in whatever century he was writing about, so he surrounded himself with a time line of dates, events, and names of those who lived during that period.

Once, a long time ago, when I asked my father to explain exactly what he did, he said it was his task to tell how it really happened. He used Ranke's wording: "*wie es eigentlich gewesen ist*—as they actually were."

I don't want to quote other people here. I don't want to sound like my father. I want to tell you my story, but I am my father's child, and sometimes we must take from the past what we can. In a monograph on Wilhelm von Humboldt, my father described the historian's task:

"There is all the more reason for the historian to concentrate so intensively upon his object that his own feelings and pretensions are dissolved. In a somewhat similar vein, Ranke once expressed his longing to extinguish his self in order better to penetrate his object."

Who knows why or when my father stopped writing history and took up his own story. Perhaps because his grandfather Joseph had. Or perhaps he really did feel guilty in the end and he wanted to rewrite his own history.

I went over to him that day as he sat surrounded by books and papers about other people. He was still humble then—still impressed with other people, not himself. I touched the edge of his cake and climbed onto his lap. He had a good lap because he had a soft paunch which provided me with something to lean into.

"Do you have to scrub the floors of your classrooms?" I asked. He laughed and shook his knees and he poked my stomach until I laughed too. He shook his knees a few more times, then he made me go away because he had one last page to finish before dinner.

I know it was spring because every spring my father's ulcers bothered him. Every year like clockwork. He said it was because he had eaten horsemeat in the trenches in Italy during the war. But he also said every individual has a weakness—his was the stomach. And, he added, every family has its weakness—ours was sight. Everyone in our family wore glasses, and later the eye troubles began. Unknowingly, my father did pass on his stomach problems, not to me but to you. So, he did leave you an inheritance, after all.

He had another ulcer attack, which I was glad of because when my father's ulcers kicked up he would read to me from the blue-covered Bible. It didn't seem like reading and the stories were as good as the Tiger Theater he did with his toes.

My father preferred the Old Testament to the New because, he claimed, the men had a better time, and he liked the idea of Noah and

Isaiah and all the rest of them actually taking walks with God. My father liked to take walks, but he usually went with Grossmama.

That night, the spring of his fourth ulcer attack, my father read me the story about Noah and his ark. I paid close attention to how God wanted the ark built. He gives the dimensions and even tells Noah what kind of wood is best for arks, cypress.

My father especially liked the part when Noah opens the window of his ark and sends the dove out, and the dove, having no dry land on which to set its feet, comes back to Noah, who simply extends his hand and brings the bird back into the ark. My father read that part twice.

Who would have known that within three years we too would be sailing away on our own ark?

"Noah could fit all those animals in his boat?" I asked my father when he had finished reading.

"It was crowded. But not for long."

"I imagine they gave nice parties," I said.

"And fine concerts," my father added. "The pigs and wolves harmonizing with the doves and the sea lions."

"Do you think they were scared?" I imagined Noah and the animals surrounded by all that water, not knowing when the rains would end.

"God was looking after them," my father said. "Remember, He made a deal with Noah. That is what 'covenant' means."

I thought about this for a moment.

"Does God still make deals?"

"Every single night of the week," my father said. "To all good girls who go to sleep on time. So." He always said "So" when there was nothing else to say.

"Are you ever afraid?" I asked him.

"Of the dark? No. Of the roof falling down? Yes."

"The roof?" I laughed. It was a funny thing to say. There we were in Hofzeile 12—a house originally built for Crown Prince Rudolf with stables that dated back to the Roman conquest. It was all so permanent. Remember, our monarchy, almost a thousand years old, was the oldest in the world.

"Sometimes I worry about those old beams," he said.

Together, my father and I looked up at the ceiling of my room. There were no cracks, no sagging. I imagined that behind the smooth surface of the ceiling, the thick, sturdy beams didn't even strain at the weight of our roof.

"Goodnight, Kara," he said and kissed the space on the pillow to the left of my head. Then he kissed the space on the pillow to the right of my head. "Goodnight, Heinzi of Gumpoldskirchen." These were the playmates my father had made up for me. Kara was my older sister, named after an aunt who had died during the 1919 flu epidemic. Heinzi I think was named after a student my father had liked. I was an only child, you see, and I had no playmates. "And goodnight to you, Pintschi-Pantsch," he said finally getting to my forehead. His nickname for me didn't mean anything. He just liked the sound of it.

In his memoirs, he wrote that I probably didn't remember Kara or Heinzi. He said that but he was wrong. I blame Isabella for that. I don't know when—before or after their visit—but Isabella convinced him that I did not remember anything about my life before we left, that I had been too young, and too spoiled.

But it was he who did not remember everything because there were more than two playmates. There were ten. He said that I would certainly grow bored of Kara and Heinzi one day, so he had invented others.

Martin Luther says your first image of God is essentially formed by your father—the idea of your father. And if you dread your father, if you fear your father, if you hate your father, that's going to influence your idea of God.

I reached up to touch my father's eyebrows. They felt like the old paintbrushes my mother had discarded after painting the birds in my room. They were not gray yet and the hairs were just beginning to grow their own way.

"Pantsch," I said.

"*Gute Nacht, mein Pintschi-Pantsch*," he said.

He was Pantsch. I was Pintschi-Pantsch.

My first memory? You asked me that once. I am lying down, covered with jackets and blankets in early spring sunlight in the upper garden by an old white wooden bench. I can see the paint peeling off the legs of the bench. I am taken indoors for fear of catching cold and I am looking up at my parents and thinking what tall people they are.

The last time I saw my father was the first time you met him. He was stooped over and his hair was thinning. He complained about the new Austria. He complained about his pension. And he complained about her—about Isabella. He had become a different man.

Just because I disliked my father in later life doesn't mean I didn't love him earlier. Even when he was no longer himself, I still called him Pantsch.

"*Gute Nacht, Pantsch*," I said.

That night I dreamed I had a guardian angel, and later, I thought I heard wings flapping. But I was very tired and I wanted to go to sleep, and the next morning I remembered that I had heard wings flapping and I had an image of layers and layers of feathers, so I looked under the bed and what do you think I saw? A white feather. One single, soft, white feather.

A spiritual adviser once asked me if I had ever had any visions. You remember? They always ask you that. Memories, visions, and "Do you see God as a man or a woman?" I imagine people say they have visions all the time. I said no, just to be on the safe side, and he just looked at me and said, "None? Are you sure?" He was terribly disappointed.

I realize now that the feather I saw under my bed had probably been from one of the down pillows, but that morning, still holding the feather, I looked out the window and saw the copper on the roof of the church down the street. It had rained during the night and the copper had that green patina in the morning sunlight. I looked from the feather to the copper roof and I decided right then and there that I had had a vision.

And very soon after breakfast and a nice chat with Cook that morning, it became my ambition to be a saint.

My father was a monarchist. He really hoped for the restoration of the monarchy in Austria. It's not a bad idea—an entity that stretched out over the Slavic nations was the greatness of the Austro-Hungarian Empire. And then there was the grand city where all the good merged: Vienna. Austria ruled over Hungary, Budapest, Czechoslovakia, Prague, what was once Yugoslavia, Bulgaria, and the German-speaking part of Poland. The Czechs had the industry; Hungary had the raw material. I don't know what the poor Bulgarians did. I guess they had their beet fields. They all supplied the capital, Vienna. They served the Austrians well, and there was a balance of power in central Europe. There was stability. I have often thought that if I'd had any sense, I should have fallen in love with a Bulgarian—they were the only ones who resisted the Germans to the end.

My father had inherited two parquet-floor factories from his father. One of the factories was in Vienna and the other was two hours away in Linz. He didn't want to have much to do with the family business. I sometimes think that my father joined the army in World War I just to get away from the factories. He got his Ph.D. while fighting the war in the trenches, and when he got back, he became a professor while he was running the factories.

Later, his mother, Grossmama, did most of the work and so did my mother. My father hated going down there—he was really only happiest reading at the university library or writing in his office. Mother kept the books for the factories. She sat at a desk off a big room filled with long wooden planks. I loved the smell of that wood. I can still smell it. And I can see her sitting there now, between two phones.

The factory in Vienna was only blocks away from where we lived at the Hofzeile. It was, in fact, right across the street from the Karl Marx Hof, where Inge lived.

One day my mother and father were walking home for lunch. It was July 25, 1934, and it was very hot, very sticky. My mother said she would never forget hearing someone's wireless from an open window. They were playing a song called "Song of Youth." It goes, "We, the young ones, stand prepared to march into grand new times." They were crossing the street and my mother was listening to this song when the Socialists started to shout, "There they are—the factory owners!" Then they started to shoot.

I know that some people never got beyond my mother's beauty. They believed, I am quite sure, that she was a silly, if not amusing woman. She always wore good hats and leather gloves. A delightful dinner companion.

Never let an American perfume touch your skin. This is what my mother told me, and this is what I tried to teach you. Use only good, French perfume no matter how poor you are. It is my understanding that a woman takes care of herself because she thinks her husband is worth keeping; still, this doesn't explain why my mother always looked so good.

When I think of her, I see a beauty—a real beauty—blond hair graying, pulled back. In my mind, she wears a hat with a net coming down over her eyes. She is distant and cool. That is the way I remember my mother.

I imagine that she wore such a hat that afternoon—the afternoon the Socialists shot at my parents. My father wanted to turn around and head back to the factory, but my mother stopped him. She said if we go back now we're going to be shot at just as much as if we go forward, so we might as well keep on going.

They held hands, ducked, and together they ran through the shotgun fire.

They did not get hit.

I'm sure they thought after that day their luck would never run out.

The following spring, we went to Rome for the term because my father was an exchange professor there. We lived in the Via Sardinia. No. 48. I went to a convent school and the teachers put me back a year because they thought my mother's Italian was so poor. Still, children catch on to languages and I slept through those classes. I remember I wrote an essay in Italian on the glory of Mussolini and the conquest of Ethiopia—a victory of civilization over barbarism. I got to read it out loud in class.

During the day my father taught at the University of Rome—he was leading a seminar on Franz Grillparzer, a nineteenth-century Viennese dramatist. Most evenings he and my mother made the rounds of diplomatic parties. They hired someone to walk me around and I played a game with myself to see how many famous people I could see.

I saw Benito Mussolini first. I was down in the street. He stood on a white balcony dressed all in black. The police pushed us into the circle below the balcony so that he would have a nice audience. When he gave his fascist salute, the crowd worked itself up into a fever. It was a beautiful scene. I practiced that night in front of the mirror, raising my arm.

I kept seeing Mussolini after that. Once, in the afternoon, I saw his silhouette. He was riding horseback near the catacombs. It was incredibly impressive.

I discovered Italian pastries—cream puffs with chocolate sauce on top, those were my favorite. Every day at three o'clock I would say,

"Mother, I'm terribly hungry." And she would say, "Are you hungry enough to eat bread?" and I would say yes, knowing darned well that the pastry shop was the only place she would think of.

We would go there for the pastry and I would time myself because, you see, every day Pope Pius XI walked in the Villa Borghese. He loved children, so you had a chance to get close. I would run down to the villa and slow down to a walk so that I could brush up against his white robes. He would always smile. Once, I gave him some forget-me-nots I had picked. He thanked me and put his hand on my head for the longest time.

I wanted very badly to imagine that at that moment in my young life the Pope was placing a halo over my head, igniting a more powerful holy spirit in me. But alas, I did not really feel more spiritual having brushed up against the Pope. All I felt was, here is Famous Person Number Two. That was what I truthfully felt.

Since then, I have come to believe that you will not find God where you expect to find Him. He might, for instance, just be the feather under your bed. In Rome I was supposed to be in pig's heaven, but I never felt as though it was such a spiritual place. On Easter Sunday at St. Peter's, I caught the flu, not the spirit of God.

But I do remember one lunch that I had with a monsignor at Vatican City. We climbed high, stone steps to get to his simple, book-filled rooms. He gave me some canceled Vatican stamps when I told him that my Grossmama collected stamps. "Here," he said. "Let her have the Vatican. She will be the only Austrian who can." Hitler and Mussolini had already met in Venice.

We ate the most wonderful risotto with lots of mushrooms. I can still see that food. Down below us the soldiers learned to goose-step. We could barely hold the food in our mouths, we laughed so hard watching their march—they all looked like the cat with boots in *Puss 'n Boots*. To the monsignor it was all a delightful Italian joke—the food, the soldiers, all that glitter of St. Peter's. In my mind, I remembered what I had heard my father tell his students: The world belongs to the few, not to the many, and least of all to all. I think he was quoting someone, but it made sense to me there on that roof with the monsignor and the rice. We were the few that day, high up on the rooftop of Vatican City.

Here, in this midwestern town where you, your father, and I now live, surrounded by all these flat, gray yards and Gothic right angles, there is no sense of humor about power. Having is as serious a notion to these young couples as the getting. Haven't you noticed? Look at the huge new homes going up in land that used to be open fields, and think of all that new, new stuff that is inside. It seems as though everything is made of cheap pine or new brick. Every now and then, I feel the need to rent a foreign movie just so I can look at old, old stone.

When we got back to Vienna, my mother took up basketball. It was 1930-something and she was in her healthy mind/healthy body phase. She organized a group of lady friends who did whatever she did. I would sit cross-legged on the floor of the gymnasium—we had a gymnasium—and watch these dignified women making fools of themselves. These were the same women who, after seeing Isadora Duncan perform one night the previous summer, had dressed up in chiffon scarves and danced around half naked out on the lawn.

My father had found out about my noodle lunches at the Neuland School and he hadn't been pleased about a schoolteacher seen scrubbing floors, so I happily attended the convent school down the street. That fall I had Sister Marie for third grade and for once I was like everybody else. That was my happiest year in school. I played piano the way you played guitar—every day, for as long as I was allowed. And then there was the day-to-day business of becoming a saint.

I thought a great deal about what it would be like on the other side. Would I see familiar faces in Heaven? Would we all eat wonderfully prepared food? Who cooked? Would everyone be leaping about in nightgowns? I imagined that saints had the prettiest nightgowns. At that time in my family's life, my mother, my father, and I each had our own agendas—just as the rest of the country had.

That year, I made my first confession with Gentz. Gentz was Father Hugo Gentz, but everyone in my family just called him Gentz. For weeks I was allowed to travel to Melk in preparation. Melk is a glorious Benedictine abbey outside Vienna. It was in the great medieval tradition and all the monks were revered scholars. The abbey had a wonderful white terrace that looked out over the Danube. Years and years later, I bought a bad picture of Melk at a house sale in Glencoe for three dollars. You've seen it. It's on the piano. Everyone thinks it's a coaster.

I remember the day I was to meet with Gentz and make my first confession. I waited for him outside and finally he came out in his long black robes and I watched as he moved across that white terrace with the blue Danube underneath.

Gentz was a big, distinguished-looking priest and a scholar and historian like my father, but Gentz stood out because of his height and build. He had a softer face than my father's—his eyes were even and he barely had any eyebrows. When I saw him walk across a room for the first time, I knew he would be important to me. This one's special, I said to myself. Besides, he looked terrific in black.

Gentz and I sat down together on a stone bench, the Danube at our feet. There were no doors or sliding screens between us and I never knelt. He asked me for my confession. He was a big, sturdy man— bigger even than my father. I ran through the Ten Commandments and he asked me what exactly I thought I was doing. I was so excited, I forgot the liturgy in Latin promising eternal life through Jesus Christ. That first time, I got things all wrong.

Gentz had such a good sense of what sin is. The important thing in your relationship to God is not necessarily your sins—for God's sake, how can you worry about keeping an accurate record? It's more important that you're moving toward God. It's your stance to God. You are, after all, reaching out to God. That's all that matters. That's all that's expected of us. And that is what Gentz communicated to me that day when I was nine years old.

I read once somewhere that the groundwork for your soul is laid by the time you are ten. If that is so, Gentz laid the first brick.

Sister Marie prepared me for my first communion. She belonged to the Poor Child of Jesus order and wore a white habit with a big, built-up thing on her head. She was very straightforward and clear, and after catechism class once I heard her tell my mother, "This one's really ripe." She knew I was more than ready.

For the picture I stood next to a girl named Inge because her braids were the same length as mine.

Inge. I don't have the picture from that day, but I do have one of Inge and me standing together outside a train station. We are both wearing our dark blue school uniforms and each of us has a big tulip stuck through the buttonhole of our white blouses. We are facing the camera, the sides of our heads touching as though we are Siamese twins connected by the brain. The sun is in our faces. Inge is smiling and I am not.

Inge lived in the Karl Marx Hof, a hideous apartment complex built for the workers. The iron gates were made to look like barbed wire, but they were painted a cheerful bright red to match the numbers outside each family's unit. My father's parquet-floor factory laid the floors with what is called "common parquet." Common parquet doesn't get the design or those extra bits of dark wood. Regardless, the Karl Marx Hof job was a very big order for my father's factory during a particularly slow time. My father often said that even though he did not agree with the politics of the Karl Marx Hof inhabitants, he was certainly glad they had come along. Inge came from a poor family. I know now that she stayed during the war and she must have suffered terribly.

Vienna was not just a city then. She was a certain taste of pine in cold, snowy air, chestnuts, and dark bittersweet chocolate.

I remember when the air changed.

After our first communion, my parents took Inge and me and Gentz to Demel's to celebrate. My mother was in her celebration-and-beauty-in-worship stage. In order to praise God, my mother found it necessary to please God, and that meant everything had to look, sound, feel, and taste beautiful. Good was never enough.

Inge and I ate *Sachertorte* and lemon ice that evening at Demel's and we laughed and made faces in the smokey mirrors. My father made us sit still and Gentz taught us the word for "divinity." When he said the words, *geistliches Leben*, which means "the spiritual life," the walls of Demel's moaned and the windows whistled. I knew it was the wind, but still, it was marvelous. Years later, when I learned English, I did not think that the word for *geistlich* was adequate. The word *geistlich* looks so much like "ghost."

I couldn't have known it then, but my confession and first communion meant a great deal to my parents. Gentz had converted my father to Catholicism. He had also married my mother and father the second time, in a Catholic ceremony. I didn't know any of that then, because my parents never told me. Like you, I had to figure it out on my own.

It had rained and the night was cool and crisp. We had the driver take us to Inge's, dropped her off, then, because it was pleasant out, we walked the rest of the way home. I remember I lagged behind my parents. I put my white veil back on my head and pretended that I was Sister Marie. I was young and good and saintly. I taught other little girls how to be the same. I was reciting the Ten Commandments when I saw a man standing in a doorway. On our street. Right at the Hofzeile.

"Look at me," the man said. His accent was guttural and distinctly German. "Look!" and then he opened his coat and he exposed himself to me.

Before I could look away, I caught sight of the glass in the doorway behind him. It was painted with a black swastika. It was the first time I had ever seen a swastika, and to me, it looked like a missing piece from a puzzle or a bad floor plan.

For a moment I couldn't breathe because I didn't want to. Right then the street—*my* street—and all of Vienna seemed to reek of rotting garbage and urine and I thought if I breathed I would taste it.

Even as I ran to catch up with my parents, I could see the long shadows of the man sprawled out on the wet street before me. In the distance, I could hear a hurdy-gurdy man grinding out some ditty.

I did not tell my mother or my father because I did not want to alarm them. Isn't it funny? I was nine years old and I was protecting their innocence.

I will always equate the German occupation with that man who exposed himself to me that night on the Hofzeile. Both were assaults. Both were obscenities.

Napoleon is supposed to have said that the day of his first communion was an important day, but not necessarily the happiest day of his life. I have that much in common with the Emperor.

That night, the night of my first communion, I dreamed that the government of Austria had crumbled and everything was in disarray and a new dictator was taking over—a foreign dictator. Everything we had was lost and my world was completely dead. And I remember I woke up and thought, this is really strange.

ELIZABETH

MY FATHER DIDN'T BOTHER TAKING OFF OUR MISSIS-
sippi license plates the summer we moved to Winnetka, Illinois, so for
months we drove around with *The Magnolia State* still stuck on the back
of our Chrysler. We had a lot on our minds. We had come north to a
better house. My father had a better job at a better firm and we were
working to make a better life for ourselves. I practiced guitar every night
so I could break into the advanced class. My mother spent weekends
buying furniture, and my father was trying hard to prepare our new
house for cold weather we didn't know too much about.

One Saturday afternoon, my father stood outside tapping against
the kitchen window. He pointed to the greenhouse. He wanted me to
come help him. I tapped back, using the tarnished silver fork my great-
grandmother had just sent from Washington, D.C. She had rolled it up
inside some yellowed, mildewy sheet music. I saw my fifteen-year-old
face, framed with short blond hair and bangs, reflected on the back of
the fork. My father smiled, pointed to the greenhouse meaning that that
was where he'd be, and I went back to reading the letter aloud to my
mother. "Dear Little Cat," my great-grandmother had written to me on

the back of a cheap paper place mat with a connect-the-dot-to-buried-treasures map on the other side.

> *Life in the Home goes quietly on. We are going to make some excursions by car and that will be a nice change. Old ladies are rather a bit dull. Now autumn has come and the roses fade but the colors of the leaves on the trees are fantastic! I hope we shall have a nice snowy winter. I thank you very much for your sweet letter. And then came your mother's. It was so kind of her to write me such a nice note, in spite her being kept so busy with settling in your new home. I'm sure you are a big help. It is good that a piano is there too. I found in my things some of your mother's sheet music. I think maybe she likes Haydn too much.*
>
> *Love,*
> *Grossmama*

I showed my mother the place mat. She said something about Great-Grandmother's strong, steady hand. The wind whistled through the front door and I said Hi to the ghost.

We had moved into a converted stable that was about ten times the size of our old home in Mississippi. My mother had fallen in love with the twelve-foot ceilings and French doors. She said the place was screaming for attention and parquet floors. The greenhouse sold my father. I was partial to the ghost.

Our ghost came only on the windy days. It was a haunted whistle through the front door. The more it blustered outside, the louder it sang, and through the long hallways and empty rooms of our new home, the songs were like exotic symphonies to me.

"You never told me you played the piano," I said.

She looked up from the fork. I had said something wrong but I wasn't sure what.

"I had a Peabody scholarship," she said, straightening.

"But you didn't go," I said.

"It was impractical," she said. "It was after the war. We hadn't been in the United States long and we needed money."

I nodded. The ghost stopped whistling and began to moan. It was hard to ignore. Only the night before, my father had spoken of the North Wind and heating bills and my mother tried gagging the ghost by pushing a rug up against the bottom of the door. But it still kept singing and my father told her to just leave it be. He'd get to it when he had the chance.

I worried for it.

I said something lame to my mother about our ghost's good sense of rhythm and I tried to sing along.

"Its C is too sharp," my mother said, giving me the silver fork in exchange for the music I was trying to read. I wondered if Haydn would translate to guitar. "Run, put this with the rest."

Like all the other pieces of silver my great-grandmother was sending every month from Washington, D.C., the fork had my mother's family crest engraved on the tip of the handle. It was a complicated seal. The lions had wild curlicue hair and the letters that spelled out *Engel* went from big to small to big.

"What's this used for?" I asked. "Pie?"

"Fish," she said, and she pointed to the tarnished fish swimming up and down the handle, to and from the seal.

We walked through our empty living room together. The piano was still the only piece of furniture in there and that wasn't even ours. The previous owner had left it behind because, he said, it wouldn't fit in his new Miami condo.

We had moved only with the basics: two beds, some bureaus my mother had pounded with a hammer and painted to make look old, and a sofa that still had my teethmarks from when I had been in need of something to gnaw on. What had filled up our cozy one-story home in Jackson, Mississippi, didn't even look right here. And we didn't have any end tables or rugs or fireplace equipment—none of that stuff Chicago people junk up their houses with to stay warm.

My mother put the sheet music inside the piano bench, glancing at the notes only for a moment before slamming the lid shut.

"Go on," she said. "There's a house sale at one o'clock and I don't want to miss it."

We never used my mother's silver. She stored it in a wooden box she got at Marshall Field's which she kept hidden underneath her bed. My great-grandmother started sending the pieces of silver when my grand-father got remarried and moved back to Vienna for good.

When the first fork came, my mother wouldn't touch it. It was black and bent, and when I asked how it got that way, she just said, "The war." When the silver kept coming, my mother began to examine it. Maybe she was checking to see if it still bore some of the marks that she remembered.

My mother never spoke of her past. She had been an only child, and, besides her father—my grandfather—she was the last of the Engel de Bazsis, the rest of whom had been killed in "the war."

I had to figure "the war" out on my own. What I read made no sense with the facts I had. My mother and her parents were Catholic but they had fled Vienna in a great hurry because Hitler had been after them. So, in elementary school, I raised my hand and corrected my teacher. "I'm sorry, Mrs. Abrams," I said. "But those death camps were for Catholics, not Jews." I often wondered, afterwards, why Mrs. Abrams never both-ered to correct me. Everything finally got straightened out when I saw *The Sound of Music* and figured that like the von Trapps, my mother and her family were noble sympathizers.

On the floor underneath my parents' bed, an arm's reach away, next to the silver box, was my grandfather's book, which lay facedown. It was my grandfather's autobiography in German, and when I asked my mother once if she would translate it, since I had never even been face to face with anybody on her side of the family, she said certainly not. She said he had only mentioned her once in the book, and since she obviously meant nothing to him, he would mean nothing to her. She wouldn't even allow space on her bookshelves for it. That part of her life was over, she said.

I didn't bother sliding the silver box out from under the bed. I reached out, flipped the lid, and put the fork inside as quickly as my mother had put away her music.

Weekdays, relatives from Mississippi would call my father to warn us about the harsh northern winters. They offered advice on weather stripping. My mother would practically hang up on them. She said all they talked about was the weather and plants. My father would try to ignore her. Then he'd turn around and say to me, "Can you believe her?," and I would follow him around the house, watching him run his hand along the floorboards and windowsills—trying to figure out where the cold might come in.

I reassured him. I told him our ghost didn't carry a draft in with it. But he always got annoyed when he couldn't pin down where the sounds came from.

When he wasn't busy making our new home fit to live in, my father was preoccupied with trying to put the greenhouse back together by sealing up the new panes of glass with putty. My mother said that wasn't her domain. She was in charge of furniture. But if we grew her some poppies and lavender, she would water them. I had tried sowing both, but all around the greenhouse were flats full of dried-up soil and the limp young seedlings that had tried but hadn't managed to make it. I told my mother that what she wanted was too complicated; we had to train ourselves on something simple and basic. Like geraniums.

"Camellias don't grow up here," I said one Saturday. My mother was somewhere across town, buying up antiques at a house sale, and my father and I were shuffling around tubs of young camellias he had ordered from some place in South Carolina.

"Now they do," he said, inspecting the dark leathery leaves.

It was an old, neglected greenhouse with a clock in the back that was stuck on four o'clock. We had already cleared away the faded carnations, the sweet peas that were the color of moth's wings, and everything else that was dead or dying.

My father handed me a package of lettuce seeds. "I read that these do well in greenhouses too," he said. "Sow them over there." He pointed to a bench he had already prepared. The mint he had uprooted from his mother's kitchen garden before we moved grew in the southwest corner, near a square of geranium cuttings I had already planted. I looked down at the package and then back up at him.

"I don't know how to do this," I said.

"I don't either," he said. "Wing it."

That afternoon, my mother came home followed by a truck full of furniture. My father was embarrassed. He said we could afford new things. But according to my mother, new things weren't the point.

We put a sofa in front of the fireplace and a set of Empire chairs between two windows. She handed me a coaster with a picture of a castle on it. The inscription read *Melk*.

"Milk?" I asked, holding up the coaster.

"Melk," she said, doing something with her tongue on the "l." She took the coaster from me and put it on the piano.

"What kind of stuff is this?"

"French mostly," my mother said.

"But you're from Vienna."

"My mother was French," she said, looking around the room. I didn't get it, but I told her how grand the place was beginning to look. She kept seeing things that were missing. My father said he liked everything, and before he went back out to the greenhouse, he asked my mother to make out a chart of what he could and could not sit on.

I had done a good job with the lettuce. My father said his hands were simply too big to handle such tiny seeds. I told him playing guitar kept mine in shape.

I was an intermediate on the verge of becoming advanced and every Monday night my mother drove me to the Grant School of Music. I would have her let me off at the corner, a block away, so I could walk. Holding my guitar like a briefcase, I felt I had a job. A purpose.

The four other intermediates in my class were the pretty, long-haired seventh and eighth graders whose mothers thought they might look even prettier holding an instrument. I hated them. I wasn't even in high school yet and already I was an exile at my new school. Nobody could understand anything I said. I still had a thick Mississippi accent even though every night I read my homework assignments out loud while I pinched my nose to practice a midwestern twang. During the day I didn't say much, but when I came home I played. I tried to convince myself that my problems didn't stem from the fact that I had short hair or couldn't talk in high-pitched giggles the way the long-haired girls did. Besides, they didn't even play well. They never practiced and how could I respect those who didn't take their work seriously? But I watched them carefully, thinking if I studied them well enough, I would learn something.

One night, one of the high school boys in the advanced class—the one with the red ski parka and dark black hair—said he had heard me and I was good.

"You should try to get into our class," he said. "We're doing ragtime."

"Ragtime?"

His collarbones were very well defined. They came forward and jutted out like wings and between them I could see the beginnings of black chest hair.

"Yeah. You'd like it. It's all fingerwork. I have a lousy voice, so it's more my style. Check it out." He gave me the sheet music and left.

Ragtime looked complicated. All ten fingers had to be doing something different at once. It looked as though it would take forever to learn.

My father was downstairs among the capos and strings talking to Carol, my guitar teacher, who wore a red wig that fell down below her waist. He was telling her to teach me the good stuff.

"You know," I heard him say. "Merle Haggard. Johnny Cash."

"Arlo Guthrie?" Carol said.

"Okay," he said. "I'll listen to some Arlo."

"What about ragtime?" I said.

The two of them looked at me standing in the doorway with my guitar. My father frowned.

"Ragtime?" he said. "You can't sing ragtime. Besides, that's for the piano."

Carol smiled and put her hand on my shoulder. Her hair fell down feathered over her eyes. "We'll see," she said. "Let's take it one step at a time."

I was glad my mother was outside waiting in the car. I told her about the ragtime boy in the ski parka. She said she wasn't raising me to run off with the first man I met in the advanced class. I told her he had given me sheet music—not a ring. She said she just didn't want me to end up like so many other girls whose sole purpose in life was to find a husband—and I thought of the girls in my guitar class. I assured her that that wasn't the case: my hair wasn't long enough. She laughed and turned around, and I was astonished at her strength as she showed me how to give an Indian burn were I ever to need a method of self-defense.

On the way home, my father had me play what I had just learned, right there in the backseat of the Chrysler. He did Peter while I sang Paul and Mary. We drove slowly, taking the long way along Lake Michigan.

He asked my mother why she never used an Indian burn on him. She thought about it for a moment.

"Give me a few years," she said, and as she turned to look at my father, I saw one half of her face smiling.

It started to snow and I didn't recognize anything even though I had been trying hard to memorize the roads going to and from our new home. Everything looked different in white.

I worried that the car would stall. Our Chrysler wasn't used to these kinds of conditions.

"Dad!" I said, scooting up between them. "Be careful. How can you see? How can you tell where the road stops and starts?" The snow was coming down thick and he had to use the wipers.

He told me he knew what he was doing and I tried to believe that he did.

"Isn't it wonderful?" my mother said, looking out at the snow. On the seat my mother's hand lay over my father's. "Our first winter together. Just the three of us."

I stared out at the leafless trees and thought about all the magnolias I had forgotten to climb in Jackson. My mother reached back over her head with her other hand and wiggled her index finger. I grabbed onto it and felt a little dopey hanging on.

Dear Little Cat,

I have still a few more bits of silver for you but they said just now that we are going to have tomorrow snow. Maybe you would like it, I have had enough of it in my lifetime. So I have to wait going to the post office which is quite far away.

Mummy must be very pleased that she has a greenhouse. Tell her she must fill it with the birds.

I am very glad to hear that guitar school pleases you. Pantsch, your grandfather, used to say when a pupil says she likes her teacher it is a sign she is good in classes. But I think it is not only the playing that you like but making contact with other nice girls. Maybe even helping some which are a little bit backward.

Love,
Grossmama

I was sick of putting away the silver. I considered those forks and knives and spoons our guests—new arrivals that I didn't want to shut up in a box cluttered with their own tarnished, neglected relatives.

"The tarnish is going to wear down that seal," I told my mother, who was preparing to go to yet another furniture sale.

"I can't do that right now," she said. "I don't have time."

"Fine," I said. "Who asked you?"

I opened up a jar of silver polish I had found under the sink and stuck in one of the spoons.

"That's not how you do it," my mother said. She took her coat off, took the spoon out, and got two sponges from a drawer.

The silver polish was the same gray as my mother's hair. But instead of turning white as her hair did year after year, the polish darkened as it soaked up tarnish. My mother always said I was lucky to have my father's hair. Hers had turned at twenty.

The spoon had polished so well that my mother wanted to do more. She worried aloud about whether by neglecting the silver for so long she had permanently damaged it. We brought out the box, carrying it between us through the living room.

The room had more furniture and that made it warmer. My mother had found a faded oriental at a house sale and two ancient-looking side tables with marble tops. I worried that the new old furniture came with other people's pasts and that their ghosts wouldn't get along with ours.

The silver was heavy and I complained to my mother that she wasn't holding up her end. We readjusted in the hall. I heard a faint whistle coming from the front door.

"It's here," I whispered.

The winds had been dying down and the sound didn't echo as well as it had because the rooms were now full.

"Ooo," my mother sang along.

"Oeee," I joined in, and for a moment, the three of us were in harmony.

"Come on," my mother said, pushing me and the box toward the kitchen. "My back can't take much more of this."

I had it in my head that while we polished, my mother would bare her soul to me—tell me, in sordid detail, about her war experiences, show me the scars that a piece of shrapnel had left behind, describe what Hitler had really looked like that time she had seen him in the dentist's office. I would know what to do if she told me those things. I would sympathize and console and maybe even feel a little exotic myself. There was so much I felt I needed to know. What they ate; what their holidays were like; how long my mother's hair had been; if she knew anybody in the mountains named Heidi or if she had ever really seen Edelweiss.

"How come Great-Grandmother wants us to fill the greenhouse up with birds?" I asked. "They'd only mess up the place."

"That's what she did with her greenhouse," she said.

"She had a greenhouse?"

"Off near one of the gardens," my mother said. "But it's funny." She put the spoon and the black-gray sponge down for a moment and stared out the kitchen window toward the greenhouse. "That's one of my last memories of Vienna. I wonder if she knows that."

"What is?" I asked. "What's your last memory?" The tarnish wasn't coming off my spoon. I rubbed harder, and my mother said, "Gently, gently."

"A month or so before we emigrated, Grandmother took me out to her greenhouse to hold a dove. She told me to think of her whenever I saw a bird. Pantsch, my father, took a picture. He was just back from Rome. I called him Pantsch, you know." My mother looked out toward the greenhouse once again, and it made me uncomfortable to see her nose turn red and her eyes get wet.

"Sometimes," she said. "Sometimes, I can still feel that bird's heart in the palm of my hand."

My mother turned on the faucet and rinsed off her spoon. The silver had polished into a mirror of designs and seals. It looked as though it came from another world. It was spectacular.

I spread all the spoons out and stared down at them as though they were pieces to a puzzle. They looked like little shovels.

"What are these for, anyway?" I asked. "Ice cream?"

"Ices," she said. "Italian ices. Lemon's the best. The more bitter the better."

I wanted to polish all the silver. I wanted to see my mother's family crest repeated over and over right there in front of me on our kitchen counter. We could have a party and use all of it. I imagined the ends of our silver disappearing into millions of mouths, though I hadn't a clue as to whom those mouths would belong. I wanted to show off all our silver. I wanted to take it to my guitar class and hand it to the long-haired girls. I would say, Look. See? This silver is priceless, and it has something to do with me.

I suggested to my mother that we display our silver—prop it up on little stands all around the house, tie up bundles of it with red and gold ribbon, scatter some on the marble-topped side tables that had once belonged to another family. She said no. That would be gauche.

"What's the first thing you remember?" I asked.

She looked at me. "Let's clean up." She washed her hands and sealed the jars and put everything back up.

When we went to put the silver box away again, my mother made me stop and put it down on top of the piano bench in the living room. She wanted me to study the legs of the Louis Quinze sofa she had bought last weekend.

"See the square nail heads?" she said. Our ghost bellowed deep and flat, then it adjusted itself and evened off into a low, muted moan. "This is no copy. Don't let anyone tell you otherwise."

"Why would anybody say it's a copy?"

"Sometimes people don't even know what they have. This owner didn't."

My mother forgot about the silver sitting there on the piano bench. Instead, she showed me the difference between a good crack and a bad one. She told me exactly where each piece of furniture came from and what it had been used for. Then she dated and priced them.

"When I die," she said, "you'll get all of this."

"Mom," I said. "We just moved."

She squinted and ran her hand along the silver box and then along the piano. She lifted the cover of the piano and pressed a key. She was worried, she said, that I would end up like her—with nothing more than a useless memory of a dove's heartbeat to remember her heritage by. I told her she needn't worry. I probably wouldn't even get the chance to touch a bird, let alone hold on to one.

For Christmas, my father set out to buy my mother a sorbet maker, but three hundred dollars seemed a bit much to spend on a machine that froze sugar water, so he bought an ice cream maker for twenty-five dollars instead.

I set the table with the little silver shovels anyway.

"What did you do for dessert in Vienna?" I asked at dessert. My mother was still a little mad because my father and I had spilt some of the salt water from the ice cream maker on the parquet floor samples she had laid out the day before.

"A gateau," she said. "Chocolate cake with lots and lots of thin layers of dark chocolate and jam." She stared down at her peach ice cream. "And we'd light the tree with candles."

"Real candles?"

"Let's do that next year," my father said.

My mother started to take a bit of ice cream, changed her mind, put her spoon back down, and poured herself another glass of wine. "It's too dangerous," she said.

"So then what did you do?" I asked.

"Everyone went off to his own room to read," she said.

"That sounds like a good idea," my father said, scooting back his chair.

"Dad," I said. "Not yet."

"I'd lie down flat under the tree—amid the presents and all that wrapping paper—and I'd look up at the branches." She laughed, she said, because now it sounded so silly, but I said no, that's what I would have done too. I thought about the treehouse my cousins and I had built in Jackson. If you laid down flat on one of the floorboards, you could spend a whole day looking up into the limbs of that oak.

"How about a concert?" my father said, getting up. I told him there was indeed a performance scheduled. A very special one. I ran to my room to get the gift I'd kept hidden underneath my bed. Carol had arranged some of my guitar music for the piano and I had rolled it up and tied it with a shiny red bow.

When my mother unrolled the sheet music in the living room, she looked at it and then at me and said, "Elizabeth Anne, what have you done?"

"Try it," my father said. He poked at the fire he had built that morning and then he settled back into the Louis Quinze. The sofa was feather-stuffed and he sank in—the cushions flipping up around his legs.

My mother sat down at the piano bench, her back rigid. She scooted the bench up, then back, then up again.

"Mom," I said. "It's just us."

She touched the pedals with her feet.

"My God," she said. "Do you know when I last played for more than one person? It was at the Hofzeile. Inge was there on the violin. Uncle Rudi was still alive and my mother served meringue."

She lifted the cover to the keys. Then she pressed down on them. A sound emerged not unlike the sounds from the music she liked listening to on Sunday afternoons when she cooked. She shifted and pressed the keys down again. One of the notes came out wrong. She tried it over, but again, the chord came out badly.

"I can't," she said, staring down at the keys. I wondered what she might be thinking of. That uncle? Her mother? Great-Grandmother? And who was Inge?

She looked up at my father and the looks they exchanged made me feel awkward.

"Mom," I said. "Just try."

"No," she said. She slid the cover back down over the keys.

"Mom. Try. Just one more time."

"Stop her, Michael," she said to my father.

"Elizabeth, leave your mother be."

"But you're not even trying," I said. I sat down next to her on the bench and lifted the cover back up. But she slipped away on the other side and ran back into the kitchen. My father followed her. I could hear them whispering. Then I heard my mother shouting.

"I don't need this," she said and I could tell she was crying. "I don't need any of you." She said she wished her mother were still alive. She said she wanted to see her father again. She missed Vienna. "I'm leaving you both," she said, and when my father asked where she would go, something ceramic broke.

When I got to the kitchen, an ice cream bowl lay broken on the floor. The brick wall was splattered with white. My mother had her back to my father. Her shoulders were shaking. Ice cream melted down her fingers and made puddles on the floor. My father's nose and cheeks were white with cream.

"Pookie," I heard him whisper.

"Don't," she said. "Just don't."

I hated my mother then. I hated her for making my father feel guilty. I hated her for not going beyond the first chord on the piano. I hated her for being hoity-toity about her gateau and her Christmas tree candles and her Viennese past. Staring down at the broken bits of china at my feet, I thought about what other households all around America were doing right then. The long-haired girls were sitting in front of their new Christmas mirrors brushing their long hair. My cousins were probably all playing Marco Polo in Grandaddy's pool—their arms reaching out to tag me, but I wasn't even there. Charlie Mae was probably in the kitchen, making fried apple pies in a skillet she never washed but wiped clean. I got a broom and swept the broken bowl into a dustpan and wondered how anything would ever fit back into place. I swore to myself that I would never ever ask another question about what was dead and gone because I was convinced my mother's past would ruin our little family.

My father laughed all at once and stuck his tongue out, trying to lick the ice cream off his nose. My mother, crying one minute and laughing the next, turned around and kissed up the mess she herself had made. I didn't know how I really felt when they went off to their room together, leaving me alone in a living room I barely recognized—straining to hear the faraway sounds of the country music my father began to play on his clock radio.

Frost covered the inside of the greenhouse and it was like an igloo when I went out there with my guitar. I crouched down beneath the benches where the heating pipes ran. I liked sitting down there amidst the dirt and the gravel, the ivy and the chickweed. In the middle of all this ice and snow and cold, I was warm again playing in Grandaddy's woods.

I was still on "The City of New Orleans" when my father came in. For a long time, neither one of us said anything. Then he grumbled over some mealybug he found on the back of his camellia leaves, and after he mixed up some insecticide in a spray tank, he moved up and down the aisles like a priest, dousing his beloveds with peppermint-scented poison.

We went for a drive to the cemetery—just the two of us—because that's what he always did with his father when either one of them wanted to get away from the house.

Real flowers marked the gravestones of the cemetery in Winnetka. No plastic ferns here. And the stones were left unpolished. The lake was only blocks away, so it was colder and we didn't get out of the car. We were the only ones there—nobody's children were playing tag around the gravestones. And there weren't any men my father's age standing in front of the markers, counting on their fingers the generations before them.

From where we were parked you could see the big stone markers of old Chicago families. A Swift. Some Armours. "Sure is a nice spot," I said, admiring the wrought-iron fence surrounding the place.

"Think so?" he said. His mind was somewhere else. "Where do you want to be buried?"

"I don't know," I said. "I hadn't really thought about it."

"Mississippi? Vienna? Take your pick."

I was a little disappointed he hadn't mentioned Illinois. I half-hoped that we would find a nice spot for three around here.

"Wherever you and Mom go, I guess."

"Well," he said, putting the Chrysler back in to drive, "I'm sure as hell not spending my eternal afterlife with a bunch of Yankee meat-packers."

On the way home, we took our time driving along Lake Shore Drive, leaning to look past the brick entranceways at the big houses beyond with grand lakefront views. We looked out at the other cars too, seeing if we could find another license plate from Mississippi. Finally, we spotted one from Missouri and called it a night.

> *Dear Little Cat,*
>
> *I did so like your paper on the planet Mars and feminism. Did you think of the topic yourself? Are you swimming in the big lake? Then you must be careful; a lake is lovely, but it can be treacherous. I had in this my experience.*
>
> *Love,*
>
> *Grossmama*

Over the next few months, Great-Grandmother's letters became briefer and more frequent. She started to repeat herself—telling the same stories over and over. She wrapped other things in the place mats besides the silver. A Teddy bear with no eyes, wearing a tattered bib that said MEIN PUZI. And a porcelain doll. Her hair was matted and she had no arms.

> *Dear Little Cat,*
>
> *The garden is white with snow. It is lovely. The birds are my friends. They know me, even take care of me. They sent me home before the thunderstorms started.*

Then one day we got the rest of the silver all at once, in a box addressed to the whole family. The letter was a mere note on the back of an envelope. "To all of you," it said in a light, shaky scrawl.

"My God," my mother said, staring down into that last box of tarnished silver. "She's dying."

Even though she said we needed some brass fireplace equipment, my mother skipped the furniture sales that Saturday. It seemed important somehow that the three of us spend that afternoon out in the greenhouse—my father watering, me taking geranium cuttings, and my mother pulling weeds.

"Mind the lettuce," I kept telling her and she said what kind of fool did I take her for, anyway? At the end of the day, she came crawling out from under a bench, covered with dirt and cobwebs that were the color of her hair.

That night, the phone rang so late, we knew something was wrong. My father answered it first. I heard him waking up my mother.

"Honey? Honey, wake up," he said. "It must be your father. I can't understand a word he's saying."

"*Allo? Allo? Ja?*" my mother screamed into the phone. "*Ja, Papa.* Speak English. What is it?"

Later, my mother explained it all to me: my grandfather in Vienna had gotten the call from a nurse at the Lisner Home in Washington, D.C., because he was the next of kin. The nurse told him that my great-grandmother had a cold that wouldn't go away. She was in bed, they thought, for the last time. My grandfather wanted my mother to go to her. He was in the middle of the second part of his autobiography, and then there were his classes.

"But surely you're going," my mother said, and then she listened, then, "*Ja, Papa*. We'll leave tomorrow." She said something else in German, then "*gute Nacht*," and she hung up.

"He's a child," I heard her say. "He's impossible. He can't look anything in the face—not even his dying mother. No. He's no child, he's just a coward."

She waited a moment and called information for United Airlines. When she asked for two round-trip tickets to Washington, I thought my father would be going with her, but, as my mother explained to me later, he had to work. "Life must go on," she said, tucking me back in to my bed. "Even in death."

When she left my room, I was terrified. What would I pack? Could I bring my guitar? I couldn't sleep. I looked to see if their light was still on.

My mother was in the kitchen making honey milk. She once said that after they had emigrated, her mother had made her warm honey milk whenever she was sleepless or sick. At the time she told me, she got all teary-eyed, and I thought it was stupid. But the smell of the steaming milk made me think how good and right it was that something was on the stove heating, with my mother there stirring in the honey.

She saw me standing in the kitchen doorway and she poured out two mugfuls and we held them between our hands, and blew into them at the kitchen table.

"Do you think she'll die while we're there?" I asked. "Or do you think she'll wait till we leave?"

My mother laughed into her mug.

"All I know is she needs us, and I need you."

When she said that, I thought I would feel more frightened and weaker than I already felt. But that wasn't the case. I felt stronger for her words and a little embarrassed at the self-important smile I tried to hide with the rim of my mug.

My mother let me crawl in bed between her and my father that night. Their room smelled of hand creams and powder, and lying under her shoulder, by her side, my mother was so soft and warm, I never wanted to move away from her again.

My father shifted, asked how old I was—"Two?"—and rolled over. His weight made me tilt toward him. But when my mother turned on her side toward me, the three of us evened out. She lifted the ends of my hair and let them fall and the tips of her cool fingers brushed against my cheeks.

"Such a pretty cat," she whispered into my ear. "Co-co-co-co."

It gave me goose bumps. I held her closer.

"Do it again," I whispered back.

"Co-co-co-co."

In her room at the Lisner Home in Washington, D.C., my great-grandmother pulled off all her clothes. The nurses tied a sheet to the hospital bars surrounding her bed to cover up her body. My great-grandmother scratched at them, screaming that she would not be caged in. My mother picked the knots away and my great-grandmother slept with nothing on.

I did not back up or look away. I drew nearer. And it was not frightening. She was beautiful. Her body was more like a child's. There were no scars or liver spots. Her skin wasn't even wrinkled past her breasts. Just loose. She was a light beige all over and whatever hair she had left was white down.

I wanted her to know that I was there, and when I bent down over her and hugged her frail body, my hands wrapped all the way around her and came back to myself. I felt the weight of what I was embracing and I did not let go.

Her chest warmed against mine. Her heartbeat was so strong and startling, I could not see how she could die. Her heart beat and beat and beat until hers made the same time as mine, and mine hers, and as I held her, I thought surely one of us was giving life to the other, though I did not know which. And as I held my great-grandmother in my arms, I felt as though I were holding on to everything my mother was losing—her family, her name, a part of who she had been.

"My littlest of all cats, how good of you to come," Great-Grandmother said, speaking so loudly a nurse came running in. My mother told the nurse everything was fine, thank you, and sent her back out. "But isn't the sun lovely?" my great-grandmother said, her eyes blue and clear. "Can you hear the birds?"

When my great-grandmother closed her eyes, my mother began tapping out piano chords across the steel guard bed rail. She whispered that my grandfather should be here. "You'd think her only son would come to her deathbed."

"It doesn't matter," I told her. "We're here."

"She said I played too much Haydn and not enough Mozart," my mother said, her nails clicking against the steel. "She loved it when I played."

My mother got up and opened a window. The cherry trees were just beginning to bud and the roses were greening.

My great-grandmother's bedroom drawers were empty, except for the clothes and the shoe boxes filled with the letters she had saved from my mother and me. What my great-grandmother had taken with her out of Europe she had already sent to us. There was a note scribbled on a white paper doily.

> To whomever it might concern:
> I prefer cremation. Send me to Wien. Pantsch will know what to do. Already I have taken up much time and space.

My grandfather's book was on her nightstand, and there inside, pressed between the pages, was a brittle black-and-white photo of my mother as a little girl. She had long black braids and she was standing in a greenhouse, holding a dove.

We had an early thaw that year, and by April most of the snow had melted and all that was left were the big dirty clumps of ice at parking lot corners. My father was busy making plans to "winterize" the house for next year.

"I don't want to be cold anymore," he said each time he spoke on the phone with another heating consultant.

He wanted to fix the whistle in the front door, too. But my mother said no.

"Leave it alone," she said. "It's comforting at night."

He switched the license plates instead. I told him it looked good. The Illinois matched the blue in the Chrysler and it was about time we had *The Land of Lincoln* behind us. Maybe, one year, we could even get a plate that spelled out *Pookie*. He told me to mind my own damned business.

By the time we had eaten up all the greenhouse lettuce, and the camellias had finished up a season of blooming, my mother threw me a party. She spent weeks planning it. She invited everyone in my intermediate class and even the advanced students came. Everyone was to perform. I made pinkish cupcakes that didn't turn out and my mother made a punch that did. She put in fat, out-of-season strawberries that floated to the top. The concoction was so bittersweet and bubbly that everyone thought it was spiked.

I wore a dress she bought brand-new for me—my first black dress— a dress, she said that, contrary to what my father thought, I was no longer too young to wear.

My mother stood in the dining room next to the punch bowl, wearing a wraparound skirt with big Rousseau-like leaves, pink berries, and bright yellow birds buzzing all around. She stood serving seconds and thirds, using the silver ladle my great-grandmother had sent. The one I had spent hours polishing the night before.

I filled the entranceway with the geraniums, which were already in first bloom.

The boy with the red parka was there.

"Great punch!" he said. "My mom won't even let me serve beer."

I told him I liked his turtleneck. He said he wasn't going to miss the snow. I said the same about the cold. And that's when I asked if he'd like to take me to Tulip Trot next week.

"Sure," he said.

"Great," I said. "Me and Dad'll pick you up around eight."

When it came time to perform, the long-haired girls went first. In groups of threes, they performed too-slow versions of "Scarborough Fair" and "If." I went solo last. I wanted everyone to hear how hard I had worked. I thought then that whatever they thought of me, they would at least have to respect my music.

And as I played, I heard the soft, uneven notes of a piano. I looked up from my fingers and strings to see my mother at the baby grand. I had not seen her go to the piano. My father stood near the fireplace. He nodded for me to go on.

My mother's notes were light and unpaced at first as she tried to make out the sheet music I had long since memorized. She was so determined, I worried for her. I knew she was attempting to do something. She was trying to save someone or something that had been put away a long time ago, and I could tell she wasn't sure if this was a good idea.

I slowed down. We started to nod our heads in time. We synchronized. For the first time, I wasn't looking down to see that my fingers were all in place, touching the right strings. They were playing on their own, so I just kept my eyes on my mother.

Her eyes were as blue as my great-grandmother's had been and when she smiled, they were barely visible. In guitar class, our teacher had once told us that when two people played together in harmony, they were in sympathy with each other. She had used that word, "sympathy." Even at the time I considered how like "sympathy" was with the word "symphony." And somehow, in an odd way, as my mother and I played it felt like that time when I held my great-grandmother. It was as though a string were running through my great-grandmother's heart and mine and now my mother's.

Just then the ghost whispered in with a spring breeze and it seemed to fill the room. And as our music evened off and my guitar teacher swung her hair in time while everyone else in the room clapped and stomped their feet to our ragtime, I could no longer tell who was leading whom or who was being led. We just kept playing on. My mother and me. Just like that.

PART II

The Gifts of Isabella

GENEVIEVE

MY MOTHER LEFT MOST OF THE PARQUET FLOORS AT the Hofzeile bare so that the sound of the piano in one room echoed in another. That was the way I first heard news of the new man from Germany. Speeches broadcast over the wireless echoed from another room, as though they were bits of a soundtrack that had gotten away from somebody else's dream.

Kristallnacht happened and nobody in my family spoke of it. Later, I realized everyone was simply embarrassed by this night—the night of broken glass, the night temples and kosher groceries were ransacked and smashed—a violent, noisy anti-Jewish riot, and still, barely anyone said a word about it.

While most people were shuffled around to different living quarters, we were not. In his memoirs, my father wrote that we were not disturbed because the Germans thought he had connections with the Pope. I imagine it pleased him to write that and read it over. He liked to barely suggest that he was vain, and then to deny it. But he did have connections—more than most—and for a time we were left alone.

That was the year Sister Gertrude was teaching me how to play the piano and Inge was learning to play the violin. I was getting quite good.

Sister Gertrude was a wonderful teacher who would play something and then say, sit down and play that, and I could. She discovered a gift in me which has since shriveled up and died.

Inge's training was less formal, and therefore more impressive. Her mother had a beautiful, polished violin which she kept hanging precariously on their living-room wall. Finally, one day, Inge took it off its hook and began teaching herself how to play.

We began playing duets. Inge stood to my right. I can still see her, her left foot planted out in front of her right for balance. She put a clean maroon cloth over her shoulder the way mothers do when they are about to burp their babies and don't want to get spit upon. Except that Inge put her violin on the cloth, rested her chin, and played.

We practiced together every day.

We were practicing one afternoon in my sitting room when Uncle Rudi came barging in, whistling through his teeth. He was back from Turkey and he had brought me a coffeemaker. Let it boil over three times, he told me. I didn't drink coffee, but I didn't say anything because it was a beautiful contraption.

Uncle Rudi got down on his knees and proceeded to roll up the one oriental area rug in the room, because, he claimed, rugs soaked up his music. A year before, he had convinced my parents to upholster the doors to keep sounds out. He got up off his knees, scooted me off my piano bench, and raced through four bars from a Mozart concerto. He really wasn't that good on the piano. His talent was with the viola d'amore.

"Show me what you are learning," he said to Inge and me. Inge had, by this time, grown quiet and shy. Uncle Rudi was a bachelor and he was very handsome, with a high, intelligent forehead, beautiful brown eyes that were set wide apart, and he had my mother's long delicate hands.

I have one picture of Rudi—still in its original frame. In this picture his arms are crossed. You can see his hands in that one.

He was a commodities trader. He sold and traded burlap. This was before plastic and paper bags, and burlap was a big deal. They wrapped beans and everything in burlap. Allegedly a lot of wealthy women were in love with Uncle Rudi, but he claimed his great love was music.

That day, the day Uncle Rudi asked Inge and me to play him a duet, I took my seat at the piano beside my uncle, and Inge picked up her violin.

It was not our best effort.

Uncle Rudi had a few suggestions for Inge—hold the bow this way, shake the left finger so. She caught on quickly. The three of us were still in my sitting room when Cook came in and asked us if we were ever going to come down for dinner.

The following afternoon, Uncle Rudi brought in the instrument he had taught himself—the viola d'amore. Inge could not take her eyes from the case lined in purple. She touched the satin, and with the tips of her finger, she felt Uncle Rudi's initials stitched in black on the side of the case. We both stared at the viola d'amore itself. Rudi went on about what a funny, impressive-looking instrument it was, with fourteen strings—seven on the bottom, seven on the top. When you saw it, you must have wondered, too. He explained to us that it was designed during a time when performing halls were getting bigger and demanded louder instruments. Inge and I each touched the blindfolded angel carved in wood at the top.

That afternoon, Uncle Rudi rolled back the oriental again. He got us playing a trio for the viola d'amore, the piano, and the violin. Maybe we would have sounded even better if I had been playing the harpsichord, but the harmony was revolutionary to me. I still to this day cannot remember the remarkable slow movement of that trio and I have not heard it since, but I can remember clearly how it felt to make such perfect music with two people I loved.

Essentially, Inge and I played backup, but this was all right because there was a part when Inge and I stopped playing and we got to listen to Uncle Rudi play on.

At times he seemed to play out of tune, but other times, the strings underneath caught the sound just right. That is the way it should be with the viola d'amore—the two rows of strings should swing in sympathy with each other. You touch one string with your bow and the air will transmit the vibrations and move the other—that is how Uncle Rudi explained it. "It's physics," he loved to say.

It was good sitting up there listening to my uncle play while the last of the day's sunlight melted out of the room. There were times when he didn't seem to be there in the same room with us. We could hear him breathing in time with the music, and saw the perspiration gathering on his forehead. Then, all at once, Inge and I would begin playing again, attempting to join him at the place one travels to when you are creating music together.

During those afternoons after school, up there in my sitting room where silent, blue birds flew immobile all around us on the walls, we were safe and very far from the streets down below where men exposed themselves and all of Europe prepared for war.

There was a time when I sat with Cook in the mornings and watched her roll dough. It was a time when oranges were hard to come by, in November, and chocolate was still considered medicinal.

Cook was Czech. She put nutmeg in rice. Her skin was flour-colored and the flesh under her upper arms waved at me whenever I sat in the kitchen and watched her roll out pastry dough. One morning when she was rolling the dough for tarts she was making for a concert Uncle Rudi was to give that afternoon, Cook let me roll smaller versions. She gave me bits of dough which I would alternately eat and roll out while she told me about St. Frances, a rich lady who didn't like being rich, because, she said, "Why should *I* be rich, when Our Lady was poor?" The sound of Cook's voice was a warm yellow, soft and sweet. Every now and then, my mother would come into the kitchen and say Cook had gotten this or that wrong in the story, but luckily, because of the nature of the dough, Cook took a long time that day to roll out her stories.

She told me about Elizabeth of Hungary, who at four years of age was sent away from her mother to be married to a prince, which, it turned out, wasn't so bad because Elizabeth got some new clothes, a velvet coat, and a silver mug with her name on it. She cared for a man with leprosy who turned out to be Our Lord and she helped feed the poor and had a lot of hospitals built in her name. Years later, when we left Vienna, I would remember the first part of Cook's story the best—how Elizabeth traveled in a silver cradle that rocked between two horses named Milk and Honey.

Just as Cook was putting the pastries into the oven, Uncle Rudi came in, looking pale. He announced to us that Mussolini was in Berlin with Hitler and that Italy had formally withdrawn from the League of Nations.

I had a vague image of a pouty Mussolini clothed in black, riding away from a big party on horseback.

"This is not a good sign," Uncle Rudi said, as my father entered the kitchen.

My father, the historian, shook his head and agreed; but then he put his arm around Rudi's shoulder, poured out two sherries, and said that we really shouldn't worry.

"Nobody will take this foolishness seriously."

I put on my coat and hat. I was to meet with Inge for our rounds with the Help Unit. Afterwards, we would practice our music.

"Where are you going?" my mother said, coming into the kitchen to join us.

"To Inge's," I said importantly. "We have a meeting."

My parents looked at each other. Uncle Rudi poured himself another glass of sherry.

"Take off your coat," my father said. "You are not going to Inge's today or any other day. We should never have allowed you to associate with that girl in the first place. The idea that you've spent so much time at the Karl Marx Hof." He spat out his "k's" and "x's." "I will not have my daughter associating with Social Democrats. They cannot be trusted. Inge cannot be trusted."

I wish I had said something then. I wish I had said, "But Inge is my friend." I wish I had said, "Haven't you been listening to us play together?" I wish I could say now that I insisted on going, but I did not even try to explain the importance of that day's Help Unit mission. I realize now that I had no recourse. I only really learned to argue with my father after my mother died, and it took years of not saying anything to get to that point.

I could not phone Inge, because she had no phone. I knew that she would be outside her red door waiting for me, her hair neatly braided, her hands to her side, and her fingers moving, always moving, forming chords on a viola d'amore that she admitted she wished she had.

I took off my coat. I went upstairs. I played a little Mozart. Then I did what I always do when I get upset or when something goes wrong. I did the same thing when you fell out of a tree in Mississippi and split your chin open, and again, years later when my father died: I went to sleep.

My father always knew when his mother-in-law had come and gone. He would come home and all the furniture would be moved and he would moan, "Oh God, Lucie has been here."

I remember the day Lucie came over and insisted on taking me to have my picture made. She fussed with my hair and had me change into all these different outfits. No sooner had she gotten me into a frilly white dress with an embroidered collar than she would pull it off and rearrange me into something else. For Lucie, I was a doll to play with. She wore a lot of jewelry—big, blue, dangly earrings and lots of gold bracelets. "We wear only real jewelry," she told me. She sounded like a chandelier in the wind whenever she moved. I think I was something of a disappointment to her. I did not have my mother's classic nose or mouth.

I have never considered myself a great beauty and I felt self-conscious that day. I over-posed. I lifted my left eyebrow and looked off to the side the way Lucie sometimes did when she put a cigarette to her mouth, then turned to blow away the smoke. Lucie shook her head and said, no no, stopped the photographer, and came over to have a word with me.

"A young girl should never consider herself good-looking," she said to me in French. "You will look conceited and draw unfavorable attention to yourself."

I smiled for the photographer after that. I was not supposed to consider myself good-looking! Well, then, I thought, I've got a head start on that game. I still have the pictures from that day. Lucie managed to get them out and now they stay tucked away in my safe deposit box at the bank. I look the way a young girl should look—terribly happy, very much surrounded by warmth and love.

I have a handful of the photographs from that period in my life, but they're all fading. You can barely see the images. Some of the pictures look like blank sheets of yellow paper. Lucie used to go through them, doctoring up any pictures of herself. She threw most of the ones of herself away—all the ones she thought made her look fat or unattractive. Then she would go over the others with a pen, drawing the hat she wore more clearly or shading her sides to make her waistline slimmer.

Now I look at those pictures and all I see are the penmarks she drew and not the image, and Lucie seems more a cartoon than the woman I remember as my glamorous grandmother. You can't see the bicycles my mother and Rudi are riding—not even their faces—but you can see the outline of a hat and the carnation in Rudi's lapel. Underneath, Lucie wrote lyrical captions such as "The Prince and Princess go riding," or under the one of them playing tennis, "*Où est le plaisir*—Where's the pleasure?"

These photographs are a lot like memory—I will remember a color, perhaps the outline, but not everything that happened. Never the whole picture or the entire image, only bits and pieces. It doesn't seem at all fair that the image disappears and all you have left is a blank sheet with a caption that reads clearly, *Où est le plaisir?*

I was having cavities filled. I don't remember how many. The dentist was a thin man in a white coat and he smelled of peppermint. I remember wondering what I smelled like to him. There was a nurse on my other side, holding up a horrible-looking weapon. She was smiling. The dentist held the drill in his hand and he asked me if I was comfortable.

I am too comfortable, I thought. The chair had been made to fit whoever sat in it—it was more comfortable than any chair I had ever sat in and that made me uncomfortable. One does not want to relax when the man standing beside you is holding a drill.

The dentist showed me where there was a button on the right side of the chair. I should push the button, he said, whenever the pain became unbearable. The button stopped the drill. Remember, they did not use novocaine back then. I was glad for the button.

I placed my finger on the button and thought, Be brave be brave be brave. Think of what Cook will serve for dinner. Think *strudel strudel strudel strudel.*

Just as the dentist began to drill, there was all this excitement outside on the street. I could hear shouting and motorcars passing. I wanted to get up and look out the window, but the dentist kept drilling.

Finally, the nurse said, "Look." She said it in such a way that it reminded me of the man in the street after my first communion.

The dentist stopped drilling and he and his nurse went over to the window. There was a lot of shouting and I heard a band playing somewhere.

I got out of the uncomfortably comfortable chair and stuck my head up between the nurse and the dentist.

I saw the motorcar with the white flag—there was always a procession of flags whenever a famous person drove through the streets of Vienna. The first motorcar carries a yellow flag and the last motorcar carries a white flag, so we knew that the next person we saw in this line of cars would be famous.

I believe he came by in a tank, and he was standing. He was short and not at all intimidating with his drooping hair and his stupid little mustache. The dentist and his drill and the nurse with her instruments of torture were much more horrifying to me.

The dentist and the nurse together opened the window. They did not say a word. There was so much shouting down on the streets and I was so relieved to have a respite from the drill that I began to clap my hands. I remember the nurse looked at me in a strange way. I thought it was simply because my cheeks were stuffed with cotton.

On the streets below, the crowds were throwing flowers at the German soldiers marching alongside the cars in their brown and black uniforms and jackboots. "Perish the Jews! Down with the Catholics!" I could hear people shout. *"Ein Volk, ein Reich, ein Führer!"* Airplanes passed overhead and later I read the pamphlets they dropped. "Nazi Germany welcomes Nazi Austria," they said.

This was March 11, 1938.

I once had to give a talk for a Catholic Women's Club in York, Pennsylvania, on "Famous People I've Known." I told them this story, but I don't think it was a great success. I think people expect more when you say the word "Hitler." I know you do.

You asked me why I think my father, a historian, didn't see it all coming. Hitler, you said, didn't come out of nowhere. You quote *Mein Kampf*. You say he said it all right there—said that he had every intention of destroying Austria, that it was the only way to safeguard "Germanism," whatever that means. What am I, my father's defender? What are you doing reading *Mein Kampf*?

Regardless, Hitler was Famous Person Number Three. After that, many many years later I would meet Richard Burton in a telephone booth in New York.

After the German troops had marched into Vienna, and the Nazi Party began to grow, after the *Anschluss*, they closed the private schools and I had to attend the public school system. Seizing control of education was one of their first steps.

I walked to and from school. I had to go past the high iron fence surrounding our garden. I walked on until the street got narrow with old buildings. At the end of the street was the Grinzinger Allee and I went up to the right toward the mountains where the new wine was made. Then down the street there was the school. The public school.

My new teacher was the niece of Hermann Goering. Her first lecture to us was about Hitler's attack—the "liberation of Czechoslovakia." I remember sitting there at my desk thinking, This is pretty one-sided. I wasn't precocious. I just knew blab when I heard it. If a ten-year-old child can evaluate somebody telling her something so carefully, you would think a whole nation of Germans would be able to evaluate their history better. Then again there is no German word for hindsight.

Anybody who still wanted to be Catholic had religion taught to them after school at the church down the street—the one with the blue-green copper roof I could see from my house. The teacher made it very embarrassing. Every day she would say in this condescending tone, "Which of you still wants to be Catholic today?"

There was no question that I would go. There were only three of us who went from my school. Combined with children from other schools, there were ten or fifteen. But our numbers decreased as time went on.

The pastor spoke to us of ancient Roman times when priests wore the Sunday robes every day. He made all these mysterious ceremonies feel like habit. Every day after school I left behind lessons on mathematical combinations and scientific theories and went to this man's church, his sacristy, his home. When I entered that church and lit a candle for my mother and Pantsch, Cook, Inge, Gentz, and Grossmama, I felt as though I was an heir to this tremendous tradition—the tradition I've raised you in.

Five of us had our confirmation that year—the year when not only Catholicism was out, but all religion. After religion classes, I walked home through the Grinzinger Allee alone, memorizing the Paternoster, the Ave Maria, and the Credo. My mother must have been in agonies waiting for me to come home safely, but I think at that point she was working on getting us out of the country. She was away all day most every day. Later, I realized she was standing in lines, trying to get all our papers. I know we were waiting for one last paper and that one seemed to take months.

Our house felt different. As Cook would have said, there was sour milk in the air.

At dinner, my mother and I would eat while we listened to my father yelling on the phone. It always had something to do with the university—the chairman of the history department wanted him to do or teach something he did not want to do or teach.

One evening, after dinner, I went up to my sitting room to practice my piano lessons and our maid, Agnes, came in to tidy up before she retired to the apartments upstairs. Agnes had gray hair, sallow skin, and a lot of wrinkles. She was a thin, prissy woman with thick ankles. She ran her dustcloth across the Biedermeier dining table and she told me what a lucky little girl I was to have such nice things. I looked all around me, at the birds my mother had painted first green then blue, and I said, "Yes, I suppose I am." Later, we found out that Agnes was a spy for the Nazis and when all our furniture was loaded onto a truck and the truck "disappeared," I thought of that afternoon when Agnes had dusted the furniture so conscientiously, commenting on the wood, the linens, and the fine curtains, and I cannot help but know where exactly that whole truckload went.

That Christmas—the last we had together in Vienna—I got two of everything. Two dark blue coats, two dresses, two pairs of socks, two pairs of shoes. One set was in one size, the other set was a size bigger. Only later did I realize that they were getting me ready to leave.

I was still small enough to squeeze between my mother and father on the love seat while we listened to the crystal set. When Wagner came on, my father got up and shut it off. "It's music that doesn't even need rehearsing," he said. "Only big gestures from the conductor. Typically German." He sneered when he said the word *Deutsch*.

It was still snowing after Christmas dinner and my mother and father retired to read their new books. I lay under the Christmas tree, eating something chocolate, staring up at the shadows the branches made from the candlelight.

Every Christmas, every year, I think back to my early Christmases. I loved that time so much because it was when I knew exactly my place in the world—under a lit Christmas tree, eating chocolates, reading a book while my mother and father were in other parts of the Hofzeile.

Once, when we were visiting in Mississippi on Christmas Eve one year, your father and I went to a Vietnamese mass. The Vietnamese and I were the only Catholics there at the time, and your father and I were the only Caucasians. From the back pew, we stared at all that shiny, straight black hair. I didn't even try to understand what it was they were saying. Their chanting was from a different time and place; but still, afterwards, we both admitted that we felt at home during that one hour—he a Presbyterian, me an Austrian Roman Catholic, sitting among strangers from Vietnam in the back pew of a small-town Irish Catholic church in the middle of Mississippi.

My mother loved *le passé simple,* an archaic form of French which is very formal and which can only be written, not spoken. It is the past tense, but it is the present as well. Harmoniously together in one moment. Faulkner, I think, had the idea. The past *is* the present, he said. Sitting in that church pew arm to arm with your father that Christmas Eve, I thought that even though you can't speak *le passé simple,* you may still be able to live it.

Rudi and I performed a duet one Sunday afternoon, and afterwards, when everyone had left the room, he chased me around the piano and I knocked over a Venetian vase. It was a vase my mother had gotten from her mother who had gotten it from her mother. It was an heirloom so incidental, it wasn't even called an heirloom—something one would miss only if it wasn't there. It lay on the floor in pieces and I stood there, wishing it back to wholeness. When I grow up, I thought to myself then, I'll remember this day and I'll miss this vase.

Rudi made me take the blame, and all night everyone went on and on about how old that vase was, how I had no sympathy, no responsibility for what was old and timeless—for my heritage. I was quite relieved when Rudi turned on the wireless and we heard that Hitler had taken yet another town or province.

Every day our teacher read out names from a list on a white sheet of paper. When a student recognized a name, he or she would raise his or her hand and tell all about that person on the list, and the teacher would smile and that student would have many people to eat with at lunch. I never knew any of the names, and it made me feel terribly lonely.

I hated lunch. There was never anyone to sit with. Everyone knew one another from something else—I had been tutored, had been to Rome for a semester, then gone to convent school, so I didn't know a soul. Here were these new people all around me and these children, I felt, weren't really my class. And I was growing too old for the imaginary friends Pantsch had assigned to me.

My mother was still in her exercise phase, though she had quit throwing the discus. She went back to formal ballet. She wasn't getting very far with me, though. I hated ballet lessons, so she let me drop them only on the condition that I take up ice skating.

I detested the cold, I detested the skating, and I detested the ice. I detested the socializing because I wasn't making any friends. I much preferred lying on my stomach on Inge's bed while she played the violin, or, on some afternoons, her imaginary viola d'amore, while I watched the sun go down, breathing in whatever her mother was cooking for dinner that evening.

There was this one young leader in our skating class—a nasty kid, kind of cute, very active and very blond. My only solace during ice-skating lessons was the hot chocolate, which you could get from the wooden booth at the rink. I was at a terrible age and I felt particularly awkward. I was taller than the other children and I just didn't fit in. I was and am still probably the only Austrian who doesn't ski and I still hate to skate.

One afternoon, when I skated or rather skidded over to the hot chocolate booth, this nasty blond boy announced very loudly that only members of the Hitler Youth Group could have hot chocolate. I knew I wasn't a member because I did not wear the white kneesocks, so I had no hot chocolate that afternoon.

When my mother picked me up at five o'clock, I asked her on the way home if I could join the Hitler Youth Group. She didn't even look at me. She stared straight ahead and she kept walking and she said quite simply, "No, you can't."

That week in school we were learning long division. I was puzzled and fascinated by it. There I was, guessing at what something can be divided into. Nobody automatically knows that 6 goes into 19 three times and you have 1 left over. You know it mentally, but 6 into 595? You've got to fiddle with it. Six will not go into 5, so you've got to tuck it into 59. I remember thinking long division was almost as unreasonable and unreal as what was happening in my daily life. Why did our teacher care who our parents ate with at night? Why did my father yell on the phone every day at noon? Where did my mother go off to during the day for such long stretches of time?

That night, Gentz came over. For some reason he was not wearing his black suit, but he was carrying a briefcase. My father was so happy to see Gentz that I asked my mother what was up. She smiled and put her finger to her lips as though she were saying *shhh*. My father led Gentz to his study and they were in there, mumbling for a long time together before dinner. When they came out, they both looked a little tired, but again, so happy that I wondered. My father held an official-looking piece of paper for my mother to see. She read it and kissed him. I said, "May I see?" They all laughed. Gentz said he had something for me, too.

He led me back into my father's study, where he gave me a prayer card of the little baby Jesus. It was a small ink sketch and the sky was a watercolor blue while Jesus was the same color as the paper—an eggshell white. Gentz knelt down next to me and said that he had drawn it himself. "Your father has found Jesus in his heart," Gentz said. "That's all that's going on. Jesus has always been there, but tonight we just made it more official." I looked back at the picture and then at him and I thanked him before my mother had even thought to ask me to.

I did wonder why Grossmama did not have dinner with us that evening. I wondered why she stayed in her rooms with her stamp collection while we made a toast first to Gentz, then to my father. For years my father had studied in the Vatican Archives, for years he held the utmost respect and adoration for the Pope and the Catholic Church—it shouldn't surprise me now that this was the night of his final conversion.

We ate a good dinner and Cook had made a kind of pastry they make at Demel's. Gentz asked my father what he thought of this character from Germany. My father said he was a silly, low-class man.

"But what of Vienna?" Gentz said. "There are such troubles."

My father stood up to go to the sitting room while my mother motioned Agnes to bring in the tray of brandies.

"We've survived two Turkish invasions," my father said cheerfully. "I don't think we have to worry about a wallpaper hanger who dropped out of high school."

I played Schubert and said goodnight and went to my room. I stood there in the doorway for a long time, trying to figure out a place to put Gentz's picture of the baby Jesus. For some reason, I didn't want Agnes to see it or admire it—I didn't want anyone to look at it and say, "What a pretty little picture." In the corner of my room, near my bed, there was the window, and I propped the picture up there on the sill behind the curtain where frost palms blossomed on the pane.

The following day, our teacher got out the white sheet of paper and read the names and one of the names was Gentz.

"Gentz!" I said and I raised my hand, saying, yes, yes, Gentz had dined with us just last night. I told them all what a nice man he was and what a good celebration we had.

"And what did you celebrate?" the teacher asked.

Everyone turned to look at me, and for the moment I felt very important.

"My father found Jesus in his heart."

The teacher squinted at me, nodded, wrote something down on her sheet of paper, then told us to get out our pencils—we were to go further with our lesson in long division. And then there were fractions. Solutions. She kept saying that word. *Solutions.* As though there was a problem—that is what I hated about math. The teacher kept making up these imaginary problems.

Now, of course, I see the connection. All around us was the geometry—my mother began to mix in new furniture with her Louis Quinze sofas and bureaus. She filled the dining room with Josef Hoffmann chairs—some had the horseshoe-shaped bases and horizontal bars in the back; others had backs with the wood bent into perfect half spheres, squares within diamonds, the sectioned rods hammered to ninety-degree angles. With all their rows of circles and the straight, even lines, those chairs reminded me of so many math dilemmas. Even the upholstery on the cushions had row upon row of gold squares and green circles—the kinds of patterns Klimt painted around his Jewish women, as though all those geometrical shapes were closing in on them and their race.

And there were the euphemisms: *die Endlösung*—the "final solution." And the question? It was *die Judenfrage*—the "Jewish question."

I have seen the numbers put before us—what is it now, six million? I stare down at that number on this piece of paper. I look at it for a long time. I think which one of those numbers was one of us? Which one could have been me?

Their aim was to exterminate European Jewry. In some ways, they were successful. That religion has certainly never been the same. Nor has my family.

In the mirror of the dressing room I see the straight, spare, geometric lines of your body in a black dress. You look like a Thonet chair or a Wagner column. Completely free of fat and ornament. You have been blessed with my mother's nose and your father's eyes. Sometimes you complain that people don't notice you. Be grateful. You are someone officials forget to look at. You will be safe.

The year I told my schoolteacher that Gentz had dined with us, my mother was studying art criticism and my father was writing about what happened to Vienna in the nineteenth century. Evenings they argued over the merits of Kandinsky and Klee; meanwhile, Hitler was in office in Germany, stirring up hatred of the Sudetens. Maybe my parents should have been studying math. Maybe they would have known sooner if they had studied geometric problems and figures.

But that day, the day I told on Gentz, I wasn't thinking of my family, or any of that. None of that mattered because at noon, I got to sit at the center table and eat lunch with the blond boy with the nice white kneesocks from ice-skating class.

I was darning my first pair of white socks. Knitting was a requirement at the public school and you couldn't graduate from the third grade until you had darned a sock. I had made these socks myself because I knew my mother would not buy them for me. And I had worn holes into both of them. My teacher was particularly eager to have me make the appropriate repairs.

I had already crocheted all of these horrors for my mother and father and I bestowed these lovely articles on them for Christmas and their birthdays. I think they were really grateful they didn't have any other feasts. I crocheted a yellow comb and brush case for each of them and I remember insisting the teacher stand next to me when I made the little loophole for the button. I always felt the teacher had to be around before I did something important with yarn.

The socks were the first handmade project I kept for myself. I kept them in my desk at school, and whenever I went to my ice-skating class, I would put them on, then take them off afterwards before my mother came to pick me up. I had grown quite fond of the socks, hot chocolate, ice skating, and a certain blond boy.

I was in the process of completing the heel when I looked out the window and saw three German soldiers taking away a man I immediately recognized. He was the shoemaker who had a shop a block away from the Hofzeile.

He was a nice man with gray eyes, and sometimes when he stood outside he would let me come in and I would go to the counter which came up to my nose and reach up to a dish where he kept candy. It was a small, dark place that smelled of good leather, and he and his wife would ask me about school and discuss among themselves my height and my long, pretty black braids.

Outside my classroom window, two soldiers had the shoemaker by his arms. The shoemaker's head was bleeding and the shoemaker's wife stood on the sidewalk, her left hand hugging herself about the waist, her right hand over her mouth. The shoemaker did not struggle, but the soldiers treated him as if he was. They pushed him and I could see that they held his arms too tightly by the way the sleeves of his coat rose past his elbows. Blood from his head dripped down on his arms, which to me seemed painfully white.

I even recognized one of the soldiers, who wasn't German after all but Austrian. I had seen him at a crossroads only weeks before. He could have been my friend just as easily as the shoemaker had been. He had been a policeman for Vienna, and now he had on a different uniform. Was it that simple? I looked down at my white socks, and I thought of the man who had exposed himself to me after my first communion. I thought of the design painted on the doorway behind him, and now, outside, the same design appeared on the arm patches of the two soldiers who were taking away my friend. For a long time I didn't know what any of this meant. I felt as though we—my father and mother, Cook, myself, and all of Vienna—were marching into a fairyland.

I looked around, but nobody else in my classroom seemed to notice what was going on just outside the window, and if they did, nobody said anything. An incident like this had already become common, but it was the first time I had actually seen someone being taken away, and at that moment I thought of Gentz and my eyes burned. I fingered the white socks in my lap and wondered if they had anything to do with anything. I thought perhaps I should raise my hand, and tell my classmates about the shoemaker—tell them that he was a nice man with a nice shop, a nice wife, and nice candy. But then I thought, what difference would it make to them that this kind man gave me a piece of candy every now and then?

"Go on," I heard in careful German. I had not noticed, but my teacher was standing looking down at me. My fist was stuck in my sock and I stared at the big hole in the heel. Quietly, my teacher moved toward the window. "Go on and make the turn," she said as she pulled the blinds.

That year, for my birthday, my parents gave me three strawberry plants and a canary. The gardener planted the strawberry plants and I kept the canary in a brown wicker cage on my balcony. I had these gifts for a few months before we left. You like to play the game of "Which was your best Christmas? What was your finest birthday?" Those were my favorite gifts, but I didn't tell you because I never did find out if the strawberry plants bore any fruit or if the canary lived.

The day Gentz disappeared, I told my mother and father everything except the part about my white socks. That would always be my secret. My father picked up the phone, then set it back down again. I tried to explain to my father that I didn't know that telling my teacher that he found Jesus in his heart was a bad thing. My mother stood up, paced, and looked out the window. "It's not, it's not," she said.

"We should have explained to her," my father said, ignoring me.

"It wouldn't have made much difference," my mother said.

I went to the closet in my room. I moved the sweaters and clothes from the top shelf and climbed up. I pulled the door closed. To hell with them, I said to myself three times, then one more for good measure.

Years later, my father found out what happened to Gentz. He was sent to Dachau. The Nazis did not like that he had been quietly and quickly converting people to Catholicism in private ceremonies. Gentz survived the camp and when he left, before the war was over, he signed something—swearing that he would never speak or write about his experiences there, and he never did.

I think back on these events now and say to myself it could have been Agnes—she was serving the night Gentz came to dinner. She could have told. But perhaps I'm making excuses—lying to myself—and that is no longer my intention. Sight may be my family's weakness, but I want to see my life clearly—even the wrongs I have done.

When Mussolini moved into Albania, Rudi began to make the arrangements to get his mother Lucie out. Things started to disappear from Rudi's place—candlesticks, good crystal, all of the things he had brought back from his trips to Turkey and elsewhere. He no longer wore his good cufflinks and watch. Only now do I realize Rudi was beginning to pawn things. His plan I think was to keep what he had in the bank, get rid of everything, and accumulate cash to pay off officials.

Grandmère Lucie went first. She carried away all the silver in her handbag—this was before guards checked. We didn't sneak it out in the hems of our clothes the way you told your classmates. At the time, it felt as though she was just going off on another trip. She kissed me good-bye, told me to be a good girl, fixed my hair one last time, and left by train, waving at us with the very papers Rudi had gotten to get her out.

I knew that we were somehow in danger but I didn't know why. I figured that our being in danger had something to do with my father and the university. I often thought of the shoemaker, and whenever I played that scene over again in my mind, I would look closer at the face and sometimes see Gentz or my father.

And what did my father, the great historian, do while Rudi was getting his mother out? It was early January 1939 and everything was covered with snow. My father was scheduled to teach a seminar on the Austrian war of 1859 as an exchange professor. Six days before his forty-fourth birthday, my father left us to return to Rome.

ELIZABETH

MY GRANDFATHER AND HIS NEW WIFE, ISABELLA, WERE
due to arrive the next afternoon, and my mother was on her hands and
knees, waxing the dulled sections of the living-room's new parquet floor.
Even though ours was called "common parquet" in the floor books my
mother showed my father and me, she didn't trust professionals to do
the waxing anymore. My mother knew about parquet floors. She told
me that common parquet in Vienna was special parquet here—it was
the same kind they had laid throughout the Karl Marx Hof in Vienna,
a Socialist tenement for "lower-class workers." I imagined sitting down
for tea with my grandfather while he spoke of oak and other more exotic
woods. I imagined him telling me exactly how his workers fitted the different kinds of wood together, then how they treated it so that it
wouldn't buckle or fall apart.

My grandfather was visiting the United States on a speaking tour.
He and Isabella would be staying with us for four days.

I wondered what my new step-grandmother, Isabella, would look
like. She was the same age as my mother and the two of them were
Viennese—would they look alike? I was always proud that my mother
looked different from the other North Shore suburban mothers, who

were flat-chested and had leathery, tanned skin and tight, yellow hair. My mother had breasts and hips—she was not thin but womanly, and on weekend nights, when she went to dinner parties with my father, she wore interesting black-and-white suits and smelled of expensive French perfume. The other women tended to smell of suntan oil, even in winter.

From what I had read of the Viennese, I imagined that my grandfather and Isabella sat around drinking champagne laced with cognac. They read books out loud to each other, wore odd undergarments, and ate with different-sized spoons and forks. They would probably be obsessed with death and headaches. They would be even more alien here in the Midwest than my mother, my father, or me.

I had never met my grandfather, but I often thought about what he looked like. For some reason, in my mind, his Austrianness translated into Jewishness—which to me was everything foreign and exotic. I read everything that I could find in the library on Austrians and Jews so that I could get some kind of picture of my grandfather. I imagined that he had the long beard and the earlocks and he kept his head covered. I even had a story for him: He was a Jewish chimney sweep who spent four years in Auschwitz and lived to tell the tale. He was a man of integrity and determination. After his incarceration, he had trekked across Europe, eating bones to stay alive, then he took a boat to get to the Statue of Liberty and the New World. I liked hearing the cackle in the Sacred Heart cafeteria die down when I started to tell about my grandfather. Each time I added to the story: That's why I'm so thin, I told them—it's in my blood. These girls had grandparents they ate with on holidays. My father's parents lived three states south. My mother's father lived an ocean away. I liked to see all those Catholic eyes widen with horror and curiosity, and finally, envy, because I had such a "different" background. I especially liked enunciating the word "Auschwitz," saying the "Au" the way a Canadian would say "out."

But my grandfather had never gone to Auschwitz. I only knew this about him: He gave up two floor factories to become a history professor at the University of Vienna. He was Catholic and married a beautiful French woman, my real grandmother, Rosette. In 1939, after the *Anschluss,* he fled Austria, followed by Rosette and my mother, leaving his mother behind. And that is what I did not understand. When I asked my mother how he could have left his mother behind in Nazi-occupied Austria, she didn't look at me when she answered, "I suppose he thought he knew what he was doing."

I was lying to myself: my thinness was not in my blood—at least not on my mother's side. I simply decided to stop eating to see what it was like. If I did have the kind of background I lied about and if I got used to being hungry, I told myself, maybe, just maybe I would be ready for the Nazis when they came the second time. And they would come again—my mother had convinced me of that much.

"What should *I* do?" I asked the day before my grandparents' arrival. I had just finished polishing all the silver and I wanted to do more to make us look good.

"Eat something," my mother said.

"Seriously," I said.

She straightened to a kneel and squinted, looking at the floor. "I *am* serious. You're too thin."

How would you know? I wanted to say. Sometimes when my mother looked at me, she looked right past me. Her mind was always somewhere else.

"Write them a welcome note," she finally said. "Tell them how excited you are that they're here." She looked at the floor, saw another scratch, and said, "Shit."

My mother had been teaching sewing in the inner city of Chicago for a year and she was learning how to swear. She said the words with relish. They were her new northern words. Her very own arsenal. "It's better in English," she explained to me once. "More satisfying."

"What do I call her?"

When my grandfather had written to my mother about his new marriage, my mother did not respond, nor did she send a wedding present. Finally, Isabella herself wrote a letter saying she certainly did not expect my mother to call her "Mutti." But they should be friends because the two of them loved the same man.

"That's assuming a lot," my mother had said after she read the letter out loud to my father and me. She pointed out all the misspellings, and said that Isabella's English was pathetic.

"Nice to see you have such an open mind," my father had said, and even my mother laughed at that.

"Dear Isabella," she said, reaching for a spot on the floor behind the sofa. "That's her name, isn't it?"

So she was to be Isabella, I thought, not Grossmama.

That night I got out the picture I kept in my closet of my great-grandmother. The day after she died, when my mother and I went to her room at the Lisner Home in Washington to collect what little she had, I had found pressed inside a book a picture someone had taken of her standing in front of a Henry Moore sculpture at a museum. She is smiling. There are three huge bronze men standing behind her. One is holding the Torah, another is reading from a book, while the third lifts his arms in praise. In her black coat and veil, my great-grandmother looks as though she is part of the procession.

"That is me!" my great-grandmother wrote on the back of the picture, and she signed it "Anna Engel de Bazsi."

I said her name out loud, then again to make it sound as though I said such a name every day all the time.

I kept this photo without showing my mother, and I hid it in a box in my closet.

Lying in bed, the covers up to my chin, I stared at my great-grandmother, then turned the picture around and looked at her name. "Engel," I said out loud. It was only one letter away from "Angel."

He was not the kind of grandfather you dream up for Christmas. He walked slowly through Customs, looking amused by the proceedings. In Miss Ott's anthropology class, I had read that in ancient Poland you kissed a person's elbow as a sign of respect. What did they do in Austria?

He was a portly, stooped-over man with gray, bushy eyebrows. He barely smiled when he saw us, but for a moment, when I saw his cheek brush against my mother's in a hit-and-miss kiss, I thought his eyes did.

It was obvious that he did not know how to greet me, nor did I know how to greet him. We ended up bowing to each other as though we were both from the Orient. My mother laughed. He looked at me, then he put out his hand.

As I shook hands with my grandfather for the first time, I thought, what a cool, dry, thick hand this is. He is not as scared as I am. It was quite clear that he was not to be my old, wrinkly *bubbe*. He was an elderly, distinguished Herr Professor. Even at the time, I remember thinking, so this is the way it will be: He will play his role and I will be the fumbling American student chasing after him, curious, but never as wise.

Isabella wore leather gloves and a fur hat. She was tall and thin and her head shook like Katharine Hepburn's. She wore thick glasses, and when she took them off to hug me, her pupils raced back and forth. She had written to me about her blind mother and said that she too sometimes had trouble with her eyes. She smelled wonderful. She was wearing, I was sure, the same French perfume my mother used when she went out at night, except I imagined Isabella wore it all the time—even on weekdays.

"My darlink Elizabeth," she said with finality. This was my new title: darlink Elizabeth. "I am so pleased to see you with my own eyes. You are such a thin, handsome young lady."

She had a better accent than my mother.

"She's too thin," my mother blurted out. "She doesn't look like herself."

He came with his memoirs, signed and dated, tucked under his arm. He gave the book to my mother as soon as he got in the car. I wanted to tell him we already had two copies—one he had sent a year ago which still lay under my parents' bed, the other from my great-grandmother's room—but my mother gave me the book and a look that said, Leave it be.

I opened the book, stared at the table of contents, and read the only words I recognized: Sigmund Freud and Ezra Pound. These were people I had only read about, but my grandfather had actually known them. I saw that there were chapters concerning both world wars and there was one chapter on Rosette, my real grandmother, and another on Isabella. I looked for my mother's name, but she was not in the table of contents. Nor was I.

"Elizabeth, you drive," my mother said, but I already had the keys. I looked at her—it wasn't like there was a choice. I always drove. I had earned my driver's license the day I turned sixteen—a day on which most teenagers rejoice with new freedom and a new life. Only I got my license not to drive myself, but to drive my mother, whose eyes were getting worse with distances.

My grandfather sat up front with me. My mother sat in the back with Isabella, her big fur hat brushing the car's ceiling. She sat straight, her legs crossed at the calf as though she were Greta Garbo posing for stills.

As I turned around to back out, I put my hand on the passenger seat the way the Adams School of Driving said to always do. My fingers grazed the back of my grandfather's neck—it was warm and oily—and I quickly pulled my hand away.

My mother scooted up between us. "Michael's at work, but he's so excited to see you." Her eyes were bright and shining with tears, but my grandfather didn't bother turning around to see.

"He must always be verking," I heard Isabella say from the back. "He is very American in this way."

When we got home, I carried their luggage and led them to their room. They looked around briefly, and then both of them noticed the photograph on the bureau at the same time and they started to speak in German.

Their German sounded stiff to my ears at first, but then the words connected together with the *unds* and the murmured *oehs* and it became like a song—a song I could hum along to, and maybe eventually learn the words.

The photo was a black-and-white of Rosette in profile taken at a studio in Vienna by a professional who had signed it in big, spidery script at the bottom right-hand corner. In the photo, Rosette sits in a skirt with an interesting Klimt-like pattern, her left hand extended, her elbow resting on her knee. The collar of her black, short-sleeved shirt is up and the only jewelry she is wearing is her wedding ring, which has two stones, not one. Her lips are parted. It looks as though she is talking to someone seated opposite her, or as if she is reaching for something or somebody.

My grandfather and Isabella were quiet for a while as they put the photo back on the bureau.

"You see," Isabella said. "She looked sick even then."

I had put out the good silver, and my grandfather stood at his place at the table for what seemed like a very long time, staring down at his place setting. I had read that in Europe, people set their tables with the fork tines down to show off the family seal, which was usually on the back of the handle. My grandfather picked up the fork to the left of his plate and stared at the Engel de Bazsi crest which I had polished to a shine.

"I remember this," my grandfather said, placing the fork crest-down on the table.

As we ate, my mother spoke German with my grandfather and Isabella spoke English with my father and I tried hard to follow both conversations.

"And what do you grow in your lovely greenhouse?" Isabella asked.

"Camellias."

"Chameleons?"

She had pressed the right button—my father went on and on about his camellias and the different kinds that grew in the South.

I heard my mother say *Grossmama* a few times. I liked when my mother spoke German, though she never called it that—it was Austrian. According to her, there was a big difference. "Go look in a history book," she would tell you, if you didn't know.

I had heard my mother speak German once before when she took me to a German delicatessen downtown in Chicago one year at Christmastime. She had a craving for a special German bread. She leaned over the glass counter that came up to her chin and ordered *Stollen*. She said the word *Stollen* slowly and with a great deal of satisfaction. What she said looked like fun to say, and I repeated the word to myself. She smiled as the woman behind the counter smiled and they began to speak. They were strangers who knew each other now because they spoke the same, different language.

At the dinner table, I heard my mother say "Lisner Home" while my father went on about his double blossoms.

Listening to my mother and grandfather talk together after such a long time, I wished I knew their language.

My mother had tried once to teach my father and me "Austrian." I was ten years old and we were still living in Mississippi. She sat us both down on the living-room sofa and had us ask each other our names and where we came from: *Wie heisst du? Woher bist du?* I answered: *Mein Name ist Elizabeth Huff. Ich komme aus Mississippi.* My father was terrible—his *woher* came out *vote hair* and his *ichs* were *itches.* The lessons lasted a week.

After we had moved and I started high school at Sacred Heart, I took French because that was the only language the nuns taught and my mother announced at the beginning of my northern education that I was not to take German. Rosette, my real grandmother, was French, after all. Yet even though my mother constantly reminded me that the language was in my blood, when it came test time, I never managed to conjure up those verb tenses that supposedly coursed through my veins.

Listening to my mother and her father speaking German thrilled me. I wanted to celebrate Yom Kippur. I wanted to run and read the Haggadah and comment on traditional verse. I wanted to raise my glass up four times right then and there at the dinner table and celebrate the exodus from Egypt. Instead, I just sat there, imagining that the pair of overalls I wore was really a dirndl.

There was an odd silence that came upon the dinner table all at once. My mother stared at her father as he wiped his mouth slowly with a white linen napkin.

"Well?" she said. "She *was* your mother. But I suppose you wanted her to die a long time ago. You could have been there. And now you want me to tell you what she said? What she did? What I found?"

"Honey," my father started.

"I *did* find a few bank receipts. You know about those, though. You managed to get to those when you visited the last time."

"Genevieve. It's the first night and I am tired. Must you?"

I had never heard anyone call my mother by her real name. It was always just Jenny.

"Elizabeth was there," my mother said.

With some difficulty, my grandfather repeated my name, looked at me, and after a moment, so did my father, my mother, and Isabella. For the first time I noticed that my grandfather's eyes were the same blue as my great-grandmother's.

My grandfather looked back down at his plate of lamb stew. I could tell Isabella now felt sorry for me—the "child" caught in a bitter family quarrel. But I was used to the way my mother fought.

"And what is your favorite subject in school, Elizabeth?" he asked, looking up from his plate.

"Anthropology," I said. It wasn't a lie. It was a near truth. "The study of man." I was sixteen years old and I had just learned the definition of anthropology and I decided that I wanted to be Margaret Mead.

"My mother loved anthropology," my mother said. She had never told me this. She never spoke of her mother. I looked at Isabella, feeling sorrier for her: she had to compete with the legend of Rosette.

"You never met Rosette," my grandfather said, finally looking up from his food. It was not a question but a statement, as though our not meeting had been my fault. I had not made the correct travel arrangements. I was not born at the right time.

"No," I said, mad at him, hating him, wishing I could do better, wishing I could have pleased him.

I sipped only the broth from the stew, and seeing the spoon, I noticed that I had missed a spot—the handle was still tarnished around the edges. I thought of all the beautiful things my mother had grown up with forty-three years ago, things that my grandfather was probably still accustomed to. I thought of all the French china and cut glass they had probably been surrounded by—the orientals, the antiques and rose prints. I thought of the clothes and dolls and I imagined what their house, the Hofzeile, must have been like, surrounded by all those fruit trees and garden statues. I stared down at the tarnished silver spoon in my stew and saw my father pouring more wine and thought of all that my mother had lost during the war—all of which my father would probably spend a lifetime trying to replace.

"I never met the great Rosette either, Elizabeth, but the first week we were married, your grandfather did say the kindest thing." Isabella took control of the moment and my father looked visibly relieved. "He was writing in his study and I asked if he needed something—some cake, perhaps—and I saw that he was looking at a photograph of Rosette at his desk. 'You know,' he said to me, 'I think you would have liked one another.' That I think is the nicest thing he could have said." Isabella's eyes were wet and her pupils had slowed down.

My mother began clearing the table. I half expected her to say, Like hell she would.

"Anthropology is not the study of man so much as it is the study of who and where we come from," my grandfather said. I wondered if he had heard Isabella's story, or if he had already heard it before and was bored. He wiped his mouth with his napkin, pushed his chair back, and said, "So."

My mother did not ask me to bring down my guitar that night after dinner, nor did I offer. It was hokey, but sometimes I played for my parents' friends after dinner, and once I started playing, they almost always ended up singing along to "Bojangles" or "Freight Train." I would look up sometimes, in between verses, and catch my mother and father smiling at each other.

My mother made tea while Isabella disappeared and came back with three small boxes wrapped in white tissue paper, tied with black ribbons. She gave my father the first, bigger box, which he unwrapped quickly. He loved presents.

"Oh wow," he said. In the palm of his hand was a porcelain horse standing on its hind legs.

"It's a Lipizzaner," my mother said. I wanted her to say the word again for me slowly.

"Lipizzaners are beautiful white stallions. They are called Lipizzaner because the Austrian stud farm used to be located at Lipizza, outside Trieste, in Italy," Isabella explained to me and my father.

"They know that," my mother said, but my father and I didn't know anything about the Lipizzaner horses or the Spanish Riding School nor did I know why these horses would be in Vienna and not in Italy. My mother sometimes thought that because I was her daughter and my father was her husband, we knew what she knew.

"Careful," my mother said as my father stood it first on the piano, then finally on the glass coffee table.

"They can dance a *pas de deux* better than your grandfather," Isabella said. "Such noble creatures danced to Mozart for royalty under chandeliers."

"But now there's no royalty left in Vienna to dance for," my mother said, the back of her hand to her forehead—playing at dramatic. "They all ran away."

"Come, come, now," my grandfather said, shaking his head at my mother as though she were a schoolgirl. She brought her hand down and, instead of swearing, she said, "Poo."

I stared at the statue on the table, wondering if royalty were the same people as nobility.

"And now I have a present for you, Elizabeth darlink, and you too, Genevieve." My mother didn't say anything more as Isabella gave us the two remaining boxes. Under the tissue paper, there were gray suede boxes and inside, rings.

Mine had a green stone. It was too small for my ring finger and even though it was too big for my pinky, I left it there. It was from Vienna and it was to be my ring. I held out my hand for my father to see.

"Oh stop it, Elizabeth. You don't understand anything."

"Well, explain it to me. Tell me."

She looked at me and her mouth opened, but nothing came out. She slid the book across the table toward me.

"Look it up," she said, getting up, leaving the room.

That day, the four of us drove into the city. My mother was quiet, and all my grandfather said from the front seat was, "So. Da Loop," when we passed through the Chicago Loop.

When we got to the Art Institute, Isabella taught me how to go through a museum. As soon as you walk into a room, she said, pick one painting that strikes you and only study that one painting. Then go to the next room—this way your eyes don't consume too much beauty all at once and your legs won't cramp.

I could feel her watching me study the paintings and I tried to make it worth her while—I tried to look pretty and intelligent in front of all that canvas and paint. Standing in front of a Seurat, I even took her hand, but only caught the cool, smooth feel of a leather glove. I felt inadequate. I wished I were as tall and long-legged and thin as she was. I wished I could get away with wearing leather gloves and a big fur hat indoors. I wished I had an accent. I wished I was Viennese.

In the afternoon, we stopped off at Holy Family. My mother wanted to drop off canned ham and a fruit basket for a family who would pick them up from the rectory where she did volunteer work.

We parked near the playground, which was really a fenced-in parking lot. There were three black girls about my age on the sidewalk getting ready to climb over the fence.

"Hey, Miss Huff," they shouted to my mother as we all piled out of the car. They wore aprons made of sequins and netting which were tied with black satin ribbons over their winter coats. I recognized the aprons—my mother had come up with the sewing project, thinking this would add glamour to their lives.

My mother waved, looking happier than I'd seen her all day.

Inside, she put the ham and the fruit basket on the receptionist's desk and introduced us all to Father Hanrahan, who proceeded to show us the Christmas cards he had painted—nude black women he called Madonnas. He had a small collection of primitive art in his office, and on each of the wooden statues, the artists had bothered to decorate the navels and sculpt the kneecaps. Isabella wanted to know where he had gotten each piece, but I couldn't keep my eyes off one. It was a pregnant woman and at the tip of her extended stomach, inside her navel, was a mirror. I could see myself in this woman's belly—her womb.

"This one is something, isn't it?" Father Hanrahan said, picking up the statue of the pregnant woman. My mother grimaced noticeably with disapproval, and he laughed and put the figure down, offering us peanut butter and jelly sandwiches. My mother said we had to get going.

"Let me show you how the inside of the church is coming along," he said, leading us to the large brick church outside.

It was one of the oldest churches in Chicago and it was falling down. The plaster was crumbling and the beams were rotted out. Father Hanrahan explained all the structural problems he and his contractors were dealing with.

"We had this problem in our house," my grandfather said. His thick eyebrows hid his eyes as he thought. "My father was always concerned about the beams. He would lay awake at night in his bed, thinking, Will they hold? Will our house collapse? He feared that he would not be able to come up with the money for repairs if the roof did cave in. The fear of rotting beams stayed with my father even in his last hours."

No one knew what to say, so we looked up, past the crucifix, at the beams that threatened to give way.

"Well, the roof didn't cave in," my mother said. She nearly spat the words out. "You left it and us. Then Hitler bombed it."

"Not before we sold it," my grandfather said. It was as though he had known what she was going to say. "Get your facts straight, Genevieve. Precision. Accuracy. We sold it first, remember? For the value of two boxcar loads of softwood."

"Not we. You. You made the decisions then. You made the noble move to sell it. *You* sold it to Goering."

"To Hermann Goering's *nephew*."

"Okay. You sold our home to the nephew of the founder of the Gestapo, then you left us behind to find our own way out, *then* Hitler bombed it. Precise enough, or shall I run through a few more facts?"

Isabella sighed and headed for the candles. I stayed near my mother. I had never heard her talk like this before. And it was getting good—my grandfather had sold his beloved house for two boxcar loads of softwood. But what was "soft" wood?

"Why did Grandfather leave before you?" My voice sounded eerie echoing in the church.

My mother didn't even hesitate. Still looking at her father, she said, "Because the oldest male of the household is always in the greatest danger." It was as though she were reciting something or quoting somebody. "For God's sake, Elizabeth. Figure it out. Your grandfather was born Jewish." She didn't look at me when she said this. She stared at her father.

It felt as though my mother had just said one of her swear words, and it was still echoing in the church.

"I was born with the Lord Jesus Christ in my heart," my grandfather said first to me, then to Father Hanrahan.

We could hear Isabella plunk a coin in the box as she lit a candle. Then she knelt. She knelt straight, her gloved hands pressed together.

She prayed the old-fashioned way—hands together, fingers up, the way I had learned to pray at St. Patrick's in Mississippi. She pressed her palms together hard too, as though her hands were a garlic press.

"Yes," Father Hanrahan said. I could feel his fingertips on my back as he led us out. "Shall we?"

After my grandfather wrote two volumes of history on the Vatican, my mother boasted that he was at the center of Catholic intelligentsia. I wondered what he thought of this priest and this church. Watching him dip his fingers in the holy water to cross himself, I wondered if he felt awkward—a man born Jewish in Vienna, Austria, standing in a Catholic church in Chicago, Illinois. I wondered if he ever felt as though he was lying.

I skipped the holy water and crossed my arms, feeling for my rib cage. My mother had once told me that every family has its weakness—that theirs, ours, was eyesight. I thought of everything I had said to my classmates about my grandfather. It was both frightening and exciting that part of a lie I had told turned out to be true. I wondered if in addition to our weak eyes, our other family weakness was dishonesty.

Outside, on the sidewalk, Isabella joined us and we all waved good-bye to Father Hanrahan.

Just as my mother got in the car, she slipped on the ice and almost fell. She grabbed on to the car door handle and said, "Mother Fuck."

I had heard my mother say this before, but my grandfather and Isabella had not. They were visibly shocked.

"Genevieve," my grandfather said. "The child. Remember the child."

It was the first time all day that I felt he noticed me.

"The child?" my mother yelled. "What would you know about any child? And what in God's name do you know about memory? I am your only child and you mention me once in your whole mother-fucking life story. *Once.*"

Isabella looked nervous, and, out here, regal and a little ridiculous with her height and her fur and her long black leather gloves.

"Ah," my grandfather said. "So. This would explain your mood."

"No wonder your mother threatened to disown you."

"Genevieve!" Isabella said. She looked at me and I waited for my mother to explain this new business about my great-grandmother disowning my grandfather, but she didn't explain anything. It was as though she and her father had some silent code. They both only told so much or maybe there wasn't any more to tell. All I knew was that it was up to me to fill in the blanks.

"These are *my* memoirs," my grandfather said. It was the first evidence I had seen that my grandfather could get flustered. He paused and turned around to look at the three black girls playing basketball in their sequined aprons. "You don't like them? Go write your own."

"Maybe I will," my mother said, getting into the car. "And if I do, I'll include *all* the facts, and maybe, just maybe, *you* won't come out the hero. Born with the Lord Jesus in your heart. What a load of crap." She slammed the door. My mother never slammed doors.

The girls quit shooting hoops to wave good-bye to my mother as we drove off. I wondered if they had been the ones who taught my mother to swear. My mother loved coming down here to teach these girls to sew and it dawned on me right then why: they were products of a war-torn inner city and so was she. I had never lived during catastrophe—not even near the edges of it—and despite all my efforts, despite my hunger strike, I would always be the spectator, not a victim. This made me sad and a bit resentful.

On the way home, my stomach growled. From the backseat, Isabella suggested we think of happy things, but her "happy" came out "hoppy" and I heard my mother whisper, "Shit."

———

During their last days with us, my grandfather read and wrote in the study. My mother was overly polite.

"Can I get you more tea?" she would ask.

"*Nein, danke schön.*"

They went on like that—my mother speaking in cool English, her left eyebrow always raised, my grandfather answering in what sounded like hoity-toity German. My father told me to stay out of it.

"There's a lot you don't know," he said, and it made me even madder because it sounded as though my mother had quietly filled him in.

Isabella and I took walks up and down our street, passing the big new houses and the smaller, older ones. I covered my mouth with my scarf and listened to stories about the Engel de Bazsis. She told me I had a cousin—or was he a kind of uncle?—who made it his life's ambition to prove Einstein's theories incorrect. He wrote to Einstein once a week, explaining his own theories.

"He could not bear to believe that everything is dependent on the existence of something else," Isabella said.

Then he was captured by the Nazis and put into Dachau. He survived the camps, but when he got out he did not write to Einstein anymore and he stopped trying to prove what was right or wrong about relativity.

We had *Wiener Schnitzel* the last night. Isabella taught me how to pound and bread the veal and she told me to always eat cucumbers with it.

"Why?" I asked.

"Because that's the Viennese way," she said, laughing and pulling me to her side. "*Und,* you *are* your grandfather's granddaughter."

This to me was the best and worst thing she could have said.

After dinner, we had tea in the living room.

"Get your guitar," my father said. He was tired of all the German—singing was as good an excuse as any to speak English.

I played and we both sang "Bojangles" and everything else I was learning in my guitar class that year. I did not have much of a voice, my father liked to remind me. I concentrated instead on the notes and what my fingers were doing.

Then I played "Leaving on a Jet Plane" without even thinking. Out of the corner of my eye, I saw my mother leave the room during the second verse, and while I sang the chorus, I heard the water in the kitchen go on. I imagined my mother standing at the sink, rinsing her silver.

I wanted to look at my grandfather but I didn't dare. I kept thinking, why doesn't he go with my mother out to the greenhouse or into the kitchen—fine places to talk about what they needed to talk about, Vienna, the great Rosette, or my great-grandmother?

I didn't stop because I didn't think any of us could bear the silence. It was a song I played well. I liked the mournful minor notes and all that sliding from A minor to G minor made my strings squeak the way James Taylor's strings did.

My mother came back on the last verse, and as I played and sang alone, it was the first time I felt them all listening. For a moment, I felt as though I was talking to my grandfather for the first time.

Isabella came to tuck me in that night. I think she liked thinking that I was younger than sixteen. She had married late and never had children.

"How did you meet Grandfather?" I could tell by the way Isabella laughed and blushed that she had been waiting for someone to ask her this all along.

"It was at a party," she began. Her "party" came out "potty."

Their meeting was straight out of a Spencer Tracy/Katharine Hepburn movie, but flipped around: she thought he was a snob. He found her frivolous.

"I was still calling him *Sie* when he did propose. In German you use *Sie* for 'you' when you are still being formal. We were sitting at a table at

Café Sacher. He said, 'Fräulein, I would like very much to marry you.' And I did say, 'But Herr Professor, have you asked your daughter?' "

Isabella's pupils were racing back and forth. For the first time, I wondered if she was telling the truth.

"You see, you come from a very important family, my darlink. Your grandfather and your mother used to live in a grand, grand house."

"And Rosette."

"Yes, Rosette too. It was called the Hofzeile, which means the little palace, but it wasn't so very little. It was big. Very big. Surely your mother has told you."

"You tell me," I said. My mother had only said the word *Hofzeile* once and that had been last Christmas.

Isabella smiled. "It was built for the Crown Prince of Austria, but he didn't want it because he claimed he could smell the fumes from a fertilizer factory in Döbling."

"It smelled?"

"No, it did not smell after all, and so your great-great-grandfather did buy it, and the Engel de Bazsis became a great, important family."

"Because of the house?"

"Because they were smart and industrious. So you see, it mattered to me what your mother thought," she went on. "I told your grandfather that I would not marry him until he asked his daughter, but then she never did respond." Isabella shook her head. "It's as though she does not care."

"She cares." I didn't like that we were talking about my mother while she was in the next room.

"I am afraid I do not understand your mother, Elizabeth darlink. Your grandfather wishes to know how it was when your great-grandmother—his Mutti—did die, and your mother vill not tell him. Vhy is dat, Elizabeth? Vhy do you think that is?" Her accent was getting thicker as she grew angrier.

Vhy. I did not know why. Maybe my mother was jealous of Isabella.

Maybe she felt he did not deserve to know, since he had not gone to
Washington himself, and keeping the details from him was her way of
paying him back. Or maybe he was keeping something from her and she
was using this as bait. My mother sometimes worked like that.

"Why is it so important for Grandfather to know?"

Isabella sighed and gave me a look that said, Oh you silly girl.

"Perhaps it is because he is Viennese," she began. "The week before
Rosette did die, he had her photographed in her hospital room. Horrible
pictures of a dying woman trying to smile for the camera. He made
postcards out of each picture and carried them around with him for
weeks, no, it was months. When I did meet him, I did gather up all these
pictures and I did destroy them. It was the only way, you see. So I think
that the only way for your grandfather to say good-bye to his mother is
to hear about how she died. How it was. Maybe even he will not feel so
badly about not being there."

Isabella's head kept time with her pupils, which were rushing back
and forth. She had a story for everything, and looking at her, I realized
that, like me, she was starving for more stories, more myths—anything
about this family she had married into. I imagined that this was what
she had to offer her husband—my grandfather. She could not talk about
books, history, or university work, but she could collect family stories,
put them on a platter, serve them up for tea. And if she did not have
these stories, she would—just as I would—make them up.

I went to my closet, reached up, and got down the box with the picture of my great-grandmother.

I put the picture in Isabella's hands and climbed back into bed,
pulling the covers up to my chin. Then I closed my eyes and thought. I
tried to remember the trip my mother and I took to Washington. It had
been my first plane ride, but I could not remember how I got from our
house to the airport to the plane to the Lisner Home. I did remember
my great-grandmother laid out naked in her bed, though, and how she

remembered me and said my name out loud when she woke up for the first and last time that spring.

I had tried telling only one other person about my great-grandmother's death—Sister Beatrice, who made me stop when I got to the part with the tubes. But that night I told Isabella how it was when my great-grandmother died exactly as I remembered it. I told her about the tubes my great-grandmother pulled out and the sheets she pushed away. I told her about the man in the lobby—the one I saw go into her room alone and who came out, an hour later, folding up a length of wine-colored cloth fringed and stitched with gold thread.

"But this was your great-grossmama's rabbi," Isabella said. I was staring at the back of the photograph—at the word "Engel"—and then, all at once, some of the pieces began to slide into place.

In Mississippi, my mother once made me promise never to tell anyone her maiden name. "It will happen all over again," she said when I asked why. "My name is a dead giveaway." She was referring to the Engel, but I was too young then to understand what she meant or to even ask why. She kept her father's book—the one which had been on my great-grandmother's nightstand—on a shelf below her spiritual books in a bookcase in the study, behind the sofa. The other volume she kept under her bed. According to my mother, what her father wrote was nobody's business. But I knew now my mother wasn't hiding the book; she was hiding her old name.

I looked at the picture of my great-grandmother again. I missed her. I missed my great-grandmother. I missed writing to her and thinking about what I would say when I visited her every spring. I missed the connection she provided me to my mother's past.

All at once I could see my great-grandmother lying naked in her bed at the Lisner Home in Washington, D.C. I was holding her all over again—but this time I floated somewhere above the scene, and looked down at an old dying woman and a young girl. I noticed something pass between the two. I tried to get a closer look. The girl was pressing so close, so close it seemed that the old woman might snap. Then the old woman opened her eyes and the young girl took in the blue of them and listened to the sound of her name: "Elizabeth," the old woman whispered. "Remember."

Just then my great-grandmother's blue eyes, the thick heavy way she whispered my name and the word "Remember," felt solid and dark purple inside me. This was it, I thought. This was what my great-grandmother left me with—a heritage—and it was up to me to find it so that I could remember it and restore it.

Staring down at the picture of my great-grandmother that night with Isabella in my room, I convinced myself to be Jewish. I knew very little about Judaism, but night after night, as I stared at my great-grandmother standing in front of the statues of three rabbis, something changed; a tie was established. "I am Jewish," I said to myself over and over, whatever this meant. At the time I did not feel as though I was betraying my mother.

"You will come to Vienna and you will learn German and you will read your grandfather's books," Isabella said, tucking the sheets and blankets under my mattress so that they stretched tight over me. For a moment I imagined myself a little Hasidic scholar in the basement of a synagogue studying the Torah, my yarmulke in place. Isabella had tears in her eyes. She cries prettily, I thought. "You are a very brave little girl." And as she said this I realized that this was precisely what I had been waiting for somebody to tell me, and it was perhaps why I told her how my great-grandmother died. It was then that I felt I had shared a secret I shouldn't have.

The next morning, as my father loaded up the car, I snapped a picture of Isabella. She was wearing the fur hat and I photographed her barely smiling, holding a purse that hung from her forearm. In the background was the sturdy roof of our house.

In the car on the way to O'Hare, I sat in the backseat, between my mother and Isabella, while my father drove and talked about Mississippi and moving north. He called the move *his* emigration.

I thought of all I still had left to ask my grandfather. If he was such a great Herr Professor of history, why hadn't he seen the war coming? How could he have left his mother behind in Nazi-occupied Austria when he fled, followed by Rosette and my mother? And how could he go back to a place that was so tainted with bad?

"You write me such clever things," Isabella said. "You told me once that you wished you were a cow. 'I want to be soft and furry and sit in the mud.' That is what you did say. *Und* now you will write to me more." I could feel my mother stiffen. "You will tell me all that you are doing and thinking. You will tell me all about your noble self."

I nodded, all seriousness. She was giving me a mission. I wanted her to go on and tell me more of what I needed to do.

I considered the letters I would write to Isabella. I would tell her how it was in my life here in the North. I would write good, grammatical English, using words she would understand. I would tell her what my father and I grew in the greenhouse, the shade of green I wanted to paint my room, and, hoping she was reading my letters out loud to my grandfather, I would tell her which anthropologists I was reading. I imagined her sitting at an antique desk in their apartment in Vienna, laughing as she read my letters, then calling for my grandfather.

"Theodor," she would shout. "Come listen to what your clever granddaughter did write."

For a while then they would waylay thoughts of headaches, history, and death, and set their minds on me.

At the international terminal, Isabella had tears in her eyes as she hugged us all—even my mother—to say good-bye. She was so dramatic, I felt as though I was in a movie.

"Can you say good-bye to your grandfather?" my mother said.

I wasn't sure how to go about it. He was a big, round man with a heavy overcoat. I approached him, but his stomach was in the way. He bent down. I put my hands on his shoulders. But then he did something wonderful—he led me through my first "European kiss." We kissed each other's cheeks once, then swung round to the other, then swung round a third time to finish off. I smiled big. I thought about the way my grandfather in Mississippi taught me how to stick a cricket onto a fishing hook—through the eye so it would keep on wiggling underwater. And now I knew a European kiss. I wondered what else this new grandfather standing before me could have taught me.

When a priest is ordained, a bishop or an archbishop puts his hands on the priest's head. Both hands. It's an important moment. Sister Beatrice told me about it once. This is what my grandfather did with me after he kissed me. He put one, then both of his hands on top of my head and then he said my name.

He could not make the "th" sound in Elizabeth and he extended his "f's" in Huff longer than what was required.

"I am glad that my mother knew you," he said.

It took me a minute to realize he was talking about my great-grandmother. My mind had been on the weight of his hands on my skull.

"Why *did* you leave my great-grandmother behind?"

For a moment I thought he was going to respond, then I felt my mother's hand on my shoulder.

"Elizabeth!" she said. "What *are* you thinking?"

It was all right for my mother to talk back to her father, but it wasn't all right for me.

"She stayed in Vienna for the same reason I returned," my grandfather said. "It was our homeland."

"Humph," I heard my mother mumble.

"Do you ever miss the United States?" I asked.

After a beat, he smiled and said, "Sometimes. Sometimes I think of the faces of those people who read late at night in the New York Public Library. They were eccentric people. A little crazy, perhaps, but they did love their books and they read all night."

That's what he missed, I thought, as I watched him hug and kiss my mother, then walk away. The faces of strangers. It was a fact hard to digest. He wasn't thinking of us at all.

On the way back, I stared out the window of the car in the backseat. The sky was turning a flat gray and I wondered, if I lived to be a hundred and five like my great-grandmother, would I remember any of this? I saw a plastic Santa lit up on somebody's balcony—its arm lifted as though he were waving at me. This is how I'll remember this day—the day my grandfather left, I thought. I'll remember a plastic Santa waving at me.

There I was, his grandchild with a name he could barely pronounce, staring out at all this flat, midwestern land, thinking in a language he didn't even know when he was my age. His Hofzeile and my great-grandmother seemed far, far away just then. Further even than Mississippi. More than anything, I wished I knew German then—a language I associated with understanding secrets.

"He's just the same," I heard my mother say. "Only now he looks old." She sounded mad and tired—the way her voice sometimes sounded when there wasn't any time left in the day.

I kicked the car door, hoping my shoe would leave a scratch. I wanted to mark this moment and this day, and I swore to myself then and there that I would do what I had to do to get back what my mother seemed hell-bent on getting rid of—her father, her family, her Europeanness, her Jewishness.

It was Sunday and that evening my mother and I went to a late mass. We both couldn't help but notice that Sister McFadden, who was most always in mean spirits, was especially kind to us, holding our hands an extra beat at the handshake of peace. I crept away after I heard her say to my mother, "Elizabeth has told us about your father and," she hesitated, "and your history."

That night, my mother came into my room. I was in bed, hiding as it were. She flicked on the light and stood at the doorway for what seemed like a long, long time.

"How dare you," she said, in a cool, clear voice. "How dare you sabotage everything we've worked for." I didn't know who the "we" was. My mother and her family? My mother and my father? Did her "we" include me? "I won't have that," she said finally and she left.

After she closed the door, I reached under my bed and got out my green ring, which I kept now with the picture of my great-grandmother in the box. Then I got out a sheet of paper. I sat down at my desk and wrote down the date the way my great-grandmother always wrote it— number of the day first, period, then the month and the year. I wrote "Dear Isabella," then I stared down at the ring. I slipped it on my finger, then off. Inside there were tiny words engraved like hieroglyphics into the gold. German words which I did not understand.

Even though I had never known my real grandmother, Rosette, I suddenly missed her. My mother told me that Rosette had seen me once, when I was a baby. She had come to Mississippi to help my mother and to meet me. Somewhere out in the greenhouse, maybe, I still had the plate she sent me with a rooster painted in the middle crowing out red letters that spelled *guten Morgen*. And she sent me dresses made of scratchy, Austrian wool—dresses too heavy to wear in Mississippi. By the time we had moved to a more suitable climate for them, they were too small.

I could hear my mother in the kitchen. It sounded as though she might be crying. I thought I heard her saying Isabella's name.

I put the ring back on and stared down at what I had written. To fall in love with Isabella was to betray my mother. I was not only required to hate Germans—all Germans—but anyone who chose to stay behind during the years of the Nazi occupation was to be feared, loathed, and otherwise avoided.

I erased "Isabella."

"Dear Grossmama," I started.

PART III

Attachments

GENEVIEVE

WHEN MY FATHER CAME BACK FROM ROME, IT WAS
still snowing and we had a big feast even though my mother looked
worried and tired. He talked a great deal that evening about his research
at the Vatican. He showed us a lump of papers with gold seals—all very
official, he said. All very important for his book.

Grossmama was quiet all during the meal. I imagined if she didn't
like to eat as much as she did, she would not have been there. Afterwards, she said she wanted to see her son, her flesh and blood, in the
library. She used these terms.

This was the first night I had ever heard my grandmother raise her
voice. "Run," I heard through the closed library doors. "Go on. Flee. But
you are not your father's son. *He* would never leave. You must not belong
to me."

My mother made me go to my room. She told me to play some
music.

My father did not write about this evening in his memoirs. Nor did
he say how or why exactly he had received clearance from the finance
commission and why we had not. He did say, however, that it was difficult for him to leave. In a flowery, sentimental passage he wrote that

when he left, he turned around and looked at it, looked at the house, the Hofzeile, one last time. He did not say that he came into my room, kissed me good-bye before the sun was up, and in the hall, outside my door, whispered to my mother, "Get to Geneva. Just get to Geneva." He did not say that his mother said she never wanted to see him again. But I suppose none of this really matters after all.

When I woke up the next morning, my father was gone.

Yes. It is true that my father got out first, and when Rudi found out, he was beside himself. At the time, I thought he was upset because my father hadn't thought to say good-bye to him, but now I realize it was beyond Rudi's comprehension that this man—my father—who had married his beloved sister had thought to save himself before his own wife or his daughter or even his mother.

"The person in danger is the male head of the family," I heard my mother say to Rudi when they thought they were alone. It was a phrase she would use later with me. Rudi could only shake his head.

Rudi disappeared for a week. My mother was terribly worried. When he turned up again, he was thinner, pale, and tired. He wore the same suit he had left in. Was it the only thing he had left? I didn't know it at the time, but he too was working on getting us out—standing in lines, paying off officials so that we all had the right documents. I don't know why, how, or when Rudi decided to take this all on himself. Why not my father?

The day he came back to the Hofzeile, Rudi shut all the doors and poured himself something from the bar. He shook his head and whispered something to my mother. Something—one of the papers—hadn't come in yet. There was more waiting and it seemed to be getting late. Did I hear him say too late? That evening Rudi sat in the sitting room with my mother, and he spoke quietly to her, gently bringing her into the situation.

The following week Rudi said that it was time our musical trio met for one last time. I had no idea what he meant, but he assembled Inge and me in the concert room at the Hofzeile and we played. Inge had become quite an accomplished violinist. I think she had simply shut out everything else and turned wholeheartedly to music. It is what I should have done. I simply plodded along making too many mistakes, but that afternoon Rudi didn't seem to mind or notice. Perhaps he didn't care. Perhaps Rudi did not hear any music that day, Perhaps he just wanted to go through the motions of creating chords, pressing his fingers down on some strings and just playing. I feel that way sometimes, don't you?

It was to be the last time the three of us would play together, but how was I to know that then?

After Inge and I had played, Rudi played on. The sounds he coaxed from his viola d'amore that afternoon were like nothing we had heard before, and when he lifted his bow, you could hear that last chord echo through the halls of our house. I can hear it now. He smiled as he carefully lay his instrument down in the purple-lined case. He shut the case, picked it up by the handle, then, without a word, without the usual ceremony one thinks every Viennese goes through, Uncle Rudi gave his viola d'amore to Inge.

"It's yours now," he said, and he kissed her first on one cheek then on the other. She looked at him and then at the case. Her mouth stayed open but nothing—not a sound emerged. Rudi nodded to Inge, then to me, then he turned and left the room.

There's no reason to wonder why Rudi gave his viola d'amore to Inge. Perhaps he wanted it out of his sight so that he wouldn't be tempted to pawn it. He had no children. Perhaps he had the urge that is in all of us to leave something—his own inheritance of music—behind to someone he knew would appreciate it more than anyone else. Or perhaps he trusted Inge. Perhaps he gave it to her for safekeeping—knowing that she felt as deeply as he about that instrument.

In the end, Rudi would pawn everything he had. Later, after we left, he stayed on with Grossmama. He saw to it that she got out. Then he was left alone, without a home, without his family, without his music.

They say when you have spots on your chest, you've got the measles. I had spots all over me. And I was glad, no, relieved to be sick. I decided that this was God's way of punishing me for telling my teacher about my parents and Gentz.

It was a warm night in April and my mother stayed with me in my room, waiting for my fever to die down. She was reading me a story so that I wouldn't think about all the school I had missed.

"Why doesn't anyone want to be around me?" I wanted to know.

"Red measles are considered very dangerous and nobody wants to catch them."

"Why don't you catch them?"

"Because I've had them and so has your Grossmama."

She read on for a bit, and, then, all at once, in the middle of a sentence, she put the book down and looked out the window. She got up, closed the doors to my room, and she told me to get out of bed. Carefully, but quickly.

I had already missed a week of school, so my teacher would not suspect. It was perfect, my mother explained. Nobody would bother to check our papers carefully because I looked awful and so terribly contagious. Up until that night nobody ever explained anything to me. It was as though they figured I understood. This was the first time my mother talked to me as her partner—she actually told me the plan. Perhaps it was because Rudi had told her his plan.

I got out of bed, and even though the night was warm and I was sweating with fever, she put me into my blue winter coat.

Cook and Agnes had already retired to their rooms—they did so every night after dinner. Grossmama had also gone to her apartments, but her light was still on.

She was in bed, her gray hair coiled up into a bun. Her stamp book was open in front of her on a little table. My mother whispered to her the plan with confidence. She had already decided: this is the way we're going to do it, now let's go.

But Grossmama shook her head. "No," she said. "This is my home."

"Don't be ridiculous," my mother said. "We can't have this argument again. Not here. Not now."

But Grossmama would not leave with us. She would not leave. How many times can I think it? How many times can I tell it? She would not leave. She felt her home was in Vienna and that was where her family was and she was going to stay. Years later, I realized that she had thought this through. Really. I think she figured that if the house was occupied, people were much less suspicious. They would not come after us.

But my Grossmama was not able to stay at Hofzeile 12 much longer after that. She had not known that my father had already sold the house to the nephew of Hermann Goering. My father was, most likely, too ashamed to tell his mother that he had sold the house his father and the father before him had been so proud to own.

Rudi got her out. He had a coterie of friends who were active in volunteer work and charities. One of these friends was involved with an orphanage in Czechoslovakia. Rudi devised a plan with this friend of his: Somebody from the orphanage would arrange for an orphan girl to come get Grossmama and escort her out of Austria.

They left in a wagon of hay. My Grossmama only wrote me the details in letters she sent to me many years later from the Lisner Home. She was so thankful to Rudi, but all during the ride she admitted that she wished the wagon was headed for France, where there was good food and hiking. But Rudi had decided that it was not wise for her to flee to France—it would be the first place the Germans would have looked—she must go deep, deep into Czechoslovakia. Who would think of looking there?

Grossmama and the orphan hid under hay for a three-day journey in this peasant's cart. It was a long contraption, she told me, with four high wheels, pulled by a single horse. The bottom was made of three wide boards. She fit the length of one.

She stayed hiding in a farmhouse in Czechoslovakia from 1940 to 1944.

The evening my mother and I left her, Grossmama promised she would see me again. She said that she knew I would be back, because, like Odysseus, I would have to come back home. I said good-bye, but I was wearing that damned dark blue coat and I couldn't hug her properly. I remember watching my Grossmama closing the door to her rooms, and seeing the sliver of light that leaked through from underneath.

I thought of her going back to her table and sitting down in front of her big red stamp book. She would open it, calmly, and then she would proceed meticulously to arrange and organize all the stamps she had in front of her. It is what anybody would have done just then. It was really all there was to do. Lodge Germany into its correct slot. Carefully place Hungary with its torn edges right up next to a nearly transparent Austria. Alone in her room that night, bent over her stamps and dishes of water, her open book filled with empty onion skin binders, my Grossmama, with her tweezers, was putting things in order, setting the world right again.

We left by taxi. I brought my big doll with me. I said that I would not emigrate without her, and that night, I remember thinking: I am going to be alone now. Inge will not be wherever we are going. I am going to need a playmate. So I brought the biggest doll I could find, thinking if I grow maybe she will still be big enough.

I don't think my mother looked back. She was very conscious of appearances, and later I realized that she knew then that there was always the possibility that the cab driver was a Nazi or a spy.

I remember the tip of her nose just barely touched the net that fell down from her hat and over her face. She wore one of those fox fur scarves and good Italian shoes.

I am sure that she knew that as we were driving away from our home at Hofzeile 12 we were driving away from everything. She had to have known. She changed after that night and everything between us changed.

Years later, when she got sick, she told me, "Don't go back. It will depress you." Only now, as I write this, do I realize she must have gone back and it must have depressed her—why else would she have warned me? This is the woman who held on to her husband's hand and walked forward in gunfire.

She didn't say anything. She didn't even turn to face me when she took my hand, and with her gloved hand, she gave me a key. I looked at her. In her hand was another key, and I recognized it to be the key to Rudi's apartment in Geneva. She opened her purse and dropped that in. Then she stared straight ahead. I looked at the key she had given me, then without a word, I put it deep inside the pocket of my doll's coat.

I still have that key to the Hofzeile. For years I kept it with that same doll that now has the face of an old woman. Now it is safe with all those yellow photographs of Lucie and Rudi in a safe deposit box at the bank.

Sometimes I wish I could remember more. Sometimes I think to myself, why didn't I look closer at my room and the streets, and why didn't I taste the food there more carefully? But of course, you never think of missing your country until you leave it.

I knew an Amish woman once who told me she had no pictures of herself, nor of her family. This was of her own choosing. I worried for that woman, and for that woman's children. They would not know what she looked like at nine or fifteen. Nobody would ever be able to look back at their own graduation or birthday party.

My mother and Rudi had arranged for the furniture and things from the Hofzeile to be shipped to Hamburg. Agnes was to be in charge. My mother had already paid for everything and she even had a permit and a receipt—a slip of paper which I still have and keep with the doll and the faded pictures at the bank. But of course when we did get to the United States and made inquiries, the Germans claimed everything had been bombed. Vans and vans of beautiful furniture.

On the train I comforted myself. I thought of Cook's sweet, yellow voice and the stories she had told me. I thought of St. Elizabeth. I am St. Elizabeth, I said to myself. I am going to a new place with new clothes and a new coat. There I will marry a prince and save the lepers and the hungry.

Later, I would learn how my mother and Rudi had tried and failed to make all the proper arrangements—that for months they went for Kafkaesque visits to government offices and stood in lines to obtain exit visas for the three of us. She and Rudi did come up with our passports, but my mother did not tell me that night that we were leaving without all the required papers.

The big crisis always comes at the border when they look at your passport and then check for all your papers—which we did not have—then maybe take you off the train to search you and God knows what else. We had been warned about that.

We had our own compartment because I was contagious.

It was raining, and from where I sat, it looked as though the whole country was weeping. I tried to cheer myself up. I thought of how my father loved trains—loved nothing more than to smoke, drink coffee, and read in the dining car of a train.

My mother got us seats on the wrong side; we sat watching everything moving away from us—we were not rushing toward anything. We only saw what we were leaving. I will always remember that—waking up on and off throughout that journey, watching my homeland slipping away, getting blurrier and blurrier, smaller and dimmer.

I wonder if it was so hard to leave because perhaps we sensed that we would never return. I wonder, if I had the chance to go back to Vienna to live, would I? Wouldn't I have done just what my father did? Leave, then, at the first opportunity, go back? Wouldn't I have?

In a letter, I think it was to his son Ernst, Freud wrote that "it is typically Jewish not to renounce anything and to replace what has been lost."

But how does one replace a country? How does one replace one's lost family?

I am always embarrassed for the American reporters when they are seen on TV interviewing the Nazi war criminals. "Aren't you ashamed?" they'll ask. "Aren't you sorry for what you did?" And those old faces will look back at the young ones and shake their heads like so many schoolteachers. The old ones always say the same thing. "You weren't there. You don't understand. It was a different world."

It is too easy for a younger, stronger generation to say, "How could they have let this happen?"

I myself am left piecing together fractions of stories and I don't know which parts are true, which parts untrue. Sometimes I wonder if it would have been better to be an orphan—to have lost both my parents in Vienna; that way, at least the picture of my past would be more complete and somehow more pleasing. And me? I would have been a blank page. I would have had an easier time of reinventing myself, my language, my history, my past. I suppose I could try and forget the stories my father told me with friends he made up for me. I suppose I could try and do this with my own story and past. My mother liked to play with reality—mixing in real fruit with the plastic, real violets with the candied. Sometimes, I'm not even sure if Inge was my real friend or one of the friends my father imagined.

We passed another train that was stalled. It didn't have any windows. I saw from the lettering on the side of one car that the train was headed for Mauthausen, Austria. I had never been there. Now I know that in Mauthausen there was a camp. I suppose none of us can watch freight trains passing in quite the same way anymore.

At the border there were the border police and the SS. They opened the door to our compartment and I could barely see. The measles had spread into my eyes and even though I did not cry when we left, there were tears.

Here is where something could have gone terribly wrong, my eye man, Dr. Smith, tells me. Here is where your vision could have been permanently altered. Maybe. Maybe. But then again, the measles that would later rob me of my eyesight saved our lives that night.

I remember seeing a blurry swastika on the guard's arm patches many times over.

My mother just looked up at the guards through the glass doors, and she said in this very loud, tense voice, "Please. The child is extraordinarily sick."

I heard one guard ask her why she was traveling with such a sick child and she made up a lie. She said my measles had gone to my eyes and we had to get to a special doctor in Geneva. We did buy some eyedrops when we got there, but they were no good. I imagine we were just sold bottled water or some such.

"She's very contagious," my mother said, shaking her head as she looked at me with great concern.

Through the closed doors, the guard yelled that we should slip our papers to them under the door. My mother nodded and opened her purse. She was completely calm. She pulled out an envelope thick with papers, one of which was sticking out. I recognized the gold Vatican seal. It was one of the papers my father had shown us after dinner. Very official, I thought I heard him say then. Very important.

My mother got up and pretended to struggle with sliding the envelope under the door. She was very slow about it and the guard became impatient.

"One by one," the guard said, referring to the papers.

I wasn't sure what my mother had in mind then, but all at once our train jolted. Outside, the train headed for Mauthausen was starting as well. It was this movement that made the guard still more impatient.

"Just slide your passports through," he said.

These we had.

We waited while he flipped through the small pages. My mother sat with me, her hand on my knee. She was the picture of a poised mother—anxious only to get her child to a doctor. From October 5, 1938, all passports issued to Jews had to have the large "J" stamp. Our passports were not stamped with the "J." So there, you see?

The man finally stamped our passports, slid them back to us under the door, and went to the next compartment.

I still have that passport dated 5 April 1939. I had long black braids then, and in the picture I am not smiling. It's a wonderful picture of me. I consider it my best. But they stamped right over my face. There on the upper part of my right cheekbone is the wing of the German eagle, and in its claws hangs a black swastika.

You ask me about the swastika. You say, "Doesn't it make you cringe? Doesn't it make you sick when you see it?" Sick? The word is not strong enough. Regretful? Weary? Fated? There are no words.

I was listed as a German citizen. Can you imagine? I was born and raised in Vienna, why couldn't I remain an Austrian citizen?

On the train I told my mother that it bothered me. My country was Austria, I said, not Germany. She said it didn't matter—that we were going to a new country where we would be new people. Then she corrected herself and said that we wouldn't be altogether new—that we would still remember and we would always be the sum total of what happens to us. I remember she used those words, "sum total," because it was like nothing she had said before. She was describing a human life in mathematical terms and it frightened me. I didn't think of anybody as a "sum total" but I did consider how we would be recreating ourselves in our new country.

I know a woman who has a scar above her upper lip. Her nose is so very small, it is obvious she had a bad nose job years ago. She is Jewish and now, in her forties, she is rediscovering the Holocaust. As a result, she told me at a cocktail party, she is not going to circumcise her newborn son. She said that her parents had her butchered, but she was not going to do the same to her son. Besides, she went on, this way nobody has any proof if "it" all happens again. I told her I understood completely and I do.

Red, white, and blue are not the colors of freedom to me; pink is. Mediterranean pink. This was the first color I could make out—the color of the outside of Rudi's apartment building in Geneva. Rudi had a pied-à-terre, and there we met up with my father, who was both happy to be in a new city and grumpy because he had been displaced. From Rudi's sitting-room window, you could see a clump of trees, part of *la vieille Genève*, a good chunk of the lake, and all that sunlight. My father allowed me in this room while he read and wrote. I spent many weeks in front of that window, rinsing my eyes morning and night with what we thought was a solution of boracic lotion, but now I know it was only water or some simple saline solution in that brown bottle. Nonetheless, slowly, my measles went away.

My mother had gone to high school in Geneva and suddenly that week it was a big party and my mother saw all her friends. When I was well enough, my father took us to the museums and to matinées—this was when I first saw Molière's *Le Médecin malgré lui*.

My father preferred to walk everywhere because, he said, Geneva was still clean and the air smelled of roses and lakewater. When it rained it was never for long and the sun shone straightaway so that eventually there was a rainbow. Once, my father and I were standing outside the café next door to the pink apartment building. We watched my mother with her schoolfriends sitting around a table, smoking, drinking coffee, and eating cakes with raisins and nuts. My father and I stood there for what seemed like a long time watching these women with my mother— their bright red lips opening and closing as they leaned forward and laughed.

"Aren't we going in?" I asked, but when I looked up at my father I wished I hadn't said anything. He looked so sad, so thoughtful, as though he was trying to figure out how to deliver bad news.

"Let's go up," my father finally said. "Let's leave them to their cakes for now."

At the end of the week, I saw my mother take my father to speak alone with him in another room. My mother who everyone thought was so frivolous. I heard her mention money. I heard her say we had to watch our pennies now—now that we were refugees.

"Perhaps we need to change the way we live," I heard her say to my father. Perhaps we were not supposed to be having so much fun. There was a war. Austria was no longer Austria. The world was collapsing all around us and we were running around to parties and to the theater, seeing the sights in Geneva, even planning a festive trip to Paris. I do not recall how my father responded.

But we did not stay in Geneva long enough for my father to change. We left for Fontaine-Lyons, a village near Lyons in France, to stay—no, I should say it—to hide in the house of my mother's cousins.

Fontaine-Lyons was a new world. I met another side of my mother's family that I had not previously known. I had no idea that I had all these aunts, uncles, and cousins who loved to talk and talk—they talked about everything and especially everyone, they talked about people who were my ancestors, people I had never even heard of before.

Henri and Ceci kept us in two rooms in the back of their house. Henri was Lucie's cousin and Rudi had made all the arrangements. In addition to traveling in Turkey and Geneva, Rudi also went frequently to Fontaine-Lyons to visit this side of the family. Henri and Ceci lived in an old stone house on a cobblestoned street with vineyards in the back. They made wine. The apricot trees were in bloom when we got there.

I developed a tremendous crush on Henri. We didn't know what to call each other, so we settled on "cousin." He played the piano and said that I played very well and we played duets on Sunday afternoons. Henri was going to be a priest but he married Ceci instead.

There was this young girl Henri and Ceci had also just taken in. Her parents had been taken away and sent to the camps and no one talked about it. I'm not even sure this girl was from Fontaine. I wanted to like her, but she barely said a word. I thought she was tremendously beautiful, but very thin.

She disappeared after every meal. I could hear what she was doing.

Every day it was the same—she would eat, then go make all that noise in the bathroom, making herself sick.

Years later, I found out from Henri and Ceci that this girl committed suicide. She had slashed her wrists in their bathtub with a straight-edged razor. When I heard, I felt quite impatient with her, then I got mad thinking about all the trouble she had put my relatives through and the mess they had had to clean up.

You ask how I know you're getting thinner. You say I wouldn't know because I don't even look at you. I don't have to see you to know. I can hear it in your voice. I can. That girl I lived with in Lyons, she did not talk at all. Now, listening to you worries me. Your sentences are getting shorter, and your words sometimes seem to disappear as though you're making yourself silent and invisible like that girl. How can I tell you? I've lost everything, I can hear myself blurting out. A house, a country, my mother, my father, and now, inch by inch, pound by pound, I am los-ing you too.

My mother had written to the Quakers, and after five months, they sent word that they had arranged for my parents and me to stay in separate homes in England. They said it was safer for me to travel first. I had never been away from my parents for more than three days at a time.

I was put up with a stockbroker who lived just outside Whitham, at a house called Testbourne in southern England. Two rivers streamed through the property—the Test and the Bourne. Orange and salmon-colored poppies grew all along those rivers and in the distance you could pick lavender. The place still exists, though I think every new house around there calls itself Testbourne.

It was a house far more modern than the ornate rococo I had left in Vienna. I remember thinking, this brick is so new. And the rugs were so light. Not an antique in the place. The whole house was done in beige and pink.

I had never seen so much beautiful land all in one place. The two rivers ran rapidly by so you could always hear the sound of that water. And the wind carried the smell of the red roses that climbed the front of the house. We had had two gardens in Vienna but they were city gardens. You had to cross the street to get to one. Here, the land and gardens seemed to roll on forever.

I got to Testbourne on September 1. It was never really very warm, never really very cold. It always felt like the season between seasons—you know the one—and I suppose that is appropriate because, for me, Testbourne was also to become the home between homes.

My first morning in Testbourne, I remember feeling Jan sitting on the edge of my bed, watching me sleep, waiting for me to open my eyes. Jan Walters was a year younger than I was. She was also shorter and a lot cuter. When the sun hit my eyes that morning and I finally woke up, Jan introduced herself and spoke in a bundle of words that came out fast and endless.

I didn't understand a word of what anybody said to me for two weeks. My father had been tutoring me in English when we knew we were going to emigrate, but the only thing I remembered from our tutoring sessions was "Silent Night, Holy Night" and that doesn't get you too far in England. Then suddenly one morning I woke up and I was able to piece some sense out of this stuff this little girl, Jan, was yakking at me.

Jan would talk about everything—*her* Father Christmas, *her* England, *their* house. How I envied her possessives! In England people know a lot about the history of their homes and they complained—complained!—about the swans that gathered in their yards.

When Jan spoke, I daydreamed. I dreamed of being back home. I dreamed of dressing up in my mother's fine silk skirts. I dreamed of walking the length of the Grinzinger Allee to market or to school, holding a stack of books filled with words I could understand.

Testbourne had once been a hennery, and every now and then, Jan and I would run out in the back and collect hen feathers. There had been a fire there a few years before. Another owner—a couple—were entertaining, giving a big, wild house party. Jan said that everyone in town said it was something called an orgy. A French prince was there. The French prince was twenty-three years old and he was having an affair with the owner's wife. At the time, neither Jan nor I knew what the word "affair" meant, but we knew that it was something to be whispered about and the word itself carried lascivious, French connotations.

The owner of the house had found out about the affair and invited the Prince for the sole purpose of shooting him, which he did or else he pushed him out a window—Jan wasn't quite sure of the particulars—but the Prince died and the owner then proceeded to set his own house on fire. All the guests, including his wife, were asleep in the house at the time. Apparently, he lit the match and left by the front door. After the fire, the place was renamed Testbourne.

Jan loved to tell this story. She would add to it: what the people wore, what they said, what they ate and drank. Sometimes the French prince became German or Italian. What delighted Jan the most, however, was not that a man would set his house and his wife on fire after killing another man, but that the Prince never told his mother where he was that night. When his mother heard the news that her son was dead, she asked the messenger what her son was doing in England.

This was the first story I ever heard and understood in English.

At night, whenever I heard the branch of a tree scraping against the side of the house or a field mouse scrambling across the roof, I would imagine, as I lay in bed, that it was the ghost of the French prince waking up in the butler's pantry, where the man was said to have dragged him. The Prince, being French in my telling, would fix himself a big bowl of coffee and steamed milk and then he would go outside, and after deciding which direction to try this time, he would proceed to stumble about the English landscape, hoping to find his way back to his own country—perhaps just to tell his mother the news of his death himself or to say what he had been doing all this time that he had been away from home.

Did I cry myself to sleep at night? I was too miserable to cry. There is no sickness like homesickness. I missed Inge and Grossmama. I missed my parents. I missed Hofzeile 12, Cook, Uncle Rudi, and Lucie. I did not know where all this moving around would lead us—would we ever be together again? Would the Quakers keep shuffling me off from one family to the next? I wanted home again, yes. Everyone goes on about how wonderful Noah must have felt when that second bird came back to the ark with the olive branch in its beak—but just consider how relieved that bird must have been.

I did want to go back to Vienna, but at the same time, I would look at Jan and her house and I was so envious. I was ashamed of my weak country and I was envious of Jan's stronger, obviously more successful monarchy.

Keats has that line about Ruth wandering around "amid the alien corn" and you know immediately that to Ruth, that blasted corn *is* alien. When I moved, beds looked alien, chairs too. When you're away, you don't sit down the way you normally do at home. You don't sleep the same way either. Everything that should have been familiar was unfamiliar. But more than anything, I wanted to be with my mother and my father. I wanted to just be with them in a room. The word "homesick" is right—you're sick with wanting to be home. I knew it was homesickness even then, which made it better because at least there was a name for it. I would tell myself, "You're going to get over this." And I would wait, systematically wait, and like sorrow, it does get less bad.

Mrs. Walters gave me my first books to read in English. She gave me a gilt and green leather copy of *Water Babies* by Charles Kingsley. The little chimney sweep, Tom, runs away from his cruel master and falls into a river. Even though I knew nothing of chimney sweeping and there had been no Mr. Grimes to beat me, when I read about Tom, I thought to myself, this is me. I am Tom. I saw that much. Tom had a passport hanging around his neck when he went to the other-end-of-Nowhere and after all, so had I.

When I read this book out loud to myself, in English, I barely recognized the sound of my voice. I felt as though I were waking up after a long, long sleep.

The chauffeur drove us to Stonehenge in a Rolls-Royce almost every afternoon for tea. Mrs. Walters would bring along a beautiful wicker hamper and lay out a picnic on one of the more level stones, and there she would tell us about Egypt.

I loved to sit and listen to Mrs. Walters, and stare off at the silhouettes of the stones against the blue summer sky.

Stonehenge wasn't roped off like it is today and no one really came from very far away to look. You could sit and eat right on top of one of the five sarsen trilithons, even nap if you liked.

It was at Stonehenge, sitting on a trilithon, staring past the Bluestone Circle, that I realized I was not going to go back to the Hofzeile. Not in the foreseeable future. Not in my childhood. Mrs. Walters was going on and on about the Pyramids, and all at once I took a deep breath as though I couldn't breathe and Mrs. Walters asked if I was all right and Jan, well, Jan just looked scared. I was all right, though. It was just something that hit me. That part is over, I thought, now what?

We went on that afternoon, collecting wild foxgloves and ferns in the woods. Mrs. Walters allowed us to cut some yellow roses from the garden and we put them in little vases on our windowsill. But I remember the feeling of understanding something so clearly—that feeling of resolve.

Years later, I was dating someone in Baltimore. He was a postman. We had been seeing each other for a whole summer, and as he helped me with my jacket after dinner one evening, I thought, hey, I'm not going to marry this man. Just like that. I suppose you can see these moments as a kind of freedom or a sense of fatality.

In October there was a harvest festival in Whitham, and there was a competition in my age group—which child could find the most flowers, press them, mount them, and label them correctly. The judge was to be some mysterious Protestant.

For weeks, Mrs. Walters had Jan and me scrambling over hill and dale every afternoon in search of cowslips and primroses, violets and snowdrops. Everything was there on their land. Jan accused me of sweating more than she did and she would often feel the backs of my knees to prove it. We started collecting butterflies then too and we had cocoons hatching.

I remember one afternoon in particular because I said that I didn't think I was going to win the competition because (a) I was not from Whitham and (b) I was a Catholic. Jan lectured me on the virtues of being a good sport.

"What do you want to be a good sport for?" I asked.

Jan could only come up with something like, "Just because."

Of course, I won the competition.

I think of that time of collecting—that time I learned how to press a flower—every year during the unnamed season somewhere between the end of summer and the beginning of fall. I remember the day in Whitchurch, the flags and the songs and the ribbon I won—and I remember my parents not being there.

Recalling my loneliness, I get lonely all over again and I'll shut the door to my room and think of my father. Is he looking out his window? I'll think to myself, and if so what is he seeing? What is he thinking? Perhaps there are trees outside changing color. Perhaps he is looking out across the Danube to the Carpathians and out further to where the plains of Asia begin and stretch as far as the eye can see. He never did go to Hong Kong; did he wonder what it looked like? Did he still have any desire at all to see me?

One day we went to the White Hart for elevenses.

"Do you know how old this building is?" Mrs. Walters asked Jan and me once we'd sat down to tea.

The walls were a glossy white, but they buckled and the floor slanted. Everyone in Whitchurch made a big deal of the White Hart. I liked it because Mrs. Walters told me that the Reverend Charles Kingsley had stayed there when he came to fish in the River Test. I liked to imagine him looking out his hotel window at the view across the town, out toward the river, thinking up a whole world full of children with the proper passports hanging round their necks—a heaven under water.

Mrs. Walters waited for an answer, but I didn't care how old the White Hart was.

"Ten sixty-six," Jan declared. We had just finished with the Battle of Hastings that week.

Mrs. Walters smiled.

"This building was built in 1492," she said. "Do you know what else happened that year?"

"Columbus!" Jan shrieked. Everyone in the tearoom looked up and smiled.

"That's right. Columbus set sail for America."

"And so will Jenny," Jan said, directing her attention to me.

"And so will Jenny," Mrs. Walters said, sitting back now. I could tell from the look on her face that she was very pleased with the lesson.

It was the first time anyone had ever called me by this name. Jenny. It made all the sense in the world really. Genevieve to Jenny. It had the short, efficient sound of a new life. America was to be my new country. Jenny was to be my new, American name. I remember I even ceremoniously took a sip from my tea as though liquid had to be included in this abbreviated form of baptism.

On the way back to Testbourne that day, we passed a window dressed with red brocade curtains on the inside. They looked somewhat like the curtains Grossmama had hanging in her room at the Hofzeile.

Two men in uniforms passed. I heard them talking about the signs they had seen in the Black Forest.

"Chocolate factory signs, but they weren't making bars of chocolate. Those factories were for ammunition," one of them said. "And *that* was way back in 'thirty-four. Those Germans have been organizing for a long, long time."

I remember this conversation because it was the first time I had actually heard people discussing the situation and it was the first time I realized what a menace Germany had become.

Looking back at the shop window, I wondered if Grossmama's curtains still hung in her room at the Hofzeile.

The door opened and an old man came out of the building. He smelled of pine and tarnish. He looked me up and down as though he were trying to guess my height. He stepped aside to make room for two men who carried a casket out of the doorway.

I backed away.

"Come along, Jenny," Mrs. Walters said, taking my hand.

I suppose Freud would have me associating my trip to the United States with death. But it is true that it was to be the end of something.

I was sitting in the bathtub with Jan in Déa, France. The Walters had taken me along with them to Normandy on holiday. My parents had written to me that I was a very lucky young girl to be included in this family holiday. I imagine it was a vacation meant to help us all forget that there was a war on. We had spent all that day on the coast and at low tide we netted for *écrivettes*—small shrimps left stranded in pools formed by the rocks.

We netted all afternoon on the same beach that was to be famous in the war that would be announced that night.

The radio was on and we just stopped splashing around in the bath water. Just like that. We just stopped. I could see Mrs. Walters's profile in the doorway. She was listening to the news. Then she came into the bathroom and told us we had to get out of the tub.

"Hitlaa has just marched into Poland," she said. You should hear the way the English say his name.

As we dried ourselves, she and her husband stood outside in the hallway. His name was Pleble Kleble—that was his name. Really. She called him P.K.

I can remember seeing them through that thick wavy bathroom glass some doors in Europe still have. I could just make out the pink blouse Mrs. Walters had on and the blue sweater P.K. wore.

They mumbled. She touched his arm. I remember that because

Mrs. Walters so rarely touched any of us. This was a woman—P.K.'s second wife—who wore tweed suits just to arrange flowers in the morning.

Jan had gone very quiet on me, and to me, this "emergency" atmosphere wasn't too logical. Why is it an emergency when he marches into Poland and not when he marched all those other times into the Rhineland, Czechoslovakia, Bohemia, Moravia, and Austria? I couldn't help but be troubled, and a little jealous of Poland—England would not go to war for Austria. That has always been something hard to forgive.

P.K. had taken a big position in the stock market at that time and I think he must have lost a tremendous amount of money that very day. Later, I found out that the Bank of England requisitioned Testbourne the following year.

We left Déa and went on to Mrs. Walters's father's house on an overnight ferry. We were to allow time for the servants at Testbourne to "ready" the house for our unexpected early arrival. Leaving at night was becoming routine for me. Jan was very excited about all the goings-on, but I wondered a little about what would happen to me. You see, nobody in England had really been affected by what was happening on the Continent yet. Chamberlain had them all believing England was okay—what was going wrong was going wrong in Europe, that's *their* problem. Chamberlain—the man who had waved his peace-in-our-time slip of paper only eleven months before.

During the Channel crossing, I stood with P.K. on deck while Mrs. Walters helped Jan with her seasickness. I looked down at the Channel between England and France—a body of water that was supposed to keep us safe. I could dive in now, I thought, and I would be safe. But he could swim it. Other people had, so could he. So could Hitler.

"We're going to Mrs. Walters's father's house. That's Jan's grandfather," P.K. said to me. His English was overly slow and careful because he didn't think I understood anything. He spoke loudly too as if I couldn't hear. "You'll like the house. It's Georgian."

I wondered, momentarily, why Mrs. Walters's father was living in a house that had come from Russia. Only later, years later, did I know that P.K. was referring to an architectural style.

I had crossed the English Channel before, but that had been with my mother and father. We were approaching the cliffs—you know the ones, the white cliffs of Dover—and I was thinking to myself, they really *are* white. And I felt safe right then. Safe again and sad. I wanted to be with my parents, but there I was with this man named Pleble Kleble.

Jan and Mrs. Walters came up on deck for air. Jan looked green, but when she saw the cliffs, she smiled and said something about how exciting it was to be fleeing the Germans.

"We are not fleeing," Mrs. Walters said. It was as though she were addressing everyone on the boat, indeed, as though she was speaking for the whole of England. But then, we all had our mantras, I suppose—we are safe, we are safe. We are England, we are England. All the really nasty business is happening over there, far far away.

But I looked down at the water. We were, I soon realized, only a boat ride away.

"No one is after *us* darling," Mrs. Walters said. She drew Jan to her side, and I could feel her trying not to look at me. Her "us" obviously no longer included me.

Mrs. Walters no longer trusted me, just as my father had stopped trusting Inge. Maybe my father was right then, I thought to myself. Maybe no one can be trusted. The ugly hate I had seen in Vienna I saw now rising up in Mrs. Walters. That kind of hate isn't just a fluke, I thought. It can happen again anywhere any time.

I thought it was because I was Viennese. Honestly, I did. I thought Hitler and his men were after all those who were not German. It makes sense, really. But at that time the facts had not been made clear. Catholicism had been and still was such an important part of our life. I did not understand that my father had not always been a Catholic.

———

After the Germans invaded Poland, I could do nothing right in Mrs. Walters's eyes. I came down with the flu. When Jan caught a cold it was, "Poor Jan. She is small and not as strong as you."

Sunday came. I knew it would be my last Sunday there—the following week I was going to Cambridge to finally meet up with my parents, who were already settled in a house there. My father had a temporary post in the history department at King's College.

I did very poorly on a math test—so poorly that Mrs. Walters notified my father. My father then wrote me a long letter on my responsibility to do my best, in short, to do my duty. If you do not fulfill your duty, he said, what have you got left? Some might ask if my father fulfilled his duty. It's beside the point, really. We are answerable and responsible for our own acts. I kept that letter for a long, long time, then I threw it out, just before I married.

Of course he was right. I know that now, but at that point in my life I didn't see what duty had to do with anything. I was mad at everyone and everything, but most of all, I was mad at England. Why should this empire be so much more successful than mine? I thought. I didn't feel like a failure, but I did feel let down by my empire, and somehow because of all this, Jan would get to stay in her pink and beige house with Mrs. Walters and the bicycles and the lovely teas and picnics at Stonehenge and I would have to move on in search of a new home. My father's letter only upset me, and, more puzzling, it did not help with understanding mathematics.

I should have stayed in bed that Sunday, but I wanted to say goodbye to a nice elderly Catholic woman who used to come by and pick me up for mass every Sunday. Mrs. Walters was surprised to see me up. She asked if I still had a cold. I said I felt fine.

That night my cold got worse, and the fact that I had denied such a possibility and went out in the rain to see the lady and made myself sicker also came to light. I was in more disgrace. Jan and I were kept away from each other. Mrs. Walters announced that Jan probably didn't have a cold, but she needed a day or so to get "caught up on her things." Luckily, I was to leave in two days.

I don't remember saying good-bye to Jan. I do remember saying good-bye to Mrs. Walters, though. One did not kiss too much in England. One brushed one's lips on the other's cheek, and this is what I did, and I could smell the powder on Mrs. Walters's cheek and I noticed a lot of soft hairs on her face.

I knew that *now* England was at war, but I couldn't help but wish Hitler would move and invade another country—maybe even England, or maybe just Testbourne, and then, maybe, my father and mother would take pity on me, forget about the math test and my sneaking out to church with a cold, and forgive me for my lie.

Upon my arrival in Cambridge, my mother insisted that I go confess my sins. She reminded me that I had done poorly on the mathematics test, thereby not fulfilling my duty. In addition, I had lied about feeling well enough to say good-bye to the Catholic lady. I was careful to pick a priest whose sermon I had liked the previous Sunday. It was Father Grant. He analyzed the problem and decided that gratitude and courtesy were important underlying motives. He became a very good friend.

We lived at 10 Harvey, a charming but small redbrick building with black trim. It was a row house and we rented two rooms. Mrs. Charlesworth was our landlady and she had a big, furry white cat with whom I had good conversations. A little boy about my age and his mother lived above us. An art historian lived next door. A Presbyterian minister lived in No. 9. Some Italians lived next to him. Word was that they had been thrown out of Italy because the father was anti-Mussolini. Then there were the two Pennington ladies, two sweet old women, who lived in the attic. The mother of the boy upstairs had more money than any of us and I think she felt sorry for me because she bought a Christmas tree for the whole house, and it was agreed that the tree would go in our flat because I was the youngest and had been away from my parents.

My mother painted bits of paper and hung them on the tree, and that Christmas, after my parents had retired with their books, and I sat under the tree looking up through the branches, I closed my eyes and imagined us back inside the Hofzeile.

The next morning, my father left for King's College, where he was preparing to teach a class. Whenever he left, my mother would rush and turn off the heat for the day.

My mother and I would then set out early every morning on some mission. My mother was very much in her religious phase. She became part of the Sword of the Spirit, a movement among the Catholic intelligentsia in London run by Maisie Ward and Frank Sheed. We would head for the library. The movement pushed study and research—this mission to be both intelligent and Catholic appealed to my mother.

We spent days and days in the library or at museums. She was studying art and archeology for God. Sometimes we went to the bakery to get lemon meringue tarts for tea and we would walk, me swinging two boxes between us—one held the tarts, the other my gas mask. Dinner, I knew, would be a tin of sardines, but it wasn't something you thought about. I just kept my eyes skyward, looking for the street sign that said Harvey.

I was in charge of the lights. The whole town was preparing for a blitz or a bombing all the time. We had those gas masks—square cardboard cartons that looked as though they were meant to hold six ripe tomatoes. There was food rationing. There were sandbags everywhere. It was my job to make sure that no chinks of light escaped from the windows during a blackout. I would plaster the windows with sticky tape and then we would have tea and biscuits in the air-raid shelter down below. This was when I was happiest. It was cold—so cold—but there was the tea and the stale poppy seed biscuits and I was with them again. I was with Mutti and Pantsch.

My father was deep into his book on the Vatican. He taught and wrote just as if there was no war. He regretted being so far away from his "primary sources." He missed his days at the archives—all those books which had been carted away and out of the country, buried under a barn at some farm in preparation for the war. Primary sources. I think back on this now—wasn't *I* a primary source?

At 5:20 P.M. on the way to Evensong one day, I let go of my mother's hand and lost track of her. I saw a nice-looking man with old, gray eyes and I asked where King's College Chapel would be.

"It would be this way," he said to me. "And would you be going to Evensong?"

I said that I would be and he took my hand.

Evensong at King's College Chapel was my favorite event every Sunday afternoon. It was better even than the *missa cantata*. The only stipulation for us was that Catholics had to sit in the roped-off section of the chapel. If you sat too close to the event, it was considered a mortal sin by the English Catholic hierarchy and absolution could be denied. My mother explained this all to me one day as we folded pamphlets with the words "Sword of the Spirit" splashed across the front.

"It would be much easier if the bells rang," the man said. "You could head towards the sound, and when they stopped, you would know you still had five minutes left." But, he explained, they had taken the bells down to make bullets.

He let go of my hand to put on a long black robe and I stopped. I just stopped. I couldn't walk any further. I could only stand there, staring at this man in the long black robe with the blue Cambridge sky in back of him. I had seen this before. Gentz. All I could think of was Gentz. Sometimes I look at you and something clicks in the same way it did that day, and it's not you standing before me, but my mother.

That day in Cambridge, there were signs all around us that said *Keep off the Grass.*

"Come on," he said, taking my hand again. "How 'bout I give you a tow and a bit of a treat then?"

Only a fellow who was with the university could set foot on that grass and this man in the black robe led me past the signs and together we stepped on the grass. It felt wonderfully good and peaceful to be thought of as a little girl, a silly little girl whose only worry was how to get to Evensong. The wind blew his robe and my dark blue coat and the hems billowed into each other and I thought we must have looked like two crows setting foot across that soft, green lawn like a King and his Queen.

Towering ahead of us, King's College Chapel stood dark and silent, and there at the door stood my mother on her toes, looking all around. She spoke French when she saw me and she did not let go of my hand even as she and the man made their introductions.

"Let's find ourselves some really good seats then," he whispered, leading us past the signs marked *Public.* He unleashed a cord that marked off the Catholic section and told me to hand it to the next "chap." Without hesitation, my mother and I followed him up the steps to the back row where the seats were highest of all.

And there we sat. Two Catholics bolt upright and the Protestant on his knees, sighing, his head on the Book of Common Prayer.

The chapel was dark then. It hadn't been cleaned. The stone was not white like it is today, and they were in the process of taking out and hiding all the fourteenth-century stained-glass windows because they didn't want them damaged. Black tar paper covered all of the big spaces where colored glass had once been, and every now and then you could hear it flapping in the wind.

I have been to King's College Chapel when the stained glass was put back in and the floors were heated. The place is altogether different. It is light, airy, warm, even cheery. But back then it was dark and cold and there was a certain coziness about the place. We were all huddled together listening to the boys' choir singing by candlelight while all that tar paper thumped against all those old, dark stones in the cold wind.

Years later, your father and I saw the west window at Winchester Cathedral. Once upon a time, the stained-glass windows there had been taken down and buried before one of Cromwell's raids, but they forgot to number the pieces of glass and they were forced to put them back up willy-nilly.

There are clumps of red here and there where someone had made an effort to piece together a picture of a saint or of Mary, but, otherwise, there is no design. Looking at it, I thought how my life was like that window—bits and pieces strewn together without making much sense.

There is beauty in the erratic style of that window. It looks like a piece of modern art—a mosaic of some kind, an artist's idea of chaos. The colors are balanced, but there is no complete picture. Just a burst of color here and there. Somehow I imagine it is even more beautiful than the original.

At King's College Chapel, as I knelt next to the man who dramatically laid his forehead on the Book of Common Prayer for the second time, I looked at the other side of the chapel. My mother sat next to me, staring up at the ceiling where the fan vaults spread out like a peacock's tail.

Later that evening, neither one of us told my father where we sat at Evensong. Even though I was only eleven years old, I knew, in my heart, that we had not committed a mortal sin by sitting in the roped-off area with the Protestants.

The boys' choir didn't need an organ to accompany them. I had been to wonderful concerts and chamber music recitals in Vienna. I myself played Handel and Chopin and Mozart, but I had never heard boys my own age singing in this way.

It was the first time in a long time that I began to think of Hofzeile 12. What had happened to Inge and to Gentz? I worried terribly about my Grossmama. I suddenly had the urge to run fast and far—all the way back to Vienna—so that I could tell them all to turn off their lights, tape up their windows, fast, so that no one would see them.

I did not know then that Gentz had been sent to Dachau. I did not know that Inge and her family were living on cold potato peels. I did not know that my Grossmama was making her escape to Czechoslovakia in a hay wagon.

"A small nation's memory is no smaller than the memory of a large one." Kafka wrote that in his diary. Vienna is a small, negligible city now, but it wasn't to those who remember her.

I have read that knowledge and memory are one and the same. Why that is I do not know. My memory of the Hofzeile brings me not knowledge but grief. I do not feel I know anything more of humanity when I think of the loss; I feel I know less.

"Is she all right?" the man in the black robe whispered to my mother.

I looked at him, then at my mother, but I did not see either one of them.

"I never said good-bye to Inge," I said in German. I had not thought that I was crying, but I was. My mother pulled me close. She kept her arm around my shoulders, and then I worried that I had gotten the big book wet, and I began wiping the cover with my sleeve.

The choir started to sing again. A little redheaded boy burped between the *A* and the *men*. Another kept his left index finger stuck in his left ear. They were all together. They were in sync and their rhythm slowed my heart so that it seemed that I too was breathing in time with their music—that we were all in fact together, pacing ourselves with one another. They ended with *Amen* and their leader allowed their *n* to echo for a long while afterwards in that dark, tall stone hall. You could hear it over the sound of the paper flapping.

A man stood up and read a story about bones turning to flesh, made into life, then becoming the twelve tribes of Israel. The choir sang again and I could hear the man next to me humming the "Alleluia" along with them.

Bless this land, I thought. Bless Inge and Gentz and Cook. Take good care of Grossmama.

I looked up at one of the only stained-glass windows left in the chapel. At the top, you could see two feet and the hem of a wine-colored robe. That's Jesus ascending into Heaven, I thought. He's going home. But those feet could be anybody's feet.

On the way out I saw a corner of the tar paper flap open. I had the sticky tape in my pocket. I always carried it with me. It was my duty, my responsibility to keep out the light. I let go of my mother's hand and taped the paper back to the stone. I think about it now, and I doubt that that heavy paper stayed stuck because of my bit of tape; but back then, when it was late at night and I lay in bed or when we were settling down in the air-raid shelter, I liked to think that I alone saved King's College Chapel from Hitler's bombs.

We left for the United States on a boat on August 4, 1942—at the height of the murdering, and the serious bombing of England was already underway. I had never finished learning how to darn a sock, but by that time, I had learned English well enough to know how to spell "arithmetic," "confession," and "right." Before we left, I started a diary. I drew a few musical notes on the cover, and on the first page, I wrote in English: "The stars are bright, packing. Deep in the heart of packing deep in the night. I am packing you in, but diary, when I shall unpack you, I will be in Washington." And when we did arrive at our new home, I wrote the address in English: 2933 Felden Street N.W., Washington, D.C. In America, everything in my new diary would be written in English. Perhaps that is why all that is in there are addresses. It was a habit I would continue. Every place we went—even hotels—I would write the address down into this diary. It is a record of numbers and streets. But never, not once, did I ever record my real home, Hofzeile 12.

It was a seven-day journey on a huge boat—my father called it our ark. I don't remember any music that day, but I do remember all the people. It's a haze, really, a haze of balloons, noise, and bodies. I remember my mother clung to a postcard she had received from a friend of hers in Geneva. The card was Joan Miró's *The Hunter*. I have seen and studied the painting since. I can recall the eye in the middle of the painting with balls and triangles, funnels, lines, ladders, and dotted paths as if they were all saying to the eye—here, go this way or there, go that way! There are fires in the picture, somebody's lost pipe, and birds flying over black lines. There's an Italian flag, and in the distance there is the French flag crossed with what looks like an American flag, but I can never really be sure because you can't see the stars or that deep, deep blue. My mother was to fall in love with all of Miró's work after that day.

Even though it was warm the spring we left, I was wearing layers and layers of clothing under my dark blue coat. You could only bring so much, so everyone wore what he or she could not carry. As we pulled away from the shores, I wanted to make a covenant with God as God had once made with Noah. God, I thought, standing on the deck between my parents as everyone around us waved at people they thought they would never see again, no matter what happens, keep us together. Keep my family together. Don't let one of us go anywhere without the other.

And just then, as we set out, as the big funnel blared and people began to weep and kiss at the air, I felt as Tom the chimney sweep must have felt when he first touched salt water. I am quite sure he was terrified and delighted all at once when he found out he could breathe in a new, foreign land and make new friends with the different fishes. I didn't think about Inge then. I didn't think of Gentz or Sister Marie—not even Grossmama. I had my thoughts set on what was ahead. A new country. I will write down everything in English, I thought to myself. I would study fashion magazines to learn how to dress like an American so that I could become an American. And if I could have, I would have done three skips out of the water, a yard high and head over heels just as Tom the chimney sweep had, just as the salmon did when they too first swam into their new world.

ELIZABETH

MY MOTHER WAS TELLING ME ABOUT A WOMAN SHE
had met at a hospital benefit who was devoting her life to God and
nutrition.

"She's very big," my mother said. Then, "Father Brown's newsletters
are getting weirder and weirder. He says he can't get out of bed. He says
he's had depressions but none so deep." She waited a beat. "I know, I
know. Don't say it."

"I didn't say anything," I said.

"You don't have to. You and your father are always making fun.
Maybe if Catholic priests didn't wear all that black they wouldn't be so
depressed all the time."

My mother had gotten into the habit of calling every Friday night
to give me updates on all that she was doing to the house. The shutters
were in and she wanted them to be just the right yellow. The beams in
the bedrooms had been exposed, and now there were the bookcases to
consider. I knew my father must have been getting tired of all the indoor
construction.

"Your voice sounds thin," she said. "Thinner even than last week.
You're still not eating, are you?"

"Mom," I said impatiently. I ran my hand over my hip bone to feel where I jutted in and where I jutted out. I leaned against the refrigerator. Stuck on the door was a copy of a photograph I had cut from a magazine. The black-and-white picture of bodies piled in heaps was taken when the concentration camps were liberated. I wanted to see this death up close, and every day, I did. Ever since I learned German, I resolved to starve myself back into the past.

"I got another letter from Isabella," I said. The name was like a fire alarm going off. I waited. "She says she and Grandfather went to Hungary in May before he went to the hospital. They visited the old factory. She says he's been asking for you. She says his heart is leaking."

"His heart. He doesn't have a heart. And if he wants to see me so badly, why doesn't he pick up a phone and call me? It's the twentieth century, for God's sake." She had on her snippy, European voice—the one she used for solicitations when people called during dinner.

"You're really not going?" I said. "This could be it. I mean he's going back to visit the factory and everything."

"I'm not going back just because that woman says I should," my mother said quickly. "You are such a fool, you really are. Why don't *you* go?"

"He's not asking for me. He has no interest in me. He's your father, Mom, and he's dying. No one should die alone."

"He has her."

"You know the situation."

There was a long pause. "It is a situation of his own making. My father made decisions all his life on his own. Isabella was one of them and I'm not discussing this anymore with you. It's none of your business."

In the kitchen the ice maker's moan echoed and turned into a whisper as I took the cellophane off a Sabbath candle. It would have been nice, I thought to myself, if I had the kind of mother who welcomed the

Sabbath with a Friday night supper of pot roast and potato pancakes. Then again, that would be the kind of mother who nursed her father while he lay dying. Without thinking, I started talking again and I started the wrong way. I started with the word "Ezra."

"Oh God," she said. "Is he your only means for a social life?" She spat out the word "he." "You're just not meeting the right people."

Whenever I mentioned Ezra's name to my mother, the conversation was ready to end and we would hang up and spend the week "recovering," only to start all over again the following Friday night. My mother had met Ezra only once, when I invited him to the suburbs for the weekend. It rained the day we got off the train and my mother picked us up. Ezra was wearing a baseball cap, and when he saw my mother, he took it off. I had never seen him do such a thing. When we got to the house, he accidentally tracked mud all over the newly polished parquet floors. He was mortified and my mother acted nonchalant. "Happens all the time," she said. But a day later, after we had left, my mother called to tell me he just wouldn't do. Who was he anyway and who in God's name were his people? He was, she said, "probably from a lower drawer of Germans."

"Marry him, and it will be a very sad day. But it won't be the first such day in my life," she had said.

"Are you there?" my mother said over the phone. "What in the world is happening to you? I *know* you're not eating. You're disappearing. You never come home. I don't even know you anymore."

I wanted to love my mother's phone calls the way I wanted to love my mother. A long time ago, when we lived in Mississippi, my mother often sat with the phone to her ear, looking down at papers, thinking with her fingers on her lips. I had loved the very sight of her—my mother on the phone, working.

But I was twenty-seven years old now and she had passed fifty and nothing was the same. I wondered why my mother and I argued more than we spoke. And why we still hadn't traded secrets like other mothers and daughters did. I wondered why she hadn't yet told me her mother's secrets about cheese soufflés, vinaigrette, and chocolate mousse.

My mother was talking again, and I felt as though my skin was coming off—not peeling off, but falling off like glass shards.

"You're wearing me out, Mom." I looked at the phone in my hand, said, "You just are," and hung up.

Then I picked up the phone again and erased all the phone numbers from Memory.

I could leave her behind, I thought, I could forget about my mother—wipe her out of my memory altogether and get on with my life. I would be better off. I would marry Ezra, grow vegetables in the summer, dry flowers and herbs in the fall, make fruitcakes at Christmas. I would give away all the sexy little black dresses she had bought me at Loehmann's, have an at-home birth with a midwife, and be at peace with myself, Ezra, and the baby.

But then, quite suddenly, my great-grandmother appeared before me. The light in the kitchen cast an orangy glow, and she was not more than ten feet from me. I could make out her blue eyes staring at me over a glass of orange juice. I could hear her breathing and the black lace dress she wore smelled musty. She took a sip of the juice, chewed the pulp, then she said my name. "Elizabet," she said.

The ice maker gargled, then I heard the clunking as it spit out ice cubes.

At Temple, Ezra and I sat in the back with all the other people without families. I could not hear much, but I liked the way the rabbi sang and the earnest way he brought his head down and his hands together in prayer. At one point he went up and down the aisle carrying the scrolls the women went to kiss. When the women rejoined their families, they smiled at their husbands as if now they knew something or had seen something no one else had, and they pulled their children close to their hips.

The following morning, Ezra played with the plaster mold of an Etruscan foot balanced on his stomach. He was in his study, lying on the futon near his desk. A Santa someone had given him hung from a screw near the window. I never knew Ezra's mother or father. They had both died when he was still in college, and his brothers and sisters were scattered in Canada and Rhode Island. His father had sold carpeting. "See?" Ezra had said, "we're destined. Your grandfather had the floors made and my father covered them up."

It was our first apartment together—my fifth in the last two years. In every place I had lived, there was a noise—the clanking furnace in one, the squeaking floors in another—which, in the end, always drove me out. This was by far the best apartment. It sat perched on the edge of Hyde Park, facing east, toward Europe.

"Look," Ezra said. "Is this not the biggest foot you've ever seen?" Fitted together, the mold looked like any ordinary big rock.

I understood Ezra's work as an archeologist. He saw a surface, then he dug and dug until that surface was broken and the undersides revealed. Sometimes there was nothing. Other times there was a whole booty of treasures.

"Check out the big toe," he said. He looked at me, then waited a beat. "You didn't tell her about us living together, did you?"

"I don't have to."

"Look, most mothers would be happy if their daughters told them they were in love."

I realized then that when I talked to my mother about Ezra, I had never used the word "love"—it was too personal to say to her.

"My mother is not most mothers."

I used to take pride in the fact that my mother was a different sort of mother. I liked that she had so much on her mind she didn't have time for cooking or cleaning. And whenever she did finally speak of Vienna, she called it her motherland. To my mother, Vienna was a "she." I used to say to anyone who would listen, "My mother is more like a friend than a mother. She's Viennese, you know," and I would think about her really being from Vienna, and for some reason I would picture red Christmas tree ornaments in a silver bowl on an old cabinet in the middle of December.

But all that had changed. My mother had turned into the kind of woman who would not go see her dying father.

"You didn't tell her that you wanted to marry me either, did you?" Ezra stood up and put the foot mold down on his desk.

"Oh, so now you're putting your foot down," I joked. Ezra shook his head and sighed. We had been engaged for over a year and each time he asked about the wedding plans, I told him I couldn't deal with them because my mother wouldn't be able to.

"We should just move to Israel," I said, resting my head on one of his broad shoulders. For a moment, I had a distant vision of myself wearing the traditional black silk and pearls, lighting Sabbath candles, making *aliyah*. "I'd wear long skirts and keep my head covered."

"Yeah. And I'd carry around a rifle. Sounds like a great life."

Outside, I knew the sun was setting from the orange cast on the brick buildings across the alley. I imagined my mother near the phone in the kitchen, staring at the crack running from the floorboard in the brick wall, waiting for a call from me, or maybe, from her father.

"You're avoiding confrontation, Elizabeth. You're scared to death of your own mother."

"Oh, cut it out. You sound like a cheap shrink."

"It's just so obvious. You and your mother. You both skirt around the issue."

I left Ezra's study and went to the kitchen. My computer, notebooks, and dictionaries all sat open on the table Ezra had built and painted yellow, blue, red, and green. On the floor all around my feet were books on *Jugendstil* which included the works of everyone my grandfather had read or known—Hugo von Hofmannstal, Rilke, Schnitzler, and of course, Freud. I had maps and pictures of every onion-shaped dome in Vienna. I was preparing myself just as my grandfather had prepared himself whenever he was about to embark on another monograph on Lord Acton or Chateaubriand.

I sat down and laid my hand on the cover of my grandfather's book. He would never know nor would he ever care that I gave his book the Talmudic attention he had never given either my mother or me.

It had been a year since my grandfather had begun to die. Isabella had called me first to say that he was not well—that he was "in hospital" because "zomzing is wrong vis his stomach." She gave no real details and his ailments sounded vague and somehow out-of-date.

Then she called my mother to say there was something wrong with his heart and there was nothing more she could do but wait, and she added that she was so sad and so tired. I know that these phone calls always came late at night and that my grandfather never got on the phone himself. Isabella always placed the call. I imagined that after my father had picked up the phone by his bed and heard the static of the overseas call, then Isabella's dramatic, quivering voice, he would quickly hand the receiver to my mother.

I picked up the phone. I knew the numbers by heart. I was the only one who still had anything to do with Isabella. We wrote to each other. We sent each other Christmas presents. I still had the wooden mousetrap-turned-paperweight she had given me when I began graduate school. Engraved in gold on the front, it read: *EILT SEHR*—Hurry it up. When I showed it to my mother, she said it was the kind of gift a commandant would give.

Isabella answered. She said she was glad to hear from me, but, no, I certainly could not talk to my grandfather. He was so very ill, and he "does hate the telephone even if just to listen." The cancer had spread to his throat and it hurt to talk. His heart? That seemed to have stopped leaking for the moment.

"Should I come?" I asked in English. "I could leave straightaway." I don't know why I said straightaway—perhaps because talking to Isabella made me feel British and movielike.

"No, no, darlink," she said. "It would be too difficult and there is now so much ice."

As I hung up the phone, Ezra stood behind me and wrapped his arms around my neck. His forearms covered my mouth. "I'm sorry," he said. "I know you've got a lot on your mind."

I leaned against him, stuck my finger in his ear, and called him by his nickname, Dirt.

"Come on," he said. "Let's go wild and order a pizza."

He reached past me, picked up the phone, pressed a button, hung up, pressed again, looked at the numbers, then hung up.

"Strange," he said. "Memory's gone."

I crossed my arms and fingered my rib cage. "I'm not hungry anyway."

The first Sunday of March, the week of Adar, I ate an apple for dinner. I was doing my best that year to follow the dietary laws—keeping meat and dairy products separate. I had read that when kept apart they are benign; together they become explosive.

"We really are from Hungary," I said out loud that evening in the middle of the kitchen. Ezra was at the museum. The ice maker let out a sigh and started its slow moans. When I first set out to translate my grandfather's memoirs, I felt like an orphan searching for clues about who her biological parents are. That feeling never did seem to go away.

I was coming to the end of the first chapter. "Does the historian have to know everything?" he had written. "Yes, we do prefer gaps to fairy tales, but the question is, which gaps?" I wondered then if my grandfather had chosen his own gaps and when exactly he had decided that my mother and I were negligible enough to fall into one.

There is a saying in the Talmud that "the omission or the addition of one letter might mean the destruction of the whole world." I was a translator, not a historian. Every letter, every word meant something. I wanted neither fairy tales nor gaps.

Even though I told my grandfather of the legitimacy of my project—that I had received grants to translate his life story—he would not discuss it. He said he would not be interpreted, that his story should remain forever in the language in which he wrote it. English would cheapen it, and, really, what did I know of Vienna? He very rarely spoke with me when I called him in Vienna. If he did choose to communicate with my mother and me, he did so through Isabella.

My mother had a theory about Isabella—that she was a saboteur. That she wanted my grandfather all to herself. My mother added that she couldn't imagine why—there wasn't any money to inherit and he was an impossible man to live with.

I looked up Pécs in the atlas and circled the town in red ink. I touched the red mark, moving my finger slowly from Pécs to Vienna, tracing the train voyage Joseph Engel and his gardener made when Joseph decided he had made enough money in the lumber business to buy a big house in a big city. Why not Budapest? I wondered. It was closer. Perhaps Joseph had not found the yellow house of his dreams in Budapest. Perhaps he saw nothing like the Hofzeile. In English, I typed while I translated from the memoir:

> The grandfather [Joseph] was determined for the Hofzeile to
> be a home for families (another, far more tasteless home for

families he had had built in Bazsi). It had a ground floor, two
upper stories fifty-five meters long, in a light yellow paint
color, with large rooms. The largest on each floor was ten
square meters with artistically inlaid Baroquelike floors from
variously colored wood. But the most beautiful feature of the
Hofzeile was the view, which looked to the north and took in
the last remnants of the Viennese woods from Hermannsko-
gel to the Leopoldsberg, in front of which the gradually rising
grape hills of Nussdorf and Grinzing are situated. I will never
forget the view in the evening light of fall and winter.

I stared down at the map of Vienna that lay open on the kitchen
floor. Döbling was north of Vienna. I had read that it was an elegant
suburb at the foot of the Vienna Woods, full of villas that housed pros-
perous artists, writers, high government employees, and the retired rich,
not to mention all those coffeehouses with the good coffee that two
Turkish invasions had left behind.

Also in the larger garden that lay behind the Hofzeile, my
grandfather had old trees—a mighty oak, birch, lilac bushes.
In a narrower passageway that went up to the Pyrkergasse
parallel behind the Hofzeile, a gate was walled in which led
to a two-story building—Devil's Castle. It was said that the
Kaiserine Maria Theresa received her lovers there with
noticeable preference for the Hungarian bodyguards.

I reread the first passage on the Hofzeile. Apparently, in the few
stories she had told me, my mother had not exaggerated about the
Hofzeile. I'd never known any details about Hungary. My mother never
told me what had happened to the house, and I wondered if my grandfather's memory of it bore any resemblance to reality, if his recollections

were like the reverse side of a tapestry—virtually the same as the front, save for a few loose threads and some knotted yarn.

I had studied my grandfather's life for the better part of two years. In my mind I clung to an image of the two of us sitting in a book-lined study, discussing all that happened in his life. He would tell me about Vienna, my great-grandmother, my real grandmother, Rosette, and my mother. We would sit knee to knee, sipping brandy, and we would both be amused and teary-eyed as he shared family secrets.

The freezer in the kitchen whined and shuttered to a wheeze.

Noises were nothing new to me, but in all of my other apartments, I had learned to place them. The furnace in one had been old. Wooden floors squeak more when the humidity level rises. I was a linguist, I told myself. It is my job to decode languages and sounds, but I wondered why I hadn't figured out the freezer.

One of Ezra's artist friends, a black man from South Bend, Indiana, once told me about sympathetic magic which he discovered when he decorated a ski mask he'd found on a street near Cabrini-Green. He sewed it with rows of spark plugs and hubcap shavings, and found that it had an angry vibe. "Objects can absorb your energy," he said. He felt that the mask had taken on the bad, violent feelings from that neighborhood in the projects.

I held my breath so I could hear where exactly the whining came from. Sometimes, it was just a whisper—so soft a sound you could barely hear it. Right then I could hear it and I wished it was louder. All it was was a sound and I wished it weighed more. I wanted to see its presence. I wanted to feel it against me.

The phone rang twice, but when I answered, nobody was on the other end.

"Ezra? Mom?" I said into the receiver. Nothing. "Grandfather?"

———

That week another letter from Isabella came in the mail, even though the address on the envelope was my address two apartments ago. It had been the one with the bad view. Now I lived in one with no view. Next to the blue airmail sticker on the envelope, Isabella had written in thick, capital letters: PLEASE MAKE FOLLOW!

Usually she wrote to me entirely in German, but this one was in English. It was dated, and after the year she had written "2:30 A.M."

My darling Elizabeth,

I want to thank you for all of your letters which touch me deeply. Thank you darling.

Yesterday I went to bed early and I did read all of the letters you had ever sent me. Afterwards I fell asleep and as it happens rather frequently got up after a few hours and started to think. A year like this particular one gives you a lot of thinking . . . But I don't want to write to you about things that happened and things that passed but of life to come.

While I was sitting in the dark near to the chimney in the living room, it came to my mind that I want to send you something—something to last. The book for instance that impressed me most in recent times is unfortunately no more available. This is your grandfather's very first book. It is a fascinating book and reveals all of his personality and his way to Catholicism. It was in this book that I found the answer to a question that has bothered me since grandfather fell ill. This "answer" will be my present for you.

One fine evening—it must have been in January, as grandfather was already suffering and very ill (although he did not know)—I mentioned something or complained about something rather unimportant at dinnertime. His answer was: "This is not according to St. Thomas." My reply: "What has this to do with St.

Thomas?" "Go and look it up," he said. I was a little angry. "Do tell me, how can I look it up right now?" It is not so easy to read St. Thomas, as you may know. Grandfather refused to answer or to explain—he seldom does.

Throughout these sad and lonesome weeks I tried in many ways to understand what he had in his mind while mentioning St. Thomas to me. I turned to his first book and there it was: magnanimity, a quality to which St. Thomas Aquinas accredited the greatest value.

Magnanimity—generosity of the heart and the spirit—this is what matters, this is what grandfather had—and still has. It was the source of his wit, his tenderness, and great understanding.

You are now past twenty years of age, Elizabeth. No more a child. You have an outlook on life and so many of its choices still open. It's wonderful and at the same time difficult and sometimes even hard. Try to compose your life from the ends and odds destiny will provide to you but always with magnanimity. This is not really my present to you. It's your grandfather's present.

I put down the letter, then picked it up and read it over again. It was written on thin, airmail paper with my grandfather's name and title on the upper left-hand corner.

In the beginning, when he first married Isabella, my grandfather had written me. He sent postcards from all over with a few sentences on the back, asking me to tell him about school. He never thanked me for previous letters the way my great-grandmother used to begin her letters. He only asked for more. I kept his cards in a separate stack, tied with thin, colorless twine. On the back of one—a photo of Alcalá's Door from Madrid—he wrote that he gave a talk and two queens and one royal highness were in the audience. The dinner, he said, was bad, and he ended by asking me to write again. On the back of another card—a black-and-white photo of the Grand Canal in Venice—he wrote that he wished he and I could watch the little boats together.

Then Isabella began to write, telling me she hoped I was collecting these beautiful postcards "they" were sending. My grandfather stopped sending his own cards and simply signed his name next to hers at the end. Isabella's cards were always clever, often romantic and affectionate messages. I kept these cards in another stack, tied together with blue twine. In one card, above her love and kisses, she wrote that twelve white horses were looking forward to seeing me. That particular postcard was from the Spanish Riding School. From Rome, she sent a photo of *The Mouth of Truth*. "My darling," she wrote. "What do you think of this little man—isn't he funny? But he is very old and very famous and he will prove immediately if you did not tell the truth. All my best wishes, Isabella." On the back of a picture of a Turkish mosque with the minaret from Pécs, she wrote that this was a very important picture. "Your grandfather's grandfather was born here," she wrote. "Many kisses, Your grandmother, Isabella." He had squeezed his initials below her name at the bottom of the card.

All through high school and college and then later in graduate school, I saved these postcards—taking in every bit of them as though they were food rations. I soaked the upper right-hand corners to get the stamps off. I looked closely at miniature pictures of the Kaiser in the palm of my hand, then I fixed them into a stamp book. I carefully taped the postcards into a big brown scrapbook, identifying each of the places in neat, black capital letters below each picture. The more stamps and picture postcards I had, the more I felt I could piece together who exactly my family was. Who my mother was. Who I was.

Who would have thrown them out?

I looked again at Isabella's big, sturdy letters. She wrote about him now as if he was already dead. I folded the thin paper and put the letter back inside the white envelope with Isabella's return address engraved in gray on the flap. I stared down at "Engel de Bazsi" and thought about my gift of magnanimity from what felt like the ghost of my grandfather, and I couldn't help but wonder what of him was left.

Eleven minutes before sundown that evening, I lit candles, put an old scarf over my head, and, not knowing really what to chant to celebrate the Sabbath, I waved my hands around. But the challah in the oven burned and made the smoke alarm go off and I had to stop in the middle of everything.

"I don't think Joseph would have liked me," I said later, staring down at the Chinese takeout Ezra had brought home. "He built his own temple next to his house so that he could pray. He didn't believe in what he called 'cheap assimilation fever.' And here I am, his great-great-whatever—just another Jewish wannabe."

"Elizabeth," Ezra said. "Eat. You look like you've been in Auschwitz."

"Very funny."

"I wasn't trying to be funny."

"I'm not hungry." And I wasn't. I didn't need lunch or even dinner anymore. I got through the day on a breakfast of corn flakes and water. My dissertation had become like meals I felt no urgency to finish. I filled myself with Austrian history and my grandfather's memoirs. I ate his German words.

"You know I can remember a time when you ate. Back when you were into the psychology of language—before you started those memoirs," Ezra said, nodding toward the papers and books on the floor.

"This is just as legitimate as anything else anybody's translating."

"Okay, okay, don't get so defensive." Ezra pushed the food around on his plate.

I had met Ezra two years before at the Oriental Museum in Hyde Park. It was my first year of graduate school at the University of

Chicago and I was still going to synagogue and eating kosher every-thing. He had just started in acquisitions.

That first week we were together, I felt as though I were wearing my right shoe on my left foot, my left shoe on my right. I must be in love, I remember thinking.

Mornings we held our breath and when we finally did speak we couldn't seem to finish sentences.

"Do you think it's because we're so . . ." I started once.

"Happy," he said. "Happy. Us."

The night I told Ezra I wanted to investigate human speech purely and deductively, he asked me to marry him. It was September, the month of Elul, and every morning I was getting up at 6:00 A.M. to blow on Ezra's old saxophone because I didn't want to spend the money on a shofar. I blew hard—the way I imagined the man in Exodus blew when Moses received the Ten Commandments on Mount Sinai. Still, I could only spew out air and spit.

Ezra had fallen out of his Judaism way back when he started col-lege, but he was willing to give it another try because he believed every-one should try to make do with the religion you're born with and he understood the need for human ceremony. "Sometimes you have to go ahead and jump in the hole and get dirty before you can get to the next, deeper level," he had said. The ceremonial act, he said in so many words, eventually led to the emotion behind it. For him, most things related back to an archeological dig.

"Is that why you want to marry me?" I had asked him at the time. "For the ceremony?"

"I want to marry you because I love you?" He said it like a question.

"You're not in love with me," I told him. "You just like that I can analyze your speech patterns."

We made an engagement of sorts. Ezra gave me a sterling silver pin shaped somewhat like the Star of David, and on Rosh Hashanah I baked a cake and Ezra decorated it with *Happy Birthday World, I Love Elizabeth* in blue.

For months I felt happy. At night we sat together on the sofa side by side, arm to arm, watching the news.

"Honey," Ezra said, looking at my empty plate. He used his chopsticks to serve me more wonton. "I think you've got a problem with food. I think you should see someone."

"This isn't a problem. I just don't want to eat right now."

"Just go talk to someone."

I slid the wonton back into the box and pushed my plate away. "I don't want to see anyone. I don't need anyone to tell me this all leads back to my mother."

"Your mother." He said it like a statement. A conclusion.

"I'm being hypothetical. There's nothing more to say," I said, getting up, rinsing my plate, putting it in the dishwasher.

I passed the table where my grandfather's memoirs lay open and saw the passage I had just translated.

My grandfather's sentences were long and complicated—it took a while to get to a verb. He had not written in a pure high German, which was what I had studied. His was a dialect-free language of high nobility. Some would have called it Schönbrunn German. My mother would have said, no, it's not German at all. It's Austrian. Then still others, with more encyclopedic concerns, would have refuted her, saying there is no such thing as the Austrian language—and if it ever did exist, it is gone now.

At meals Mahler was the center of attention. Justi sat next to him. Grandfather next to Bruno Walter, who sported a black, pointed beard. Once Arnold Schoenberg came. Mahler introduced him as his most talented student and he played for us that afternoon.

I came from a family who ate with Mahler. I had a great-grandfather who took walks with Ibsen and who performed after-dinner séances with Mahler's sister, Frau Professor Rose. I had a grandfather who visited Ezra Pound at St. Elizabeth's, had a twenty-five-minute audience with Pope Pius XII in 1958, and almost wrote a book of jokes organized by country with Sigmund Freud. And I'm going to ask my mother if it's okay to marry a guy who's nickname is Dirt? She hadn't said anything, but already I was wondering if my mother was right.

I marked the page with a pencil, closed the book, and left the kitchen.

"Maybe she'll be happy you're getting married," Ezra shouted from the other room. "Maybe she'll learn to like me."

"I'm late," I said, stuffing my sweatpants into a bag with my aerobic shoes. I touched the mezuzah on the doorpost and left.

At the end of Fatburners, our aerobics instructor commanded us to do the scissors on the floor. In the mirror I watched as we worked our legs in time.

"I've just had the pity-est day," Kathy said, lifting her leg next to me. We turned on our sides, holding our legs up to the count of ten. "You know how some people can just sit around and talk about vegetarianism and shoot the whole day? That drives me nuts."

Kathy called herself my high-impact, long-duration, low-intensity friend. We never saw each other outside of aerobics. Usually, we only talked during the floor stretches at the end of our ninety-minute workouts. Kathy was in real estate, but she wanted to start her own bakery. She actually wore purple eyeshadow because a computer told her to.

"It's your mother again, isn't it?" she said.

"It's everything this time. My grandfather's dying and he won't see

me. I don't know how to tell my mother about Ezra or how to really fill
Ezra in about my mother."

A little boy tumbling on a blue mat nearby crawled next to me and
asked, "Where's my mommy?"

"I don't know, what does she look like?" I looked around at all the
women in black tights and white T-shirts. I wondered why he was asking me and not Kathy. Kathy looked friendlier and had better teeth.

After a moment of consideration, the little boy leaned and whispered in my ear, "Like a ghost." Then he set off again, crawling back to
his blue mat.

"What do you care what your mother thinks anyway?" Kathy said.
"Ezra's a great guy. Just marry him and be happy. You'll both have the
same initials, you're meant to be. Come on, you're, what, twenty-seven
years old for chrissakes."

For a moment, as Kathy and I raised our legs and air-biked, I pic-
tured my future with Ezra. There we were on another dig in a hot
place—he with his paintbrush, dusting off a vase; me with a pocket English to Hieroglyphics/Hieroglyphics to English dictionary looking up
the ancient words printed on the vase. REM's "Shiny Happy People"
would be playing on our portable radio, and we *would* feel like shiny
happy people, except that we we'd be covered with dust.

We stood up and did as our instructor commanded—reaching for
the track lighting in the ceiling.

"What? Do you wanna be one of those boomerang kids? Leave
home, then keep going back there to live? Spend the rest of your life
going to disease parties with your mother? One week it'll be a charity
for lupus. Another week it's M.S. That what you want?"

We looked to the left for a beat, then to the right. Neck stretches.

"But I don't want to end up like those couples, you know, who get
married after they've lived together for three years. You ask them how

they are after their wedding and it's always, 'It's the same, but it's different.' You know?"

"Do you always think like that?" Kathy said, making like Raggedy-
Ann, flopping toward the floor. "I guess you get sick of being brainy all
day. I mean, I'm thirty years old and I think I'm finally ready to take the
SATs." Kathy stood up straight, then stood next to me, comparing our
thighs in the mirror in front of us. "You know, you're lucky with Ezra. I
was engaged to this guy once, and all of a sudden, in the middle of the
night, I wake up and see him on the bedroom floor, crouched down,
spinning on the balls of his feet, shouting, 'Get off me! Get off me!'
Turns out he'd been abused by his father. He never told me that. I got
out of that like that." She snapped her fingers. "I hate it when they keep
big secrets."

That week I ate only spinach, and I translated the most affectionate passage I had yet come across in my grandfather's memoirs. Using vague
but delicate wording which made very little grammatical sense when
translated into English, he wrote about his first love, a "great" and
"strong" love, with a boy he never named.

> The events of puberty caused me a lot of trouble; I found
> no one who could or would talk about the burning question
> with me. A house doctor who was trusted with this task
> proved to be grotesquely inept at doing it. A great love I
> had for a colleague of my class and which he reciprocated
> helped me get over much; it was a strong love and I
> remember quite exactly the content of the letters which we
> wrote to each other, and I see his clear, brown eyes, the cut
> of his mouth, his light, somewhat shy laughing, and his
> hands with long, not at all weak fingers. Smiling—Hands—

innumerable variations about a beautiful, not known topic. I
lost sight of him soon after the final exam. I know where he
lives; he married a rich woman, and I hope I never see him
again.

I had read enough about fin-de-siècle Vienna to know that experi-
ments with homosexuality were not at all uncommon, but what was
unusual about the passage was my grandfather's unembarrassed, almost
haughty declaration of love. *Eiene grosse Liebe. Eine starke Liebe. Liebe,*
the word for "love," never came up again in his book—even when he
wrote of my mother, or anybody else in his family, for that matter.

I wondered what would have happened later if he had been found
out. Many homosexual Jews and non-Jews went to Sachsenhausen in
East Berlin, which had the reputation for its gardens and beautiful
flower beds, tended, of course, by the prisoners, who were given pink tri-
angle patches to be sewn over the left breast pocket of their regulation
uniforms and worn point-down.

"Aren't you coming to bed?" Ezra stood squinting in the doorway.
His hair was tousled the way it appeared in pictures taken at dig sites
every summer.

After Ezra had given me the pin shaped like the Star of David, I
went out to lunch with my father to ask him for his blessing.

"I want to be sure this is okay with you and Mom," I had said.

Our tuna plates arrived and as the waitress set his down, he smiled.
At the time I hadn't been sure if my father was smiling at the idea of my
marrying Ezra, that I was asking for his blessing, or if he was just glad to
see his lunch. "Have at it," he said, raising his fork.

"We should go on a dig together," I told Ezra.

He knelt and kissed my knee. "I thought you said you weren't the
dig type."

I put my hand on his head. "I'd do anything for you, you know."

"Are you just saying this because I held your hand for nine hours during *Shoah*?"

"Hold me again," I said, kneeling on the floor in front of him. "For nine more."

That month on Rosh Chodesh, my mother called and told me that Father Brown had asked about me after mass. "You should come for Easter. That's what he told me. 'Elizabeth should come for Easter.'"

"I told you, Mom. I don't celebrate Easter anymore."

"Elizabeth. You're not Jewish, you're Catholic."

"I don't *feel* Catholic." I waited a beat. "Jesus was a Jew, at least on his mother's side."

"How dare you. Just how dare you. Where do you get this? That boy you're living with?"

"Let's leave Ezra out of this, okay?"

"The Nazis wouldn't have even bothered with you—you're that watered down."

"Wait a minute," I said. "You don't want to be Jewish, but then it's something to be proud of?"

"I never should have told you anything. You never should have met my father. I should have just kept my mouth shut, shouldn't I? Then you wouldn't be living with this ridiculous boy." My mother sighed. "Look, you're not a survivor. You're not even a survivor's child. It doesn't concern you."

"But it does concern me. Even if I was completely non-Jewish, it would concern me. You shouldn't negate something just because it doesn't concern you or because it happened to 'them.'"

"Don't tell me what I should and shouldn't do. I'm tired."

"That's just wrong," I went on. I was righteous from a morning's worth of reading and I felt compelled to lecture her. "It's not 'their' tragedy, it's ours. It's yours and mine. It's everybody's. This was a human event—done *by* people *to* people. I *want* to own up to it."

"Own up?" my mother said.

I looked up and Ezra was standing in the doorway with a sack of groceries. We were going to celebrate our first Seder together. He put the sack down and made like an audience, silently clapping, cheering, whistling—all exaggerated.

"Fine," my mother said into the phone. "So go. Go own up to your make-believe Jewishness. What does it matter anyway? I am appalled by you, Elizabeth. You grow up to become what? Nothing. You have come from everything and now you are a nothing. It's as though you don't really belong to me. I don't understand you and I certainly don't understand whatever you have going with this silly boy. What is his awful name? Ezra. You are nothing and you are certainly not my daughter."

When I heard the dial tone, I could still hear her voice and I must have looked different because Ezra asked if I was all right.

"It's no big deal," I said, walking to the sink, putting my hand on the faucet, holding my wrists under the cold running water so that I would stop shaking. "Maybe . . . " I swallowed back the urge to cry, then took a drink of water straight from the faucet. "I don't know. Maybe she's bothered by your name."

"I'll have you know that Lichen is a great, great name," Ezra said, putting his chin on my shoulder. "A lichen can survive anywhere—even in places where nothing else will. There are fifteen thousand kinds of lichen, and they can live up to five thousand years. We are second only to the Bristol pine. We are survivors. We will never face extinction."

I turned off the water.

"I was thinking of your first name. Ezra."

"Oh," Ezra said, letting go. "So, my little psycholinguist, *she's* bothered. Not you?"

For a moment I remembered how my mother had often cut her

name in half whenever she filled in documents asking for her maiden name. She would write Bazsi, leaving out the Engel de. I had read in a newspaper article that scientists had developed a way to cut out the "good" cholesterol genes of people to be put into the livers of other people who produced too much "bad" cholesterol. What else could be cut out and replaced as quickly as that? I wondered if my mother was ever bothered by what she did—writing down only a part of her name. It seemed to me, if you took away something that had been there for a long time, there would be a hole left. A gap. An omission that might mean the destruction of the whole world.

"Forget it," I said. "What does it matter, anyway." I turned away from the sink, got my coat off a chair, and left.

I stopped at a bakery and bought a sack of day-old danish. I walked toward the lake and sat on a bench facing the water. I ate. Systematically, I ate all six danish in the sack. I wasn't full enough, so I went back to the bakery, got another six, came back to the bench, and ate those. I got up and brushed the crumbs from my lap. I picked up a stone and threw it into the lake. Then I went to the public restroom. I shut and locked the stall door. I took off my coat and hung it on the hook on the back of the door. Then I leaned over and made myself throw up.

It was, I knew, a last resort—a habit I thought I no longer had, but whenever I felt myself getting emptier and emptier, even smaller, I felt as though I was purging myself of whatever part of me I was not interested in keeping. Sometimes it was the Catholicism I had accidentally acquired at birth. But today, today I was attempting to get rid of the twelve danish and my mother's utter shame and disappointment in me. Maybe I was meant to be nothing. Empty.

Afterwards, I put on my coat, rinsed my mouth, chewed gum, and caught a cab to Michigan Avenue.

At the Spertus Museum of Judaica on South Michigan Avenue in Chicago there is a touch screen computer that you can sit in front of whenever you want to talk to a rabbi. The only problem is you usually have to wait in line and you can only ask the computer questions about the beginning of life or how to allocate your time. You cannot ask if your attempts at assimilation into Judaism are working. You cannot ask if you should marry a man named Ezra. You cannot ask why your grandfather won't communicate with you. You cannot ask how to stop making yourself sick or how to talk to your mother.

There is another machine in the museum and this is where I sat. On that computer screen, the names of relatives lost during World War II by Chicago area families appear and disappear. It takes a full day to get through the list, and that list is incomplete. I know because we are not on it.

A woman in a light green coat sat down next to me in front of the screen. She asked a guard how long she should wait for the "M's." The guard said he had turned the computer on at ten that morning and that it would be a while for the "M's."

The woman took out some knitting from her purse. She would wait, she said.

When I got to the discussion of his conversion in the memoirs, I expected to read that my grandfather had been dragged kicking and screaming down the Karntnerstrasse to St. Stephen's cathedral the way Gustav Mahler had been forced to be baptized—the only way he could be elected *Hofoperndirektor*, chief conductor of the court opera. But no. My grandfather invited his priest friend over and had a quiet ceremony at the Hofzeile before dinner—as though his conversion were cocktails.

Later, when he told his mother, she threatened to disown him.

At the rate the computer screen flashed the names of Chicago area people killed in the Holocaust, it would take some six years to honor each individual Jew and non-Jew who had died. I wondered then how long it would take me to grieve for all the relatives I never knew.

In the Spertus Museum of Judaica there are questions everywhere you turn, questions, you are told, a Jew must ask him- or herself. How can we survive without independence? How can we worship? What laws should be followed? What should be assimilated from other cultures? What rejected?

My grandfather's high school graduation project was called "What you inherit from your fathers and how you earn it in order to possess it." He even wrote a poem at the end of the paper entitled "The Fairy Tale of Good Fortune," which he said was destroyed in 1938 along with everything else.

We were up to the "L's." I thought of Ezra's name, Lichen. Second only to the Bristol pine. They were survivors. They would never face extinction.

The name Engel de Bazsi does not appear on the computer screen at the Spertus Museum of Judaica. I know because I have sat in front of the screen and waited and waited, all the while thinking, if we assimilated and assimilated and assimilated, could there be any Engel de Bazsi left in me?

My mother had often told me that her family never was Jewish, not really. There was no mezuzah near their front door and the men certainly never wore homburgs. They never heard the ram's horn blown for the New Year in a synagogue and her father never taught her what to do when death was near. He never told her to cover her head and say in a loud voice, *Shema Yisrael, Adonai elocheinu, Alonai echad*—Hear O Israel, the Lord thy God the Lord is One. These were the words to say so that you would not die alone. These were the words that would join your death to all those who had come before and were still to come. I doubted very much that my grandfather would say these words at his own death because I doubted that in death, as in life, he really wanted to be in the company of his ancestors. Not the way I did.

There is a part in the Epistle to the Hebrews about faith: ". . . faith is the assurance of things hoped for, the conviction of things not seen." There are things I do know but never saw: that the Nazis chose to hold selections at the camps during Passover; that they cremated the dead, knowing that Jews did not believe in cremation as a burial act. I know that at the *Natzweiler* camp in Struthof, Germany, they used to put some women's bodies in tubs to "pickle" them after their deaths so that their bodies could be sent to the nearby University of Strasbourg for "study."

What do you do with such facts? Scream them out? Thumb-tack them onto an imaginary bulletin board next to your heart? Find a refrigerator and some magnets—post them all over, up and down, then never eat again?

Just then "Melzinski" appeared on the screen and the woman put down her knitting. We both stared for a beat. Then "Melzowi" appeared, and the woman put her knitting back into her purse, got her coat, and left.

It snowed that night—a late, solid, big-flaked snow—and Hyde Park went mute and white.

Ezra had gotten into the habit of going to his lab at the Oriental Museum whenever we fought, which was getting to be more and more frequent. Sometimes he stayed there all night.

Sitting back at the table in the kitchen, I read about a great-uncle I had never heard of—Joska. He rewrote *The Merchant of Venice*, retitling it *The Merchant of Rome or Shylock's Original Figure* so that it was friendlier to Jews. He had a son he named after Richard Wagner. After the Socialists burned his manuscript in Leipzig, the SS took him to the concentration camp at Dachau, where he went on a hunger strike to protest mistreatment, and there, of course, he died.

That night, lying awake alone in bed, I thought of Joska. It felt as though I had known about Joska all along. There was a professor of linguistics at the University of Chicago. Everyone knew that he was a survivor of Mauthausen. I knew because I had taken his class and seen him rolling up his sleeve as though he wanted to make sure his students saw the tattooed numbers there on his forearm. Some said he even rubbed olive oil into the numbers at night, so that they would not disappear.

In his memoirs, my grandfather wrote that when his wife, Rosette, was pregnant, he mentioned to Joska that he wanted a girl. "Don't talk nonsense!" Joska had screamed. Maybe Joska knew something then that no one else did. Did he know that the family would face hardship? Was it possible he suspected that a girl—my mother—would be the last of them and would be unable to carry on the family name?

Joska. Did he put cheese in his coffee or wear noisy shoes? I worried for his spirit—he had died away from home, in a camp. My great-grandmother had died away from Vienna, in a home in Washington, D.C., for the elderly. Elie Wiesel wrote that God is in exile—He's everywhere, so He's never home. I supposed Joska and my great-grandmother were all right, then; they weren't alone.

Joska. I said the word out loud and thought on it hard—maybe the air around me would catch the good, hard, two-syllable sound of his name and carry his ghost, the ghost of Joska, to me. Maybe Joska would be my messenger—my Hermes—and go back and forth between my mother and me. Tell her she's not alone, I thought hard. Tell all of them, they're not going to be alone.

That night I sat at the kitchen table and finished translating my grandfather's memoirs. I did not read what I had expected and half-hoped to find. He had a few good World War I chapters. He told a funny story about how he "held" his position in the trenches during a particularly brutal Russian attack because he was so immersed in reading von Hof-mannstal. For this he received a silver metal.

But there was so little about World War II and not even one Hitler sighting—only wistful descriptions of the Vienna Woods at twilight and the sounds of the Hofzeile settling in. There was the one incident when he was in high school and a student called out *Sou Jud* or "Jew pig," to which my grandfather responded *Sou Christian*; but, otherwise, no witnessed brutal attacks upon my mother and her family. In between the lines, I could sense the slow, patient workings of a new German bureaucracy whittling its way toward the landholdings and the houses.

Had I been a reviewer, I would have said that it was a self-pitying, sad book. The story of a man who had to flee his country, and who returned expecting prizes and compensation for his losses. Alas, upon his return, he never did get the salary, pension, or position he felt he was entitled to at the University of Vienna. He was not selected to be the director of the Austrian Cultural Institute in Rome, the only position for which he had ever strived. His was the story of the prodigal son returning to his motherland, but when he got there, nobody was left to welcome him home. His Vienna was a nasty place. Freud and Kokoschka were wise to have left and stayed away.

As a reviewer, I would have lamented that this author did not write more about the intriguing *personal* element of his life—his family—and that it was unfortunate that this particular historian spent so much page space name-dropping.

As his granddaughter, for all that I wanted to find out—Why had he left Vienna in 1939 without his own mother, whose papers were stamped with *Juden*? And how could he have gone back to the very city that had turned against him?—the answers were not there. Instead, I read the most about people he never really knew and the least about those closest. I now knew how many times he had seen Mussolini (three) and how many times he had visited Ezra Pound at St. Elizabeth's in Washington, D.C. (twelve). He wrote a whole chapter on the "Negro question" in America, but not a word about the "Jewish problem" in Europe. He used delicate wording for concentration camps—"places of shame"—the way a Nazi would have called them "work camps."

He mentioned that he had met one of Rasputin's murderers at a dinner party in the late thirties, but he never mentioned that he had dined with me, his only granddaughter. He didn't write about my mother when she was ten, moving to a new country.

"Writing history is beautiful and is an occupation worthy of a man," my grandfather wrote near the end of his book. "It was, it is a preparation. It is not a result. In retrospect, I have nothing to be ashamed of, with errors, failures, and regrets, yes, but nothing to be ashamed of. This is something even if it is not that much." I realized that his "it" referred not only to the writing of history but to how he lived his life.

On the last page of his book, my grandfather wrote: "and now that I have been given the path to the 'high age,' I hope that I will keep the discontent with myself." When I finally closed his book, I knew then that his hope had failed.

We were approaching Seder and I was eating mostly salted matzoh to remind myself that my ancestors, in their haste to leave Egypt, didn't have time to let their bread rise. I wanted to be reminded of quick departures, and I often wondered what I would have packed if I had a forty-year walk through the desert ahead of me.

"What is it?" Ezra said when he saw me. "You're pale."

"I keep seeing her," I said. "I keep seeing my great-grandmother."

"That's because you're not eating enough."

"It's the Sabbath before Seder," I said. "I forgot to look up exactly what to do."

He was standing at the kitchen counter next to a blender full of green goo. "Presto," he said. "Pesto. Lots of iron. You need that."

I had put a fish bowl in the room to represent the parting of the Sea of Reeds, and I had planned to dress in traveling clothes to act out the Exodus, but that evening, we just lit some candles and prayed before dinner.

We used to do everything right, or at least we tried. In October, on the first day of Tishri, we had eaten apples dipped in honey to get the new year off to a sweet start. Staring at the candle in front of me, I couldn't help but think that I should have been in Vienna or in Jerusalem in the Old City pressing a *Kvitel* into the cracks of the Western Wall.

"This isn't working," I said, taking the white shawl off my head, blowing out the candles.

"Sure it is," Ezra said. He used to stand, but now he sat, a fork in one hand.

"Not this," I said. "Us."

Once, he told me that when he saw Simon and Garfunkel perform in concert in Central Park, he thought they looked like two goldfish. "I want that kind of synchronicity between us," he had said.

"*We're* not working," I said.

"What are you talking about?"

As we stared at each other, neither one of us moving, I felt something slamming shut in my heart.

"My family wouldn't understand all this." I looked around the room at the table and the blender and the cinder-block bookcases.

"I'm not living with your family, I'm living with *you*." Ezra got up and paced a circle around the kitchen. "What we have here is obscene." He gritted his teeth. "We're too close *not* to be married. It's the next logical step for us. It's the next emotional level."

"Jesus, Ezra, this isn't a dig. We don't have to keep shoveling to the next level."

He turned on the blender, then he turned it off.

"It's not finished," I said, looking at the basil inside the blender. "The leaves are still whole."

"What's the point? If you do finally eat it, you'll only throw it up." He took a deep breath. "Oh God, Elizabeth. I'm sorry, but it's not so complicated. You've got a problem with food. You've got a problem with your mother. And you've got a problem with me."

He went to the closet and took out his coat. The wire hangers jingled, and for a moment, they sounded like the wind chimes outside my aunt Pauline's house whenever someone came or left and closed the sliding glass doors. Even then, growing up in Mississippi, I remember thinking that leaving shouldn't sound as sweet as arriving.

"I love you," he said, with one arm through the sleeve of his coat. "I want to marry you. You, and all your God-damned problems." He put his other arm through the other sleeve. Then he sighed and wrapped his neck with a bright red scarf once, twice, three times. "I wish that was enough for you."

Already I was thinking of him in the past tense. I thought of the way he had once looked at me while he ground pepper over a salad he had made for the two of us, and the way he had buried his face into the crook of my neck that same night, mouthing "I love you so much" so that I could still feel the words on my shoulder afterwards.

"What was it that Pat Nixon whispered to her husband in the helicopter as they were leaving the White House for the last time?" Ezra said. "Oh yeah. 'It's so sad.' That's what she said. 'It's so sad.'" He shook his head. "It's so sad, Lizzy."

He closed the door, then opened it again.

"Just do me one favor," he said. "Call me when you think you need to."

I looked at him, then I nodded.

In India, those who handle the dead are the Untouchables. They are considered dirty, and in some towns they are not allowed into the marketplace during daylight. I wondered right then what the Indians did with those haunted by the dead. I should move to India, I thought. That way, I would be tagged an Untouchable and no one would have to deal with me. She is the one steeped in the past, they would whisper as I passed, shopping for my vegetable Biryani. See the cloud over her head? She is the one immersed in death and memory. And when I finally left with my bags of groceries, I would sweep away my own footprints as though I had never come, as though I did not exist in their world.

I stood staring at the closed door after Ezra left. I looked and looked and looked at the door and realized that it was not real. It was not made of wood, but of aluminum. It was only made to look like a door made of wood.

My mother liked things made to look like what they were not—new furniture made to look old. Me. I imagined all of what she had grown up with at the Hofzeile—parlor rooms filled with Prussian helmets used as ashtrays perhaps; a knight in armor for an umbrella stand; a Turkish dagger used to cut the Sunday roast. All the surfaces she had known as a child had been stuccoed or covered with tortoise shell and ivory. The pianos and sofas had probably been swathed with oriental rugs—everything was covered with something else. It all seemed so impossibly heavy, too heavy for one person to bear.

She says they were all Catholics—her mother, her father. And she went to convent schools all her life, yet her great-grandfather had built a temple near his home so that he could worship there at his convenience.

How is it that she lived like that?

In his memoirs, my grandfather wrote that Ezra Pound sat and stared down at Washington from his hill in St. Elizabeth's for long periods of time. Looking out my window to the chip of a view of Hyde Park, I wondered what Pound had thought about. Had he felt the thundercloud splitting open above his head as I felt then? Had he tasted the blackness surrounding him as I did? Had he heard his heart tighten up as though it were hardened sugar? Had he seen the ice in the air? Had he worried if he would ever be warm again?

That night, I had a dream I was on a train. As it headed through a tunnel, I heard my great-grandmother say my name. I looked around at all the passengers in the train, and through chinks of light I saw businessmen mostly, reading papers. In the dream, I closed my eyes and tried to sleep, but my great-grandmother woke me up with her blue eyes. She mouthed my name. She is reminding me to do something, I thought in my dream and in my sleep. I thought of what my grandfather had said of her advice in his book: don't eat black meat, don't smoke cigars, and get lots of exercise—that's how you live long. But I knew that wasn't why she was staring at me with her blue eyes, keeping me awake.

At dawn, I woke up, thinking I heard a floorboard creak.

"Who's there?" I said. "Ezra?"

A siren sounded down the street. I got up and reread a section from the book.

> Today it seems to me as the correct expression of these years that they were dominated at home by the ever-growing concern of my father regarding the Dippel trees of the Hofzeile, which he had inherited after the death of my grandfather. How long would they remain standing? The concern grew in him that the beams in the roof supports would become damaged and he would not be able to come up with the high costs of repairs. The fear of the rotting beams never left Father, even in his last hours. But the beams were still intact and the monarchy long since fallen when the house was sold. And the roof construction

remained sturdy and the beams were unharmed when the bombs of the Second World War began to topple the old house.

"When the house was sold." It is interesting to note, I wrote in the margins, my grandfather's consistent use of the passive voice.

At 8:00 A.M. I called my mother.

"Don't we need to buy some clothes today?" I asked.

Standing in front of the dresses at Loehmann's, my mother shouted out, "What are you today, an eight or a six?"

I moved out of Blouses toward her.

"Eight," I said. "I like them big and baggy."

"I miss this," she said, putting her arm around my neck. All the clothes hanging over our arms came between us. "We never get to play anymore. You shouldn't hang up on your mother." Two women speaking Polish to one another excused themselves and reached between us to get to the fourteens, and my mother had to let go.

In the communal dressing room, my mother was quick to take off her clothes.

"I bought a lovely new underthing and you have to say something about it," she said. Standing in front of me in a champagne-colored camisole and control-top pantyhose, my mother managed to maintain a particular kind of coquettish dignity. She smelled vaguely of good perfume, and as she smiled, the crow's-feet flew out from the corners of her eyes like firecrackers.

"Nice," I said.

I put a skirt on first, but my mother saw the girdle I wore anyway.

"What are you trying to do, hold your bones in?"

"I'm fat," I said.

"How can you say that?" We looked at each other in the mirror. I'm fat with two religions, two languages, and too much past, I wanted to say. One body can't fit all that in.

"You look like a Schiele woman. One of his charcoal drawings— those studies in bones and shadows. Is *he* making you like this? You shouldn't have to lose weight for any man."

"I'm not seeing Ezra anymore, Mom." I zipped up a skirt, looked in the mirror, then zipped it off. My mother didn't look pleased by what I had just said. She looked concerned. "I don't like this plaid, do you?" I said.

"What is it you want?" she asked. Even though we both knew she wasn't referring to clothes, it still wasn't one of those meaningful moments a daughter looks back on, gratefully acknowledging that, yes, once upon a time, her mother *had* in fact asked her what she most wanted. This was nothing out of the ordinary. My mother always asked the big questions.

I supposed I wanted Ezra back. I supposed I wanted a smallish house and a serious perennial garden. I wanted to finish what I had started. I wanted to swallow what I ate and have the ability to keep it down, hold it in, make something of it so that it was good for me. I wanted my mother to see herself in me and like it.

We looked at each other in the mirror. "Nothing much," I said. "Just something."

I changed into a baggy sack dress.

"So *that's* the way you feel about your life," my mother said.

I stared in the mirror and saw what she saw.

"I just don't want to wrinkle," I said.

"It's a ghostly color on you." She held up a short red cocktail dress— a size six. "You look so good in red. Try this one on." I held the dress up to my chin while she stood back. "You have my mother's nose," she said, fluffing my bangs. "Most women would die for that nose. You're a beautiful woman with this huge shadow hovering over you. You don't eat and you wear old, shabby clothes that are too big for you."

She took a few steps back. In front of the mirror, she posed, putting one foot in front of the other, straightening the jacket of a black wool suit she had just put on. An elegant mourning ensemble. She arched her left eyebrow and did not smile. My father and I always called this her "European" look. She used it when someone was being nasty to her. It was also the look she had in her engagement photos.

I wondered how my mother had first said good-bye to her father. There was a wedding photograph of my grandfather kissing my mother's forehead before or after the wedding—I could never tell. She has her eyes closed and she is smiling. Her mother, Rosette, stands aside, looking on.

"Too severe?" My mother held the collar of the jacket closed with two fingers. There we were, I thought, standing next to her. She in her mourning suit. Me, looking half dead.

I saw a mother elephant with her stillborn baby on TV once. The mother elephant stood over the dead calf, lifted one leg, and passed the sole of her foot over the length of her dead offspring. She lifted each of her feet in this manner, her soles never touching, but hovering over her dead baby. It was an eerie moment and I wondered what exactly was happening. Perhaps this was the mother elephant's burial ceremony— her way of saying good-bye. Perhaps she was blessing it, preparing it for its elephant afterlife. When the mother elephant had patiently passed her four feet over her baby, she left the dead heap and headed out back to her herd.

"Yeah," I said. "It's too severe. Maybe something softer."

She looked at me, and brushed the hair away from my face. "Such a pretty cat." She had her co-co voice on.

"Mom."

"I'm trying to say I'm sorry," she said, all serious now. "I'm sorry for blowing up at you. It's just that I want so much for you. The best for you."

"Let me ask you a question," I said. She nodded. "Why don't you ever talk about Grandfather?" I started to say "your father" but that seemed too personal.

My mother sighed and let go of the collar, revealing her camisole. She sat down on one of the benches. "You know, when he visited that one time, he accidentally called me Kara. I can understand that, but still. He did not know who I was even if it was for a minute and it hurt."

I nodded. Kara I knew now was my grandfather's sister, who had died during the influenza epidemic in the winter of 1919. In his book, he explained her death in an adverbial clause. His brother, Cosima, who died on the battlefield at Konyuchy, got a paragraph. My mother earned three sentences—the first one concerned her stealing the squirrels' winter storage, the second had to do with her "wrong" decision not to visit Ezra Pound anymore when he was incarcerated at St. Elizabeth's because she was, at the time, trying to get a governmental position in Washington, and the third claimed that she had had a tough time coming to America and that even after twenty years there she was still homesick for Vienna.

My mother had once told me that my father's father tended to hurt those he loved the most. Maybe this was also true of her father. Maybe this was why my parents were always saying or whispering to each other, "I love you," three, sometimes four times a day. Their parents had never told them.

"Mom, why didn't you go back to Vienna to live?"

"I had a husband," she started.

"Before that," I said.

She shook her head. "It wasn't an option." I sat down on the bench beside her. The two Polish women stood across the room trying on red spandex dresses that zipped up in front.

"When my mother was dying, I left you with your father to be with her. I flew to Vienna from Jackson. I nursed her while your grandfather was in Rome researching. His wife was dying, and he was researching the holy Vatican." My mother was talking now as much to herself as she was to me.

"Did you go back to the Hofzeile?"

She took a deep breath.

"I wanted to, but Mother said it wasn't a good idea. She said she had once. She wouldn't talk about it. She just made me promise never to go back. She said it would depress me."

"You really don't want to see him?" I said, half whispering. "Not at all?"

"Oh Elizabeth, you're making me so tired I can't see straight." She stared at the Polish women posing in their spandex dresses.

"Can I go?" I said this just as the thought came to me, and as I said the words, I knew I *had* to go.

"I don't know why you'd want to," my mother said, though she did not sound surprised. It occurred to me then that she may have been expecting this, maybe even hoping for this, all along. "It won't do you any good. He's not the same man, and Vienna is certainly not the same place." Across the room, the two Polish women put their clothes back on and left with the spandex dresses. "I don't think it even exists anymore."

My mother and I looked at each other in the mirrors. For years she kept me posted on what material things I would inherit when she died—furniture we had gotten together at house sales, silver her mother had managed to smuggle across borders. But my mother never spoke of the other things she would pass down to me.

I thought of how it would be if my mother died. People who knew her would look at me and most likely remark on our resemblance. "I'm not sure how," they would say. "Maybe around the eyes." But I would know what they were seeing was not the similarity between our foreheads or our eyebrows. What they saw was my real inheritance—the anger and regret my mother had left with me to polish and covet.

"Do you think I'd be too much like the angel of death?" I asked.

My mother laughed and put her arm around me. "You do manage to always pop up at the crucial death scenes," she said. "That's not necessarily a bad thing." She let go of me. "But just know that you won't find anything." It was exactly what she had said when I told her I was translating her father's memoirs.

A large Hispanic woman with red hair took off her clothes next to us and stepped into a pair of white leather pants with fringe sewn in at the seams.

My mother opened her purse and took out her car keys. She looked pale.

"Are you hungry?" I said. "We can go get something to eat."

"Come with me first," she said, looking at her keys.

It was the first time we left a discount clothing store together without bags. Without a word, we drove straight out of the parking lot and to the bank. Once inside, my mother led me into the basement to her safe deposit box.

It was the kind of silent ceremony I suppose I had wanted all along. My mother found her safe deposit box, set it on one of the gray-black marble counters, and carefully took out each item until the box was empty. There were some letters I didn't ask about, and a cheesy little light blue hand-painted picture of Jesus as a baby. There was an old, worn light brown leather box, which she unfastened. I caught sight of some old jewelry—pearl earrings with interesting, tarnished fasteners, brooches, and necklaces I vaguely remembered my great-grandmother wearing in Washington. My mother refastened the lid to the box and slid it next to the letters. There were some papers and another box which she did not open. Then she brought out a doll.

It was a good-sized doll about the size of an old Thumbelina I used to have, but it did not have the face of a baby. The painted eyes were chipped as she looked straight ahead, unsmiling. Her braids were loosening and coming unfixed from her head, and it looked as though she was going bald. My mother pulled the little blue hat down tighter over her head, fixing what looked like the remains of a feather in the rim. The puffy white sleeves of her dress were water-stained red-green and her blue apron was torn in half and unraveling. As my mother pulled up the doll's dress in the back, I saw that she had on a pair of graying cotton bloomers and that one of her shoes was missing.

"Here," my mother said, laying a rusty key in the palm of my hand. She had pulled the key from somewhere inside the doll. The key was one of the big, old-fashioned kind, and it looked fake somehow—as though it were the key to a cartoon city mayors give to honored guests.

Then it occurred to me. This was the key to the yellow house in the golden land. This was the key to the Hofzeile.

My mother put the doll and all the rest back inside her safe deposit box. Then she slid the box back and we left the bank. She didn't say another word about the Hofzeile or my chances of finding it still intact.

"Let's not go to the Pie Pan today," my mother finally did say that afternoon. "I'm too old to be eating in mediocre restaurants."

And we did eat. We had big Greek salads and bialys, and, afterwards, I didn't go to the ladies' room to throw up.

PART IV

Ghost of a Nation

GENEVIEVE

MY FIRST FRIEND IN AMERICA WAS A PRIEST. AT SCHOOL
there was a competition—whoever sold the most subscriptions to the
diocesan paper would get five dollars. I thought the parish priest was a
good prospect, so I called on him. Father Green was amused and bought
a subscription. Then he came to call on us.

We started having a "priest dinner party" once a month, always with
Father Green. My mother had about two or three standard dishes she
served; she used to cut out the recipes from the society pages.

We knew a lot of white Russians when we lived in D.C. and we
usually invited them to the priest parties. A princess living down the
street from us made a living trading the old books and musical instruments she had smuggled out. She stopped me on the street every day to
remind me that she had known Alexander I and Napoleon I. Your father
gets disgusted when people make such a big deal out of fallen Russian
aristocracy. I tell him people make a big deal just because aristocrats are
different, and they usually have better taste in furniture.

I remember my father being mad once when the three of us went to
a concert and the program was Wagner. They were still teaching German in the schools, he complained, now Wagner. Why weren't the

Americans more anti-German? They were at war with that nation, were they not?

In Washington, I missed Grossmama. I missed having tea with her. She always served me fruit crackers. In Vienna, when I went down to the factory, I had seen Grossmama amid those long wooden planks and my mother very far away between two phones. Now all that was gone.

In Washington, the three of us clung to the church. It was where we felt most at home. Mass was still in Latin, so we could forget about struggling with American English for at least an hour. More important, we knew the procedure. We knew the language, the movements, the prayers—we knew where our hands were supposed to go, we knew when to kneel, sit, bow. When you have the ritual down, the rest usually follows.

For the first time I made a novena for Grossmama to come to America. Every day I said the Magnificat, which was the hymn that Elizabeth said when she saw Mary—or was it Mary who said it? "My soul does magnify the Lord, and my spirit has rejoiced in God my Saviour. For He has seen the humility of His handmaiden." Go look it up—it's in Luke. For it to work, you're supposed to say it nine times a day for nine days. I just kept saying it every morning, noon, and night for months. Then I wrote a letter to President Roosevelt.

I told him that we had left my Grossmama at Hofzeile 12 in Vienna. I drew a small map and I told him where he could find our yellow house. It is not hard to locate, I wrote him. It is a palace. I told him how we were enjoying our new life in this new world of America, and I knew that my Grossmama would enjoy it too.

I received a very courteous letter back from the White House assuring me that the President had handed the letter off to the proper authorities. Then I said my novena again.

Grossmama came wearing all her good lace dresses, one on top of the other, and a coat over all of them. She had a hat on, too. Her face was pale and drawn. She was so much thinner and smaller.

My mother had gotten in contact with her through the American Red Cross, and we had received our first letter from her in a refugee camp at Bergen-Belsen, Germany, dated August 9, 1942. She wrote to us in English on American Army stationery. She wrote that Munich wasn't much fun and that it looked even worse then Vienna. There wasn't much social life at the former concentration camp. She didn't mention the Hofzeile. She sounded relatively chipper and she worried that she was going to be a burden on us.

My father went up to New York to meet her and bring her to Washington. She then proceeded to drive my mother and me wild. She got the back part of the house. We had no rugs, which was a problem because she wore these very loud, hard shoes with these little heels. Grossmama was a hyper woman—you're so much like her. What should I do next? What should I do next? She would rush from one corner of the room to the other, and we could hear those shoes!

My father decided that since my mother was working, and I was going to school, Grossmama should do the cooking. He assumed she wouldn't mind and she didn't. She had a scout's attitude, but the meals weren't very well balanced. We would have one meal that was just too much food and then the next meal wouldn't be enough. I remember the first dinner. There was a roasted chicken with paprika, a heap of roasted potatoes and spears of broccoli, two kinds of hard, sharp cheeses, and a bowl of hard-boiled eggs. I looked at my mother and she shook her head and said, "Shhh."

"Grossmama," I said, ignoring my mother. "You must be very hungry."

And she came round the table and held me. "Oh yes. I am hungry."

She must have been about sixty-five at that point. Later I learned that, like most, she had survived on potato skins.

She had changed somewhat since Vienna. She still walked a great deal and brewed her own teas, but she was edgy and she had trouble sleeping. We could always hear her pacing in her rooms.

On Christmas Eve that year, we splurged and bought a tree. It was a small one, but my mother painted little ornaments on cardboard and I made cookies and milk punch. Each of us had wrapped presents and put them next to the tree. My mother and I were so pleased. When we were ready to go to midnight mass, my father called Grossmama down.

She looked pale and had a black fringed shawl around her shoulders. When I kissed her, her face had the distinct sulfuric odor of candlesmoke. I think she had been praying.

"Why is this?" she said when she saw the tree and the presents.

My mother and I went on ahead. Then my father came out of the house alone. When we returned from midnight mass, the tree was out on the sidewalk on its side with the ornaments still hanging on. Inside, all the presents were gone. The three of us stood quiet for a long, long time, our coats still on. Then we heard the little heels of Grossmama's shoes on the floor upstairs as she began to pace.

Right after the war ended, my father went back to Vienna every summer to continue his research. We couldn't afford to go with him, so my mother and I spent those three months together in Washington. I worked at the library at Catholic University while my mother taught summer school.

We gave parties together—for the first time—and we would continue this habit all during my high school years, through college, and graduate school, right up until I met your father. Together, we did what

Cook and Agnes had always done without us. My mother didn't believe in doing anything ahead of time—"The more time you spend on a party, the more time it will take." She drove me wild, working peacefully on an article about the new postwar New York abstract impressionists until late afternoon when we were giving a dinner for twelve at seven.

Of course, everything would turn out fine. But there was the time the roast slipped on the floor in the kitchen and my mother blanched. The floor consisted of stripped wood planks. I instinctively picked the roast up, dusted it off, put it on a platter, and served it. Nobody ever knew the difference.

She went to the embassy parties alone, usually in a dress I had bought her. She wouldn't worry about meeting important people or being alone. "Don't ever be afraid to be alone at a party," she told me. And of course, she always met interesting people.

"I met someone really nice today," she told me one evening when she came home from one of these parties. This was after college even and I had gotten a job at a Washington newspaper. "He is Catholic," she told me, "from Massachusetts, quite good-looking, and not married. You really should start going to these embassy parties again, Genevieve." His name was John Kennedy.

Whether she wanted to be or not, I made her my confidante. I told her about the dances I went to, and I would keep her posted on the progress of a latest crush. Later, though, she would tease me, "How about keeping *some* secrets from me!" But that didn't stop me. "I had the most wonderful time," I would say, sitting on her bed at one-thirty in the morning. You used to do the same and I recognize the same, sleepy half interest I have that my mother had.

The parties I attended were a bit of a struggle because we had no money. It was a good thing I had a Sacred Heart uniform because we couldn't afford clothes. I would wear a lightweight, dark blue sweater with the dark blue skirt and roll up the waistband to make it resemble a dark blue cocktail dress. Later, when I had made enough money to buy my parents a house and a car, I bought them each a new set of clothes.

I know you think I am too concerned—too caught up in things. I can practically *hear* you thinking, "Mom, why do you make such a big deal out of clothes and furniture and houses?" I do not want you to know what it is to live in a house you don't want your friends to see, or to have to make a school uniform look like a chic little cocktail dress. I don't want you to know.

My mother? You never ask about Mutti. There was a painting of her in our Vienna living room. In it you saw all that fantastic chiseling—the cheekbones, the forehead, and her nose, which was better than a classical Greek nose because, really, that nose is too strong. She did not have the ideal American figure, which, of course, made her more interesting.

My father felt that women had to have a pursuit other than children and the kitchen—that this was one of the foremost problems in America, this and a lack of good household help. There was a need for Mutti's second salary to supplement my father's from Catholic University, but the solution for my mother was ridiculous. She had five, sometimes even seven part-time jobs. Later, she had the train ride to Baltimore and her hour rides to Marymount—till I bought them the car. She wrote articles, got her master's degree in art history, entertained once a month, and went to concerts and gallery openings every two weeks. We did have a maid once a week. "I can't stand to clean," Mutti would say. An hour's housework and she would have to lie down. We made fun of her then, but now I wonder—was that already the leukemia? She exhausted herself and she started taking pills to get to sleep.

When we moved to Washington, my mother and father found their own spiritual advisers first, way before they even thought about acquiring a family physician. My father would ignore the dark rings under my mother's eyes and discuss at length the expertise of the Jesuits.

When I asked, my mother responded to my questions about God, but she sure didn't volunteer any information. When she spoke of these things, she spoke through clenched teeth—not really enunciating, as though one shouldn't talk about something that mattered this much.

They tell you faith is a gift, and essentially, your stance toward God is a gift, but I worked my way into spirituality through memorization and lists. I memorized what Father Green told me about the ideal girl— she knows her destiny and from that knowledge she carries her calmness. As she approaches that goal through prayer, she gains in wisdom. Every other day I was making lists of resolutions to study more, pray more, sew more, and to shroud myself with Jesus Christ so that I could—as one nun put it—"radiate Christ." I read Teresa of Avila and memorized parts of that. "Imagine this Lord himself at your side. . . . Stay with this good friend as long as you can. . . . You need not be concerned about conversing."

My mother used to pray in the chapel during her free periods—two hours a day. My father said that was why Sacred Heart let her go—the nuns got jealous.

A mystic is somebody who has a degree of union with God. People said that my mother had that union. Once, a priest who had known my mother said to your father's mother, "Well, you know, Jenny's mother was a mystic." Your grandmother didn't even blink when she said in that lovely southern accent of hers, "And she had the prettiest skin, too."

I think that being an only child makes you closer to your parents because you don't have that other childish world in which to live. When I decided that I wasn't going to go away to college on a scholarship and piece together a life for myself elsewhere, I seriously wondered if I was too close to my parents. Is that why you have no inclination to marry or move away? I finally decided, though, that I was getting such a good education in Washington and I was meeting all these interesting people—none of which I could have done on my own at another college.

College came and went, and in 1950 if a woman was graduating and she wasn't getting married, she was considering the "sisterhood."

Father Green, who had become my spiritual adviser, talked me out of it. He said that the conditions of most religious orders for women in the United States were such that it would be fairly hard to progress spiritually and that there would be major upheavals in the near future. I think he knew Vatican II was in the making. He said that I would "go further" in my spiritual quests if I did not become a nun. He also thought I should consider buying a house.

My mother thought I should get married. "I don't think having a career is that good for a woman," she said. At this point she had just taken on her sixth part-time position.

My father felt I should go on with my education. "Get a graduate degree at Johns Hopkins," he said. He was still writing *The Growth of German Historicism* and teaching at Hopkins and all his colleagues assured him I could get a scholarship. I think he had it all planned really. I would get a master's in history, which I did, then become his secretary.

At graduate school, when I took classes from my father, my feelings for him changed. Standing behind his lectern, he read from notes, but he often stopped, looked out a window, and thought—sometimes out loud or sometimes there was just this moment of quiet—and we *witnessed* him thinking. Those were very emotional moments and I don't think they were at all staged. When he spoke of recent historical events, namely, the *Anschluss*, his attitude behind the lectern was that of a supreme father: Look at the mess we humans have made! No, *really* look at it. Now. Don't let it happen again.

I can recall the afternoon he lectured on the eighteenth-century German historian Johann Gottfried von Herder. He said that for Herder, the early national spirit of a country was purer because it had developed by itself, free of foreign influence. My father said that Herder chose to emphasize these beginnings because he could perceive in these earlier periods the purer form of the "national spirit," which can be more easily grasped by the historian. My father went on to explain one of Herder's ideas: If the task of a nation is to develop its own spirit and form, then a foreign influence will, almost inevitably, prove to be detrimental.

My father never actually came out and said how important a nation's independence was to its national spirit. He didn't have to.

It occurred to me that afternoon, sitting in the auditorium at Hopkins, that my father probably viewed people as countries. He had been so attentive to my early development—telling me stories, asking about my friends and schooling—but now he was really no longer concerned about how and what I was experiencing or who I was meeting. Perhaps he thought I had been too polluted by "foreign influences." I was twenty-one and already I had lived in five countries outside my motherland. Maybe to him my national spirit was dead.

I think if my father were a country he would be Austria herself, where tradition thrived. What appalled my father the most about the Austrian *Anschluss* was the idea that Austria would now no longer be pure. I don't think my father liked what America did to him or for him. Some would have said that America's size and scope intimidated my father and that's why he wanted so desperately to go back to Vienna, but I think he was merely attempting to protect his own national identity those summers he kept going back.

When Austria lost her independence to Germany, she forfeited her future forever; and so it went that when my father married Isabella and lost his independence, he forfeited his future with me.

We still had not heard from Uncle Rudi, but we were in contact with Grandmother Lucie, whom Rudi had gotten out early. She had set herself up in a tiny apartment near New York, in Scarsdale. She had all these friends and they would come over and she would make them fresh mushroom omelettes and little delicacies. She had a great talent for winning the love of people. Her idea of life was a good party.

While I was at graduate school, Lucie took me one summer weekend to Shelter Island and she arranged dates for me with impossible men. Each night I came back to our little cabin and she and I would laugh about how ridiculous they all were.

She had developed a horrible smoker's hack and her doctor decided the Scarsdale climate was bad for her. She hit upon Charlottesville, Virginia, and moved into this chic little place down there. Here's this French woman, catapulted in her late seventies to Charlottesville, Virginia, and it didn't seem to bother her a bit.

She made bundles of friends and she gave lovely parties. She said I absolutely *had* to come there every chance I could—there were the nicest men going to the University of Virginia.

But while I was attending my father's lectures, typing his notes, organizing his papers, I had fallen in a sort of love with a man named David. He was a graduate student in history as well, and he worked part-time in the post office. He was brilliant and I do think he pulled me through most of my classes. We were together one year. The reason we broke up seems medieval today. He did not want our future children to be raised Catholic. He was concerned whether being married to a Catholic would hurt his career, not as a postal clerk but as a Presbyterian minister.

It was the worst and best time to break up with him. I was in the middle of my dissertation about the *Anschluss*. He had said he would help me with the format and the footnotes but then he would come over and it would always be so discouraging. He would say things like, "But nobody in the West cares about Austria! You have to *make* it relevant." It was always more work and worry, but then, his questions always made me rethink everything.

I finished the dissertation alone. I read one section over and over:

> Since even a popular will to resist would have been overcome by Germany's armed might, and since Austria could not have defended herself for any length of time, the intervention of the Western Powers would have been the only effective factor in preventing the *Anschluss*.

In my mind I kept hearing David say, "But nobody in the West cares about Austria!"

There is an expression your father uses sometimes: "Woulda, shoulda, coulda." It's all the same. If, if, if . . .

After I received my master's, I was exhausted and Grandmother Lucie insisted I come and visit her in Virginia.

My mother thought this David of mine was so preposterous she had absolutely no sympathy for me or for my broken heart. She just wouldn't talk to me about it. But Lucie wanted to know everything. She made me lots of chocolate mousse when I got to her house, and after I told her everything, she held my hand and said, "Tomorrow, we go shopping." She got herself a new silk dress, and for me, she bought a lamp for next to nothing. Then she set me up with a Mormon. I still have the lamp.

I returned to Washington renewed. I wanted desperately to work for the State Department. It was my dream to work to make the world safe for democracy, but I still had an accent people mistook for a German one and I was, quite simply, from "someplace else." I finally secured a job as a copy girl for *The Evening Star*.

For eight months I felt dead inside, but I never stopped working. I used to sit in the kitchen of my parents' rented house, looking at the oven door tied closed with string, and think to myself that I must make enough money to buy them a new oven, a car, clothes, and a house none of us will be ashamed of.

During one of our meetings on spiritual matters, Father Green, who was terrific with practical matters—the only priest I have known to be so—told me that now was the time to invest in Washington real estate. He convinced me and he was right. That evening, I announced to my mother and father that I was going to buy them a house. Grossmama was delighted by this, but I remember the way she looked at my father that night. It was a this-is-your-role-not-hers look. She said that she too was looking at a place of her own—the Lisner Home—and that she had made plans to move. It was what she wanted to do, I was convinced of that.

My mother took an immediate interest in my proposal—she had a feel for houses. We found one very soon afterwards and I made the down payment.

The Mormon Lucie had fixed me up with came up to Washington to help us move. I decided I wanted to paint the back porch bright watermelon pink and he said he'd help with that, too. He proposed marriage to me the day we were painting. He said I was such a good painter that surely I would be as good at missionizing. It was like a business deal. I asked him how many wives he was planning on having. He said not many—that on the average, his Mormon friends had seven wives, but he was thinking more along the lines of five. We painted all that day until we were finished. Later, I put black curtains up with pink stripes. He was especially good with all the detail work around the windows, so I waited until he had finished. Then I said I really didn't want to be one of seven, six, or even five. He seemed to understand.

My mother and I began to furnish the place. We discussed "attachment to things" as we hunted through Georgetown for damask to cover a chair we had found in the basement of our new home.

"No," she said, holding out a busy bolt of cloth in one store. "We need a nicer background."

My mother was tireless when it came to her belief in backgrounds. She convinced me that all of this was a part of making a new home—a nice place for me perhaps to marry from. "I don't think having a career is that good for a woman," she told me again that day.

We took a break at a coffee shop—it was cheaper than lunch. We talked about what color we should paint the living room, and she regretted not having her rose prints.

"But what about your saintly indifference to things?" I asked. I thought of the sapphire ring she wore at dinners. It was a showy thing, something her mother Lucie had given her. I remember I saw a man, her dinner partner, bend over it, murmuring words of appreciation in French of its beauty, its quality, its value. My mother only feigned polite interest. My father cut in and said what he always loved to say solemnly at dinner parties, "We lost everything in the war." He always emphasized the *everything*.

My mother did not tell me her feelings toward things that day, but she imparted this idea—a kind of quality of living which I could see she had a particular gift for. If you're heading for ultimate beauty, enjoy what there is along the way, yes. Don't get caught up in the little things, though, because you have to keep going for the ultimate. That is what she imparted to me. No rose prints, no furniture, no books. These were not what my mother left me. No. I have a much more significant, much less tangible inheritance.

The furniture we assembled were memories of our togetherness— our first real togetherness in a new world. She loved the chairs and the sofas, I think because we had gotten them together. She would see something—a print—that reminded her of Vienna, and even if we did not buy the object, she would tell me her memory and I would leave a store or a house sale a little richer with that. This is how I came to know my mother. Each time I go to a house sale now, I feel my mother there with me. She stands not more than two feet from me, just as she used to, wearing a silk skirt, her hair brushed up and away from that high, noble forehead. She leans so close I can smell her good French perfume, and she will whisper her advice.

My father would claim that mother love is the most selfish love there is—the mother loves the child as a former part of her. Whatever. I felt that my mother's love had a strength, a tenacity, a ferocity under all that calm, cool, gentle humor, and that the day I married was a death for her—but one she knew she had to go through.

When Lucie died of lung cancer, we all went down to Charlottesville for the funeral. Her husband was buried in Vienna, but she told my mother to bury her there, in a cemetery near Monticello that looks out over the mountains.

My mother was set back. It didn't help that she still had heard nothing from Rudi. My father and I both were concerned about her. She didn't say much then or when we got back to Washington. She worked. She just quietly worked, and smiled less.

After a year, I decided to join the Young Democrats because they dressed better than the Young Republicans. I went to every meeting, and there, I met a strange, wonderful man from Mississippi. I was disappointed when I found out that he was married, but he invited me to a party and he said his wife's brother was coming into town.

Ruth Ellen served only vodka that night and I think I was standing near the bar, talking to a senator—was it Stennis?—about something or other—was it alligators?—when your father came into that room that night in Washington. I said to God, "I didn't think you made them like that anymore. Thank you." He was five years younger than I was, he was tall and blond, and he had this way of walking which was absolutely presidential.

He still denies it, but I'm sure he told me that night that he was related to Faulkner. I did not stay long, but the next day he called and asked me to *West Side Story.* Then he sent roses. I think there was a dinner or some such in between. Then he borrowed Senator Stennis's car. I remember I was staring at the cigar in the ashtray in the front seat when your father said something like, "What would you think if I asked you to marry me?" And I do think he was genuinely shocked that I didn't say no right away.

He came over to meet with my father. They went into my father's study for all of fifteen minutes. They came out smiling, but later, I found out that neither one of them understood what the other had said. That night, when Michael had left, my father said that this man didn't have a penny, but he was honest and he knew what he wanted: me.

I didn't want to give up my job—it had taken so long to secure. They wanted to send me to India when I gave them notice. "Mississippi?" I heard over and over. It was 1958. "Don't you know what's going on down there?" And they were right. I would have been safer in India.

You've heard your father's side of the family retell the he-proposed-to-Jenny-on-the-third-date story far too often, I'm sure. It has become myth, but at the time, it was all fast slow motion, and even though so many people told me I was crazy to give up Washington, marry Michael, and move to Mississippi, which was essentially a Third World nation, I was so sure. I think now maybe it *was* his eyes. They are the courageous blue of a sailor's. I've seen that blue in some policemen's eyes. It is the same blue as Grossmama's eyes.

———

The wedding photographs are frightening. My mother stands behind my father as he kisses me good-bye. She is pale and she looks exhausted—was she already getting ill?

We had the reception in the home I had bought. My mother and I made everything. It was a party I did not want to leave. All day it snowed and I—along with all of Washington—was covered and immobile in white.

The mother's place is at the side of her daughter when the first child is born. This is what my mother always said. Your arrival coincided with my mother's vacation as well as with mine, but birth and death can't be timed exactly. There is a great deal of waiting, and sometimes, fear is necessary. During the thirty-six hour labor, my mother wasn't calm. She called our funny Austrian doctor in Washington, who, of course, was no help.

When you were born, I shouldn't have hesitated. I should have gone on and named you after my mother. But I had wanted to name my child after the tale Cook had told me in the kitchen once at the Hofzeile—after Elizabeth of Hungary—and as soon as I had written "Elizabeth" on the dotted line, your father said, "What about 'Rosette'?," and I knew immediately he was right, but it would have cost five dollars to change it and we couldn't afford that, so we left it. Elizabeth.

Yours was not an easy birth. It was as though you were putting off the inevitable—I'll have no part of this, I imagined you thinking, because you certainly weren't any help. And later, when we got home, you cried and cried and cried.

"She really cries a lot," my mother said the morning after the first night home. "I didn't sleep too well."

I was frantically reading Dr. Spock while I fed you. "What about all those maternal instincts of yours?" I asked.

"This is the time a young girl's mother is supposed to get up with the baby," my mother said, and with that, she made an omelette and arrangements to leave early.

I was proud that my mother wasn't the type of woman to stay and hover—that she had some kind of a career. She was still beautiful and alive with thought. Now of course I worry that she was working much too hard.

I went to Washington to be with my mother and father before they moved back to Vienna. I helped them pack. My father sold the house and the car, and even though I had bought them these things, he kept the money. He neglected to mention this in his book.

I sought out Father Green. He had been so wise about real estate before (when my father sold the house, he came out with a nice profit), I thought he could help me again with an equally practical matter: birth control. I had already had you the first year of my marriage and I didn't believe in overpopulating the world. But Father Green was at the lofty level of playing spiritual adviser to somebody important in Woodstock, New York, and he gave me all of two minutes on the phone. "You are out of my province," he said. That was that. I would not see Father Green after that, though I would write to him often and even call. Who knows how, why, or when people decide a friendship's up. "You are out of my province," he said. My first American friend. I was out of his province.

My father refused to believe that my mother had leukemia, even after it was diagnosed shortly after they had moved to an apartment on Barenhartgasse in Vienna. For a long time the doctor made me promise not to tell him. "Your father is the biggest child I've ever met," he wrote to me in a letter. He thought the knowledge that my mother had no hope of surviving would kill my father.

I wrote them once, sometimes twice a week. I knew how they needed letters. I wrote mainly about you. I thanked them for all the French, German, even Italian books Mutti sent you. You called them "bucks" and you touched each picture, saying, "pity, pity," meaning pretty, pretty. I worried that you were not learning to talk—having so many languages coming at you at once. I thanked Mutti for the ashtrays she sent, a corkscrew, long white gloves for me, ties for your father, and little dresses she sent you. Once my father sent you a "buck" for Christmas and you wouldn't let it go. I went into the living room and there you were, sitting under the tree in your little chair, "reading." You even slept with the book—a habit which did not improve its condition, since at times it got rather moist. You also loved church. I sat and prayed for my mother with you on my lap. Once, halfway through mass, you discovered the infant of Prague statue up front. You shouted, "baby, baby," at the offertory. I tried to explain but you only yelled again, "baby, baby," and "pity" at the chalice.

My father would write back, always signing his letters with a big black "F." Was that for Father? Always, always my mother wrote letters that started with *Liebling*. I asked for pictures and she did send one.

The two of them are standing in front of a bridge somewhere. He has one leg crossed in front of the other, and, smiling, his hat tilted at a cocky angle, his hands in his coat pocket, he looks terribly pleased with himself, confident. So caught up was he in the moment of the camera, the view off the bridge, the pleasing sense that one has after giving a fine lecture then eating lunch. He looks straight at the camera. My mother stands behind him, her feet together as though she is standing at attention. She looks past the camera—toward the right—she's thinking about something altogether different; she's barely there and she's not smiling. She's very pale and thin and there are dark circles under her eyes.

You want to shout at this man: Take her home! Put her to bed. Take care. Can't you see that she's dying? In this picture you don't wonder so much what he is thinking. You wonder about the woman standing at attention. You wonder what is on her mind.

Then my father wrote that my mother was in the hospital, getting a blood transfusion, and I heard nothing for two weeks. I wrote and wrote: What is the news with Mutti? Is she in pain? How are the transfusions taking? Will the system return to normal, or does she get shots, pills? Please inform—being a heaving ocean away doesn't lessen one's thoughts. Finally, I got a postcard from Mutti. It was a Miró, and on the back she said: Come. Please come.

I flew from Jackson, Mississippi, to Vienna. Your father's parents took care of you while your father worked.

My parents were living in a new apartment building far away from the city, out in the hills. It was not beautiful or scenic or chic. It was depressing. They had a car, but my mother could not drive a stick shift, so she felt stuck. She was away from what was good about Vienna—the concerts, plays, and all the art museums that she loved. I looked around at those white walls and the small rooms and thought: why did they come back?

Pantsch wasn't there—he was in Rome. He had left before I arrived. More research. Just as Austria had feigned ignorance once upon a time, my father was pretending not to know his wife was dying.

I blame my father for many things. He alone had decided that they should go back to Vienna, and now I think I know why. For the prestige—not theirs, but his. As he perceived it, he was returning from the United States and now he would have the high status of being a full professor at the University of Vienna. He didn't know that at the university he would encounter our old friend Father Gentz as the chairman of the history department. My father never told me exactly what happened between the two of them, but I do know this: Gentz, for whatever reasons, provided only the minimal salary and pension plan for my father. In fact, he kept my father scrambling for money. Was it revenge? Had Gentz bought into German propaganda? Perhaps Gentz said to himself, I—a born Catholic—went to Dachau, and this . . . man . . . got away virtually unharmed and now he has the nerve to come back. My father never argued with Gentz, but he did complain.

The trip back to Vienna was the beginning of the end for my mother.

When I was there she said, "I think I'm going to make something positive out of this illness. I'm going to get myself some really glamorous negligées."

I asked her if she wanted to see the village priest and she had this inexpressively sweet smile on her face. She said the Austrian priests were so out of date, so backward. "I've stopped going to church," she said.

Of course I think about her sanctity, but she was not really what you think of as a saint. She was like you in some ways—once she made up her mind to do something she was determined to do it, and she would have these long silences when she really got mad. Just freeze you out. She used to get mad at my father. She got mad at me. She wasn't speaking to me when I was dating the postman.

She still wasn't talking to me when I first met your father. They were leaving for Scarsdale and I said, "I've met someone and he's really impressive." She paused, her hand on the doorknob as my father took their luggage out to the car. She looked at me as she put on her gloves and she just said, "Oh? Yes?," and she whirled out and left. It was as though she were telling me, this is your deal, I've given up. I realize now that that must have been a more difficult time for her than I had guessed.

The day after I arrived, she arranged for us to have dinner at Sacher's. It was as though she were trying to convince me that she was okay with what we both knew was happening.

She ordered a big, old-fashioned Viennese dinner and she paid for everything ahead of time, so all we had to do was sit down in our costumes, look good, laugh, and eat. It was what she did magnificently.

I knew that she had not wanted to leave the United States. She wanted to be near me, yes, but, more important, she wanted to be near her grandchild. She had looked forward to that—looked forward to knowing and caring for you.

She had found out the truth all at once when she moved back to Vienna, and sometimes I wonder if that's what killed her. She told me she had been at a museum looking at the newest modern art when she recognized neighbors—people who had lived near us when we lived at the Hofzeile. They told her what had happened to Rudi.

After he had gotten his mother safely out of the country, and after he had put Grossmama safely into hiding, he pawned everything else he had and got others out as well—friends, colleagues. He moved back into the Hofzeile, sneaking down into it through a tunnel from the garden that came back up into the basement under the kitchen. Meanwhile, above him, Hermann Goering's nephew moved in with his family. Then one day this family of Goerings left and didn't come back. Rudi moved upstairs. The neighbors knew this because every now and then they could see a sliver of candlelight coming from the sealed windows of the concert room.

I suppose there's no way of knowing whose bomb finally came down on our Hofzeile—Russian, British, American, German? It was a direct hit.

I can't help but wonder which dark room Rudi had been in at the time. He did not have his sheet music or his instruments, but he could have pretended to play his viola d'amore as I had seen Inge often do. Surely he was in the concert room, where the floors were bare and the walls insulated so that no outside noise came in. And surely the imaginary music he played was loud enough in his mind to drown out the sounds of that nameless bomb.

My mother said she thanked these neighbors who told her of her brother's fate. She left the museum, went to the market, went home, and made dinner. That night I imagine my mother stared at her husband— my father—from across the dinner table. Perhaps she thought of what he had once said of Rudi—that he was the silly, irresponsible member of her family, and he would never grow up. Perhaps my mother seriously wondered if she had made a terrible mistake in marrying my father.

It was late April and the chestnut tree blossoms were out when she finally had to go into the hospital. From her bed, she complained that modern art was not the same. A pile of white flour in the middle of an empty room. A gallery window stacked high with white bread. Food art, she called it. She preferred the kind of artists who tinkered with paint.

On the last day that I was with my mother, she didn't say much— only that she wished she had something to give me because she knew that my father would forget. At the time we both laughed at the mention of my father, but it was as though she knew that he was incapable of doing the right thing. I knew then that leaving this time was going to be harder because I was older and more aware of what I was saying good-bye to—not a house this time, no. Not even a country. I was saying good-bye to my mother.

There was a view outside her hospital window, and that morning she looked out and said that it was heartbreakingly beautiful. I thought it was such a sentimental, mushy thing for her to say, and my mother was neither sentimental nor mushy. She was wearing a new bed jacket, and she said that she wanted to talk about furniture. She was never one to mince her words.

The hospital stood on a hill and outside the window you could see that the gardens were terraced all the way down the hillside. There were the linden trees there, and flowers and vegetables grew up and down the hill. The townspeople who had done all that planting were cultivating the plots with hoes and picks. It was a sight that was very common and very beautiful, especially just then.

Sometimes when you come home, you bring out the photos from my wedding. In them, my mother looks beautiful, but thin, tired, and pale. Now I recognize the look on my mother's face. It is the look she had that day in the hospital. In one photograph she stands behind my father as he kisses me on the forehead good-bye. In the picture she wears a satin dress and a lovely hat with a veil. But you can see the dark shadows under her eyes, and the sadness at the corners of her mouth. She holds her gloved hands together as she looks on. My only daughter's wedding, I imagined she thought. My only daughter's wedding. She knew what was happening.

In the Bible, people are never said to be just mean or unjust; they're never just plain wrong. No, it is always said that their hearts harden.

When I am with you, you don't have to tell me; I know. I know that you are getting further and further away from me and my heart doesn't harden; it breaks.

I know now what my mother meant by "heartbreakingly." She did not want to say good-bye to that everyday beauty she saw outside her hospital window, and she knew that she had to. It would not be the first time for such good-byes.

After I met your father, married him, and moved to Mississippi— then later when my mother left Washington with my father to live in Vienna, and my parents and I were not in different states but different countries—I felt the kind of homesickness I had felt in Whitham with the English family. I told myself that maybe my parents and I needed that kind of distance between us, maybe it would be to our benefit to have the Atlantic Ocean as our boundary. Surely the kind of closeness the three of us felt as a family would never be altered. Surely. But the distance was too great, and when I flew back to be with my mother as she lay dying in a sad, newly built concrete hospital room in Vienna, I wished I had been with her every day all along.

We looked out that window for a long time that morning. We

watched until whole sheets of rain came down and dribbled on the sill until at last she said, "Close the window."

After the funeral, I went back to Mississippi. People in the South know what to do when someone dies; they cook and they bring over food for you. They make sure that you don't spend your time taking care of business so that you allow yourself to grieve. They wrote me lovely sympathy notes:

> *Dear Jenny:*
>
> *I have thought of you so much. You and Michael are two of my favorite people and you have been very brave and wonderful coming to a completely new part of the world, so far from your family . . .*

> *Dear Jenny:*
>
> *I want to tell you how often I have thought of you these past weeks. Your mother must have been a very lovely, intelligent woman from all that I have heard of her, and I can see those same qualities carried on in you. Your loss is one all of us are facing and I'm sure it must take a great deal of courage to get through the initial shock . . .*

The initial shock. It took forever to write thank-you's. I would start:

> *Dear so-and-so,*
>
> *Your thoughtful note did become of so much help to me when my mother did die, that I have been wishing I would write something which would be so much comfort to you and me . . .*

I got lost in the words. In the English words. It was the first time in a long time the English language felt really foreign in my mouth, in my mind, on the page.

You speak your version of German. I can even hear you thinking and dreaming in it. You've put on that language as though it were a new mink coat. I felt that way when I first learned English. But the year my mother died, I had to take off my American-English. It didn't fit—it felt tight and scratchy and I stored it away in the back closet of my mind with the Italian and the French.

Luckily, I was teaching German that year, and I made the announcement in class that we were only to speak German. That semester, I would hurry to school. Your father thought I was burying myself in my work to hold off my grief, but teaching German was the only time, the only place I felt I could think and talk like myself.

Less than a year after my mother's death, your father and I left you with your grandparents and we spent part of our savings to fly to New York. We went on a fact-finding mission. Your father wanted to see how he could get into the brokerage business and he had written to the head of the New York Stock Exchange, who wrote back saying research was the field. Your father said, forget research, I'm going into sales, and he lined up a series of meetings with various prospects.

One afternoon, while your father went to one of these meetings, I went to a poetry reading and there was this pockmarked man reading Dylan Thomas. At this point in my life I had attended hundreds of poetry readings. I had heard Frost, Pound, Eliot, Auden, and everybody else in between. At this particular reading, I kept thinking to myself, I've heard Dylan Thomas reading Dylan Thomas, why do I have to listen to this other Welshman? He did get my attention, though, when he looked up and said that one line about raging against the dying of the light. I thought of my mother then and I thought of my father.

It hadn't even been a year since my mother died, and already my father was seeing another woman—a woman my age. You have to laugh. But still. Still.

My father didn't ask me about Isabella, rather, he told me. He said in German, "I'm going to marry her." For me it was another *Anschluss*. She took this man over—infiltrating him. She worked her way so far into his life—cooking, cleaning, playing hostess—he became convinced he needed her to survive. I suppose I should have been grateful, but lines from my dissertation kept popping up in my mind: "It might well be asked whether Austria's chances for maintaining her independence could have been improved had her domestic conditions been different." My father was a child; he needed a nursemaid. And like Austria herself, my father let the *Anschluss* happen. Worse yet, he proposed marriage. Come on in! Take me over! At least Austria never extended an invitation to Nazi Germany—there was *some* pretense of resistance. I thought of another line from my dissertation. I had typed it and read it over again so many times, I had it memorized: ". . . since Austria could not have defended herself for any length of time, the intervention of the Western Powers would have been the only effective factor in preventing the *Anschluss*." In my mind, I was the West. But nobody cared about Austria, I could hear the postman, David, say.

Of this I would not be accused. I cared. I cared deeply about my father and his future.

I called. I wrote letters. I invited my father to come live with us, but he didn't have the imagination to live any place outside Vienna.

So, as my father would have said. So. I *did* feel I had been betrayed by my own motherland . . . and now by my own father.

When I looked up again during the poetry reading, the pockmarked man read out his "rage" again and our eyes met.

At intermission I got up to call your father, and coming out of the phone booth was the pockmarked man. He was shorter than me and his skin really was very bad, but he did have stunning black hair that hung in his eyes and he asked me if I wanted his autograph. I said, "Why in the world would I want your autograph?" and he smiled and said that all the other women seemed to want it and I said, well, then, go to the other women!

That evening, after I told your father, he said, "You saw Richard Burton?" I remembered my list and who was on it. Mussolini. Pope Pius XI. Hitler. And now Richard Burton? It was hard to comprehend, but still, that was how much my life had changed.

Not but a year later, my father wrote to me in English, "She has never read Aquinas. She can make soups, liver dumplings, cakes, but she can't think on her own. She gossips. All the time she gossips and she has no friends of her own. She complains bitterly about first my salary then my pension. She says nasty things about you." In summation, he wrote, he was no longer happy with who he saw across his tea table—she was like a student who had not done her homework. As I read the letter, I recalled a time when my father had once made fun of grade-school teachers who, after a while, began to talk in the high-pitched squeals of their pupils. Perhaps my father was afraid that being around Isabella would make him stupid. "This is no kind of life for me," he said at the end of his letter. "Is divorce out of the question?"

I wrote back and said that he could not marry a woman, then leave her a year later. He had to work it out. I wrote that he, too, was a difficult man to live with, and that he should be more kind, and more patient. That is what I wrote to him. I suppose I was fulfilling the Western prophecy: The Germans have marched in, now you have to make do with them. In other words: You let it happen.

Afterwards, I heard from him less and less until finally he came to visit here. He was by that time in his seventies and stooped over. I barely recognized him. Isabella proclaimed proudly that she had gotten him off coffee and onto tea. For his stomach, she said. He called me Kara and told me the same story twice in one week. He was an altogether different country.

ELIZABETH

"IT'S A PITY YOU DIDN'T KNOW HIM," GRETA SAID, pouring me tea. Greta was tall and vague and she talked in high-pitched, singsongy clichés. She said things like, "I remember the humanity of your grandfather" and, "It's a pity." Her lips lingered on the "p" in "pity" until finally she spat the word out. Greta had been one of my grandfather's students and Isabella's friend. I had been in Vienna a week. I had missed my grandfather's death by one week and his funeral by three days.

When Isabella called my mother to say that my grandfather had died and his funeral would be held in two days' time, my mother was furious with her for not including us in the funeral plans. She sent word to Isabella that she would not be coming to Vienna, and she told me to stay in Hyde Park, forget about the trip to Vienna, and forget about her family. "They're all impossible," she said. As a kind of compromise, I didn't go to the funeral, but I did go to Vienna.

I had come to this country certain I would love and respect it. It was older, more traditional, and more prestigious than me or my country, and yet, and yet, I thought that surely it would see me as one of its own, take me, welcome me even—not as a daughter, but as a granddaughter who appreciated it for all that it is and once was. Sure, it had been taken over by the Germans. Once. But was that really the fault of the Austrians? Why blame Austria—she was a country worth having, didn't that make her even more desirable? So what if she lay passive and unresponsive? That was then; couldn't I now admire her without judging her by her past actions or inactions?

Not really knowing what else to do with me, Isabella thought it would be a good idea if I met Greta. "She is someone close to your own age," Isabella told me, as though Greta and I were five years old and needed playmates.

Greta sat across from me, sprinkling still more powdered sugar over the already powdered apple strudel, and she insisted on speaking in English.

We were in her apartment, which looked out over the Karlsplatz. If you stood at the window, you could see a slice of the Secession Building with its gilded sphere of laurel leaves and berries. I knew it was one of my mother's favorite buildings. She once told me she wished she had an evening dress that had the same tone. Isabella called it "the Golden Cabbage"—a building she considered much too full of artifice.

"We were like his children. His family," Greta said. She wanted to talk about my grandfather. "He had nobody else, really. There was us and there was Isabella." She looked at me long enough, and then she cut the strudel, the powdered sugar sprinkling out on the glass coffee table and on the bejeweled Arabian knife shaped like a sword. "You're probably so tired of our pastries by now."

"Not at all," I said, smiling. At that moment I felt fat in my German—my "r" didn't roll off my tongue the way Greta's did. I put down my fork. He *had* a family, I wanted to say. He didn't need any people like his children. He had a child—a daughter. My mother. And he had me.

She wanted to talk about the funeral.

"It was a dark, rainy day," she said.

The word for funeral in German means "a lovely corpse" and apparently the Viennese make such a big deal out of the sick and the dead it is as though they are celebrating their own grief. As Greta ate her piece of strudel, she went on and on, talking about the rain only in poetic terms.

"Sigmund Freud didn't go to his mother's funeral," I cut in. "He didn't believe in ceremonies."

She shrugged. "I'm a Jungian," she said, putting down her plate, going on about the time she wore a red wig to one of my grandfather's seminars on "The History of Political Thought" while she was seeing a "shrink" because she was interested in psychoanalysis. She had trouble with the word "psychoanalysis."

"So many people were there." I gathered by the way Greta sighed that she was back on my grandfather's funeral. "A few of his colleagues, though, were—oh, what is the word?"

She got up and looked through her bookcase.

"Perhaps I can help," I said.

"No, no," she said. "I want to practice my English. The old world is over, the new world is here. Everyone must have good English." She said this with irony, as though I represented the big, ugly American who had just bought Europe with a Gold card.

Greta's living-room wall was lined with books, where Greta now stood, flipping frantically through the pages of a dictionary. She seemed nervous and impatient. I wondered if she had ever gotten on my grandfather's nerves.

"I can't find it," she said.

On the bookshelf, framed in hammered silver, was a photo of Greta standing next to an Arabian man I assumed was her husband. Next to this was another photo, of Isabella with my grandfather. They were both in the middle of a good laugh and they stood with their arms around each other's substantial waists. There was an orange table in front of them set for tea and the Danube flowed blue in the background. I wondered why Greta had this photograph and I didn't.

"Oh that," Greta said, seeing me staring at the photograph. "Do not think that I put that there for your sake. I always have it there. We were like family." Greta put her hands on her thighs and bent down to look at the photograph with me. "Isabella," she said, "always so chic. And dear, dear Theodor. I felt like his daughter, or his granddaughter, really."

For a moment we stood quietly next to each other, looking at the photo. Her bare arm smelled of sweat and curry. My grandfather had taught Greta; she had been his student for four years. She had sat in his classroom, drank and ate with him.

"What's the word?" I asked, wanting to get out of the room.

Greta looked at the open dictionary in her hands, sighed, slammed it shut, and tucked it back in the bookcase.

"*Neidisch*," she said.

We looked at one another, and I thought I saw her left eyebrow arch.

"*Neidisch*," I repeated. "Jealousy. Envy."

There is a sense of fatigue in Vienna, and eventually, despite yourself, by the end of the day you develop a taste for Isabella's plum brandy, even though on first tasting it, you might have found it too thick and sweet.

From Greta's street, I found the subway that took me to the Alte Danau, where Isabella lived with her blind, crippled mother. At the Stadtpark subway station, a postman stood next to me on the platform and told me about three marathons he had run. He had four grandchildren, he said, and it was his intention to leave each of them a marathon medal when he died.

I nodded and said this was a nice thing to do. At times like this one, I wished that what my grandfather died of had been contagious. It could have been one of those diseases that skips generations and goes straight to granddaughters. At least it would have been something we shared.

Getting on the train, I realized I had come to Vienna hoping that my grandfather had left something for me and that at some point—some special moment—during my stay, Isabella would present it to me in a very fine way.

"He had pain here." Isabella pointed to her upper thigh. "The cancer had moved to his bones. I did tell the doctor to keep him from pains and not to tell him the truth because I knew he would be terribly worried about me. This is why I was not anxious for you to talk with him. I thought you would blab." She put her hands out on the table between us, palms down. I picked up my glass of plum brandy. I wore the ring Isabella had given me, the green half of my grandmother's wedding ring. Every now and then you could hear it clinking against the glass.

She smiled, coquettishly. "At first the doctor thought I am Theodor's daughter and I could have easily been. Sometimes I think of your grandfather as my closest girlfriend." Isabella laughed. "Don't mistake me. He was a man. A wonderful man. But wasn't it Jung who said that there is the male and female in all of us? Your grandfather had all the niceties of the female."

I could imagine what my mother would have said if she had seen Isabella: Well, he certainly didn't leave her much. She's wearing clothes that look like she's making do—black pants and a black sweater, green Keds sneakers. Except for the bracelet—a silver bracelet that looked like a piece of modern sculpture. Isabella always had interesting jewelry.

We were sitting outside on a white porch in orange chairs, the same chairs I had seen in the picture at Greta's. On the table there was yet another strudel—Isabella's strudel. From the porch you could see a chunk of the Danube, which was not at all blue but mocha-colored, and every now and then, Sunday strollers stopped and peeked through the opening in the fence. I considered what we must look like together. Did they imagine that we were grandmother and grandchild? Mother and daughter?

Opposite the house, on the Prater, there was a twenty-story building with a sixty-foot tower that told the Viennese every night what tomorrow's weather would likely be: if the tower's light was yellow, it would be fair. White meant cloudy. Blue was rain and red was stormy. Isabella acted somewhat hoity-toity about the tower—as though it were some unique European invention. Clever and quaint like the blue-green paint that was peeling and chipping on her outside shutters. But when I looked across the water at the tower, I thought of the porcelain poodle my grandmother in Mississippi had once sent me for Christmas. It too had predicted the weather by changing colors, only its colors translated differently, and after a while, the poodle just stayed a light blue all the time.

Isabella told me about the time my grandfather and "the great Rosette" were in the hospital at the same time. She knew the story as though she had been a part of it.

"They were in the same hospital room at the same time. He had an operation on his stomach. She had a rare blood disease." It was leukemia, I wanted to shout. It's not so rare. People on television get it, for Christ's sake.

"Neither one of them spoke of their ailments. Each to save the other."

Then Isabella brought up my grandfather's recent and final illness and the operation, saying that it went well, but the weather had changed.

"The weather?"

"Didn't Mummy tell you about the weather?" Whenever Isabella referred to my mother, she said "Mummy."

Before Isabella phoned to say that he was dead, my mother had already taken to bed. My mother is like that—when someone in the family is ill, her body takes in that illness and she takes to bed. Then, when the phone rang late one night, and after my mother heard Isabella's voice, she gave the receiver to my father and went back to bed. She lay there until my father came and told her what she already knew.

When I invited my mother to come along with me to Vienna, she had said no, she would never go back. She took me to the airport, though, and on the sidewalk at O'Hare, my father tipped the skycap and put his hand back in his pocket. He was never one to jingle change in his pocket—was noiseless with his money. But just then, he took out a pile of bills neatly folded into a silver money clip. "Need any money?"

"Na," I had said.

He nodded, hugged me, and got back in the car as I looked toward my mother, squinting against the sunlight.

My mother hugged me tightly and whispered into my neck: "Tell that bitch Isabella she can just go to hell."

"A body changes when the weather changes," Isabella said. "When the day is bad your heart feels bad. If it rains, your arthritis kicks up. When your grandfather came out of operation, it got cold. He told me not to bother him. I thought that was a sign that he was well, so I did leave the room. And then . . ."

Isabella pushed the strudel toward me, and I shook my head.

"It's a pity you missed the funeral," she said.

"You didn't give us much time."

"Yes, but, darlink, it was impossible to postpone." She said this smiling. Isabella enjoyed saying the p-words the way Greta did. For a moment I imagined classrooms filled with Viennese women learning English, spitting out "pity," "impossible," and "postpone."

From the back of the house I could hear Isabella's mother yelling for her. She wanted some brandy herself, she yelled in German. Isabella's mother was ninety-something, and she had no interest in me, nor I in her. She stayed in her room in the back of the house.

Isabella poured a third glass of brandy, sliced a piece of strudel, and brought those to her. I heard some mumbling and a "sh, sh." I heard Isabella whisper in German: "Soon we'll have the applesauce I make from the little apples that fall from the tree."

Even though I knew that my great-grandmother used to go to the Klosterneuburg Meadows to swim in the Danube, I liked sitting out on Isabella's porch, imagining my great-grandmother in her younger years, swimming in the muddy waters here, wearing a baggy cotton swimming ensemble, or maybe, just maybe, nothing at all.

I got up, went to another room, and changed into my bathing suit. Down near the banks of the Danube, I stepped lightly into the chilly, mucky water. I didn't want to go in, but I knew I had to now that I was there. The only good part of the whole ordeal was once I was in, I could feel I was being watched by Isabella, who might have been whispering to her mother, "There she goes again, that silly girl," or some other older person either disgusted, overwhelmed, or impressed by my icy immersion.

I stepped, then sunk in deep, head and all. I swam fast to warm up, then slowed to a steady pace. Swimming in the Danube reminded me of the way it felt to hear my mother speaking to her father in German. The current of the water went up and down all around me the way the rhythm of their voices had that time he had come to our house the week after Christmas.

I was treading water when I saw that the light in the tower on the Prater across the river had changed from yellow to red.

For two weeks I slept in the room my grandfather had used as a study during his months off from teaching. The house had always belonged to

Isabella. Some said that while she got an older, better name when they married, he got the cottage by the Danube. The chair at his desk creaked in a comfortable way and the room smelled brown-green somehow— like musty bread. There were books in French, German, and English, and in every one of them, there were his marginal notes.

Every night, after a swim and a dinner of maybe liver dumpling soup or crepes made with apricot jam, I went to my room and shut the door. In Isabella's Danube house, there was a bed in every room but the dining room, and screens to hide the beds. In the room where I stayed, the bed was a small daybed which was good for reading and napping.

Every evening I read from books that had belonged to my grandfather. In black ink next to paragraphs which were not intended to be funny, he had scribbled "Ha's" and, every now and then, there was a *Nein* next to some factual information. In the space below the *Nein* was my grandfather's version of what had happened, including the supposedly correct dates.

To my surprise, my grandfather was not included in any of the books about Vienna, the University of Vienna, or the Vatican. He wasn't even in any of the indexes—indexes that seemed to include everyone but him. So, as my grandfather would have said, when there was nothing left to say. So. Just as my grandfather had not included my mother or me in his own personal history, so history had not included him. Then again there was nothing in any book about the Hofzeile either, but I still had the key.

One night, I stopped reading. For a long time, I stared across the room at an armoire. There weren't any closets in Isabella's house, but there was an armoire which contained a few of my grandfather's old black and gray suits and jackets.

I got out of the bed, walked across the room, and opened the armoire. I held the sleeve of a black suit jacket. I touched the lapel of a gray tweed coat. Over my nightgown, I put on a shirt I found hanging inside one of the darker suits. Then I put on the suit. It had not been cleaned and I stood there breathing in the smells of old tobacco, tea, a plum tart perhaps, newspaper ink, maybe even a bit of cologne or was that Isabella's good perfume?

I stood in front of a framed mirror hanging by the door. I straightened the collar. He had stood face to face with Pope Pius XII—had he worn this suit?

So he met with the Pope. So? Two men who kept quiet during World War II. Neither were heroes. Two men who could have and should have saved more than their own lives stood before one another face to face for twenty-five minutes on September 15, 1958. And what came of this profound meeting? The Pope said this: "You know, Professor, at that time before the war I was so happy. So happy."

I found a tie hanging on a hook, and I put that on. It was striped and somewhat elegant. I wondered if he had selected his own clothes or if Isabella had anything to do with it. I wondered what Freud said about men who wore striped ties.

I tightened the knotted tie around my neck.

Ezra once told me that when an archeologist reconstructed the *Homo erectus* larynx, he discovered that the species probably couldn't make most of the sounds we do. That same archeologist lamented the fact that speech from that far back could never really be studied. Many speech patterns are altogether dead. Speech, he said, leaves no direct fossil remains. Looking at myself in the mirror, I had the feeling that there was so much I didn't know—so much I would never be able to piece together, no matter how hard I tried to reconstruct their lives and translate the meaning.

"Elizabeth!" Isabella stood in the doorway. "You strange child. This is obscene. Come, come." She spoke to me in English and she came over to me and began untying the tie, and unbuttoning the shirt. Her breath smelled of cigarette smoke. I backed away from her, rebuttoning the shirt.

She left the room. I heard a drawer open, then shut. Then she came back, sat on the edge of the bed, and lit a cigarette.

"You make me smoke," she said, inhaling deeply, then exhaling. Her head began to shake.

"When Rosette did die, your grandfather showed everyone pictures of her. He kept them in his wallet, in his notebooks, and in his briefcase. Rosette was a very beautiful woman. Everyone told me so." Isabella sighed. "After dinner, he would show them to his host and friends. It was quite pathetic. And a little bit obscene." She looked at me as she inhaled deeply from her cigarette. "When he showed me those pictures, I said to him, 'You had a happy life for forty years, now what about the rest?' And when we married, I took those pictures away from him and I got rid of them. Every single one of them. I got rid of them. I burned them."

I put my hands in the pockets of my grandfather's pants pockets. My knees felt wobbly.

"That suit," she said. "He wore it the week before he did die. He wanted to take a walk and he wore that suit. Someone should have gotten rid of it for me. But no one did. I had no one. There was no one here for me." She backed out of the room. "Take it off. Hang it up back where you did find it."

Outside my open window, a couple passed. They were having an argument—something about an alarm clock. A dog barked and the man told her to hush. "Shh," he tried to shout.

If you ask Isabella about the funeral, she will remember that she wore a black suit and a black veil, that the weather was stormy, and that my mother was not there.

"I don't know why she wasn't," she will say. "Really. I don't know why." She will put her hand to your face, woefully, her fingers smelling of garlic and nutmeg.

At moments like these you will think she will do something important. You think perhaps that, remembering something, she will leave the room and come back with a box.

"Here," she will say at that time. "I wanted you to have a little zomzing with which to remember your grandfather."

Instead she says, "It's a pity really. Your mother never really knew her mother or her father and now she misses them."

When Isabella left, I put my hands in the pockets of my grandfather's suit jacket and pulled out a postcard from the right pocket. It was a cheesy drawing of the post office in Jackson, Mississippi, dated 1963.

> *Dear Pantsch:*
>
> *I took the Little Cat to church this morning—have you ever prayed with the sweet smell of your only daughter around you and her soft hair under your chin? When she saw the baby Jesus in the crib, she said "baby" and proceeded to chew on her shoes. When she got restless before the consecration, I whispered to her: "God is coming" and held her up to see the raised host and she exclaimed, "Oh pity." Every day she grows to be more and more like her Grosspapa—she does love the ceremony of religion.*
>
> *We hope you come soon. Michael still wears the Tyrolean hat you sent even though it's in the high 90's here now. Elizabeth likes to play with the little chamois brush that sticks up from the band.*
>
> > *Love,*
> > *Pintschi-*
> > *Pantsch*

I kept the suit on. I walked around and around the very room he had once worked in when he was alive. My grandfather had read an old postcard my mother had written to him about me the week before he died. Maybe, just maybe, he missed her. Yes, he must have missed my mother and maybe he even missed knowing me. I sat in his chair. I looked out the window as I knew he would have. Somehow, it seemed as though if I moved around enough wearing my grandfather's old clothes, that maybe, just maybe I could bring him back from the dead.

That spring there was a poster all around Vienna of a fey-looking middle-aged man in a black turtleneck sweater, his left eyebrow raised in an arc. He stared at you from poles near the underground, and on fences near coffee shops. He whizzed past you on the side of a bus. He looked at you all the time every day, as though he were saying what my grandfather had always said: "So." Except that his "So" ended with a question mark. So? As in: What do you make of it?

I passed this poster every day when I took the train out to Unter-Döbling first thing. The train stopped right across the street from the Karl Marx Hof, where I got off and walked past the colored doors, admired the gardens that each tenant kept across the street, and walked down the Grinzinger Allee toward the Hofzeile.

The Hofzeile was a street now—just a street of concrete apartment buildings where mostly refugees lived. Every day it was the same thing: I stood across the street from the apartment building with the number 12 in blue and white tile letters and I stared and stared and stared, making a fist around the key my mother had given me from the doll in her safe deposit box.

It had been so much worse for so many other people, I told myself. This was just one yellow house. Now it is gone and it is a gray, concrete apartment complex. Think of all the lives lost—not buildings. Whole villages founded by Jews in the eleventh century often had no Jews left in them today. So why did I linger on this too-new street?

I suppose I stayed, looking for some kind of evidence that my mother had lived there—markings on a stone wall that showed her height through the years, a piece of rotted kite string stuck in a tree, anything. Today, I promised myself, today would be the last time.

I sat on the curb opposite No. 12, took some bread and an apple from my backpack, and ate while I read a letter from Ezra. I had been in Vienna long enough to receive mail, and it made me feel as though I were not a tourist seeking relics or monuments but an inhabitant. A dweller. Seeing those envelopes addressed to me in Vienna, Austria, made me feel—for the moment—as though I really lived in Vienna, Austria.

He was on a dig at Dun Aengus on Inishmore, one of the Aran Islands, a three-hour boat ride from Galway, Ireland. He wrote that the fort was enormous and D-shaped, on a 300-foot-high cliff. The fort's dates were unknown, but the cliff edge in the burren was early Christian. He wrote that Dun Aengus had to be much older, and he said it was sad how little people knew about such a huge, spectacular old site. In his letter, he asked how it was possible for a people to have erected such great and mighty walls only to forget about them. What of past glories? he asked. And what about us?

I knew then what I was going to write to Ezra. I would tell him that I for one did not forget or neglect "past glories." I would say that if he didn't mind, I would very much like to see him—that I had something to tell him. To ask him, really. I would tell him to meet me at a restaurant; yes, that was it. We would eat, then maybe I would pull out a silly plastic ring, and ask him in a serious but chatty way: Marry me?

I looked across the street. Something in Turkish written on bedsheets with pinking shear edges hung outside a window of Hofzeile 12.

From the window's ledge, two Turkish men laughed, saw me sitting on the curb on an otherwise empty street, then slammed the window shut.

All around, the city was teeming with exiles and refugees from Bosnia-Herzegovina, Turkey, and Pakistan. Like me, they were flocking to Vienna as though it were still the center—the golden center—where there was one ruler, control, law and order. But of course, all that was left of that world was the Ringstrasse and a few bombed-out buildings.

Down the street to the right of me there was a church, and there was another to the left. Everywhere I looked, there were church steeples. I wondered if these had replaced temples. After my grandfather had returned from the fighting along the Piave River near San Donà during World War I, he stood with his father in the ruined gardens of the Hofzeile. All the plants and trees were without leaves and most of the garden statues had toppled over and crumbled. His father said then that one thing was for sure: "There will and must always be a Vienna."

I looked all around and thought, this city is mean the way a person can be mean—the way Isabella can be mean. It burns anybody and anything that gets in its way. But surely, the city wasn't always that way.

There is a cliché that the "golden heart" beats in the breasts of every Viennese and that their joviality, or whichever translation may be attempted of the word *Gemutlichkeit*, is perpetuated despite their history—despite the *Anschluss* and its aftermath. There is a saying, or rather, a dialogue that is supposed to illustrate the character of the Viennese: In Vienna everything is *gemutlich* except the wind. But the wind only comes here because of Vienna's *Gemutlichkeit*.

I felt to make sure the key was still in my pocket. For any other traveler in search of her roots, I thought, this was where and when I was supposed to cry. I swallowed hard, staring across the street at the concrete building in front of me.

"It's a very private thing, a house." I whispered this to no one and to everyone. "My mother's house. It's a very personal thing." If only I had seen the yellow of it, I thought to myself.

I walked down the street a bit, toward a museum where stables had once been—stables that dated back to the first Turkish invasion. The outside of the building was mustard-colored, partially covered by ivy. The window trim and gutters were green and big pots of pink oleanders stood out in front all in a row.

It was a museum for everything that had been found in the stables—mostly bridles and old haylofts. Nothing of importance. Nothing that showed that generations of people—not horses—had lived nearby.

I thought of all the relatives I had never known who had stood, slept, eaten, and danced under the roofs of the Hofzeile, which no longer existed: Joseph, Rudi, Lucie, my real grandmother Rosette, and Joska. I thought of my grandfather's sister, Kara, and the tennis courts a gardener transformed into an ice-skating rink every winter just for her. Once upon a time, the Nazis had a plan to create a museum to commemorate the "extinct race" of Jews. Sitting in front of the concrete apartment house on the Hofzeile, I thought to myself that I would like a museum of my mother's family. I wouldn't even care who had created it. At least she and I would have that.

Outside the museum stood a stone statue between the potted oleanders. It was of a boy leaning into a pailful of stone grapes. He had no legs and his right arm was missing. His left arm held the pail like a crutch. I thought for a moment that this ruin of a boy might have been among the statues my great-great-grandfather had kept in his garden, and I thought of somehow taking him with me, giving him to my mother as a Christmas present. But then I realized the boy was not of aristocratic or even heroic origins—even though he had lost limbs—and his mere charm would not have placed him in the company of Franz Josef and the Kaiser. This boy looked glum, thirsty even, with a vine of real ivy growing across his brow. Yellow water stains discolored his bare chest. Still, I wondered what my ancestors would have thought of this sad little boy. I wondered what they would have thought of me.

Since I had come to Vienna, worn my grandfather's clothes, and slept in his study, I was no longer angry. I felt only a deep sense of regret—regret at never having known my mother's mother. At never having known any of them. Hitler didn't lose the war, I thought to myself. He got so much of what he wanted. Too much.

The Midrash says that any person, family, or community to whom a miracle has happened may establish its own local Purim to celebrate deliverance. We will have an Engel de Bazsis Purim, I thought. My mother, my father, Ezra, and I. We will dress up and celebrate with a Purim parade and we will make and eat rice cakes shaped like Purim people—making sure to design one like Hitler himself with peanut butter skin, raisin eyes, and a carrot mustache. This we will devour ourselves until every last crumb of him, and not us, has disappeared.

I walked down the hill, which led to a street filled with shops. In a pastry shop, I sat down and ordered coffee, and noticed two elderly women sitting at the table next to mine. They stared and I stared back. Excuse me, I wanted to say, but weren't you around when they took away my family? Did you or your relatives give any of my relatives the gas that killed so many in those showers, Zyklon B?

In the mirror across the room, I caught sight of myself drinking coffee. I do not have a problem with food, I thought to myself, because I know now that I am thin. Too thin. An anorexic looks at herself and sees a fat person. I looked at myself just then and saw a drawn, too-thin girl/woman with hair the color of a storm cloud. I put my cup of coffee back in its saucer as a bus passed, and taped to its side was the poster of the man in the black turtleneck, his eyebrow arched, asking *So?*

So, I will return to the United States, I thought to myself. I will make my home there. I will marry the one I realize I love and I will go to my mother and tell her everything I've seen, and maybe she will do the same with me. So.

My mother had once said to me almost accusingly, "Look, you're not a survivor. You're not even a survivor's child." But just then I felt I was a survivor, and in a way, I was. I was never intended to exist. I thought: I am the ghost of all those who have died.

Since I had been in Vienna I had noticed that there weren't many kosher restaurants. So many towns in Europe—small and large—were nearly *Judenrein*, free of Jews. I wondered if these same towns were free of ghosts.

The two women whispered something to one another, and they both looked at me again. Like most of the people in Vienna, these two women looked to be without guilt, and I wanted to change that. One woman put her finger to her lips and I thought I heard her say, "Sh." They looked at me as though I was a ghost. Their ghost, or perhaps Vienna's ghost, and I stayed there longer than I should have, knowing that I haunted them.

That afternoon I went to the University of Vienna to meet with Henrich, a man who had once been my grandfather's student, and who now held my grandfather's former position. Greta had called him to say that I was in town and he called me immediately to say that he wanted to meet me—that he had something for me.

Henrich was a balding, energetic man my age who wore Birkenstock sandals with black socks. He was on his way to a hiking expedition. He reached into his desk drawer and handed me a new legal pad, telling me I could take notes if I liked. "Your grandfather was very Austrian," he said right away. "He was a traditionalist. A monarchist. I, on the other hand, was raised a Socialist."

Henrich spoke in a lecturer's tone about the characteristics of his former Herr Professor. Like Greta, he insisted on speaking in English because he said he needed to practice. He was getting an honorary degree at an American institution in the fall and he wanted his English to be flawless.

"He liked the ladies—quite typical. He liked clever, self-assured women like, well, like yourself. You would have liked him, I think."

"I knew him." I wished I didn't sound so defensive. I wanted to tell this man to mind his own business, but I couldn't tell him that because I wanted to hear more.

All I really knew about my grandfather was that he was a historian—a man who remembered the garden and the creaking beams of the Hofzeile, the tennis court in Cortina, and Sunday afternoons in the Pribram villa in the Billrothstrasse. At the end of his memoirs, he recalled a stick of cherrywood, but no mention of my mother. He remembered reading in the Lombard Bank, discussing the possibility of objective history at Johns Hopkins, and lectures on Machiavelli in auditorium No. 41 in Vienna, but not once did he recall any of my letters or the few talks I had with him when I met him once.

"I don't think he cared much for me," he went on. "He could be very precise. He was so—oh, what is the word?—*verletzend*."

"Cutting?"

"Cutting? Yes, he could make cutting remarks. Not cynical, not quite bitter, but almost. I remember in a seminar once, I was talking about the war of 1859. Your grandfather said I was not exact enough. He was very blunt about it. I remember this too very well. He knew me, you see. And I knew him."

"How do you mean?"

Henrich pulled out the bottom drawer of his desk, where he rested his feet. "My mother had told me about the great Theodor Engel de Bazsi long before I became his student. My mother knew your mother when they were children growing up in Vienna. They were best friends."

"My mother and your mother?" I said. "Best friends?"

"For just a short time, but I feel sure that your mother would remember her. My mother's name was Inge."

I tried to think of who Inge might be and shook my head. I couldn't even imagine my mother with a childhood friend—my mother didn't trust anyone enough. "Inge. My mother may have mentioned her once."

"Ask her. Ask her," he said, smiling. "The way my mother went on about your mother's family—I think she wished she was your mother's sister and that Theodor had been her father. She admired everything that they were and stood for. When I finally did come to the university, it saddened me that he and I could never talk of the past, but I understood. He had left Vienna during the war. My mother had not." He paused to clear his throat. "It's funny, no? We could not talk of our own personal histories, but there were to be no limits on talk of the world's history."

Henrich pulled out his own legal pad from his desk drawer and read from something he said he had looked up about the logistics of my grandfather selling the Hofzeile. At the time, there was a temporary loophole in the Nazis' anti-Jewish regulations: Jewish veterans of World War I could avoid internment if they agreed to surrender their property and leave the country.

"This is what your grandfather did do," Henrich said, giving me the sheet of paper. The lines on the page were scrawled, but it was clear enough. I stood up, thanking Henrich for his time.

"Oh no," he said. "But this is not what I had to give you."

He lifted his feet from the drawer, got up, and reached behind me where there was what looked to be a fat black violin case leaning in the corner. He put the case on top of his desk and opened it.

It was essentially a violin with two rows of strings—one on the bottom, one on the top. There was a blindfolded angel carved at the top.

The case was lined with water-stained purple satin that was torn along the edges.

"It's a viola d'amore," he said, strumming the strings. "My mother played this every afternoon for as long as I can remember. It makes a beautiful sound, yes? The strings underneath, here, echo the strings on top, here."

He put his hand over the strings to silence them. "If she was in the mood after she played, my mother would tell me some story about her childhood and about how Vienna used to be. Your mother had an uncle—a dashing young man. My mother said she had a schoolgirl crush on him. His name was Rudi and he did the most wonderful thing. He gave my mother a reason to stay alive during the war years."

Henrich looked past me. "Your mother—she left early, but my mother stayed."

Henrich told me the story of the day Rudi gave Inge his viola d'amore and later, after my mother and her family were all gone, and Inge and her family struggled to survive on bones and potato skins, how she learned to play the viola d'amore and she played and played while everything around her exploded.

"I never did learn to play, and now that I want to, it's really too late," he said, closing and then locking the case. "My mother wanted me to give it to your mother personally. Can you?"

"Yes, of course." I wanted to lift the instrument out and pluck a few strings, but it looked too delicate.

"It's pretty beat-up, I know, but it's a miracle that it's still in one piece."

"Is your mother still with you?" I asked.

"She died several years ago."

"I'm sorry," I said.

Henrich shook his head. "She was never a physically strong woman and so many who stayed suffered from malnutrition. Even if they did survive those years, they died soon after. When she caught a cold that last year, it quickly turned to pneumonia. She was in hospital for only a short time."

He gave me the case, then apologized for not being able to show me my grandfather's old office. It was being renovated.

As we walked out of his office and down the hall, the viola d'amore case gently swinging between us, Henrich told me about the way my grandfather moved. "He was a proud man and the way he walked, well, you felt there was a distinguished personality moving about."

I thought of all the great thinkers from this university who had been forced to leave. Most of them did not want to be known as Jewish this or Jewish that, but as Austrians. Still, Vienna could not think of them as such and did not back them when it came time. Now the city and the university profit from their memory and successes. And my grandfather still chose to return to such a university in such a city, trusting it and its inhabitants.

It is not palpable at first, but one feels the effects of Vienna eventually. Where was God? they ask of the Holocaust. And the answer is always: Where was man? Well, where the hell was the country of Austria? The Germans called their native country their *Vaterland*. For them, their land was masculine. For my mother and, most likely, for Inge, Austria was their home and their motherland. My mother had always referred to the city of Vienna as a "she," and her country as her *Mutterland*. What kind of motherland doesn't protect its own children?

I wished then that my grandfather had been more bitter. Maybe then he would have stayed in the United States, and maybe then I would have known him.

Outside, we stood on a few broken and chipped steps to the university. All around us were the buildings of the Ringstrasse with the sort of windows Vienna is famous for—windows with little porticos that reminded people of eyebrows. I looked up for a moment. It is an odd sensation, standing in a place where you know what happened but see little sign of it left. I felt then that I was standing in a ruined city and that all around me there were eyes watching me.

Church bells started to ring.

"I rather had the impression that your grandfather was devout, if this is the correct word," Henrich said. "The Austrian Catholic is not like the American Catholic. It's something quite conservative here, but that did not exist for your grandfather. He was, quite simply, fascinated with two monarchies—the Papacy or the Vatican and the Austro-Hungarian Empire. I imagine he felt every empire needed a father, and since there was none left here, he pretended to be it."

I nodded. The church bells stopped.

"Aren't you a member of what they call Generation X?"

Henrich was almost the same age as Ezra, and he had the same long brown eyelashes.

"Missed it by a year. I'm older. I think I'm in the Shampoo Generation. We've spent the most money on hair care products."

He laughed, then quickly stuck a cigarette in his mouth and lit it. "You look like her. You look like Rosette." He inhaled deeply, looked at some students coming up the steps, then turned to me. He must have seen the expression on my face. "You mean, no one has ever told you that?"

For a long time Isabella sat at the table in front of the window looking out past the porch.

"I think that he knew damn well he was dying," she said. It was the first time I had ever heard her swear in English or in German. She looked out toward the Danube and lit a cigarette. "You make me smoke."

That day the Danube was green.

"On his eighty-fifth birthday, I asked him, 'Do you want them to come?'" In her tellings, Isabella was always the heroine. "The weather was very bad, and he did say no, I don't want them to run the risk. There was *so* much ice."

I considered how our lives had changed as a result of Isabella's almanac. "Did he mention Mom? Did he say he wanted to see her?"

I didn't want to sound too eager. I didn't want to appear desperate.

She nodded with her eyes closed.

"He called for Gentz. He was a friend of your grandfather's who had died two years earlier. I found Gentz an arrogant man who was no good to your grandfather, but your grandfather kept saying, 'I need to talk to Gentz. I must talk to Gentz.' And he did say, 'Genevieve mustn't come to the funeral,' and that's what I told your mother. I was helpless, you see. I could do nothing. I had to warm up my food three, sometimes four times because of the phone calls. I would be eating and then the phone would ring. We called her Genevieve, which is much nicer than Jenny. And you know what she said to me? She said, 'Take it easy.'"

I could hear my mother saying this. She said this when she needed time to think. It was a lot like her father saying, "So." I supposed it was easy to misinterpret.

"Take it easy," Isabella said. "Can you imagine? I spoke mostly to your father. I could always speak more easily to your father than I could with her."

For a moment we looked at each other, her eyes racing back and forth, her head shaking. Isabella was still a tall, straight woman, but whenever she said or even thought my mother's name, her head shook.

At times like these, with her salt and pepper hair drawn up in a gentle bun, she looked more like Katharine Hepburn than Katharine Hepburn.

Looking at her, so undone by the very thought of my mother, I suddenly felt terribly wise. Isabella didn't get my mother and I think I finally did.

"Your German is very bad," she said. "So—oh, what is the word? So day-to-day. You are not your grandfather's grandchild." She got up from her chair. "You may think that because you can translate languages, you can translate me." She crossed the room, circled the dining-room table, then stood in the doorway. "You are not your grandfather's granddaughter."

That night, after we had eaten a sort of Viennese pot roast with rice into which she had grated fresh nutmeg, Isabella, smiling now and still smoking, told me about relatives I never knew existed. They were distant cousins of my grandmother Rosette's and they lived in France.

"They hid your grandfather and grandmother. And Mummy." Isabella had already gone through half a pack of cigarettes. "They did come to Vienna. The whole family, without notice. They couldn't stay with us because there wasn't enough room, but we took them to the opera and then we never heard from them." Isabella turned to me then. "Just like Mummy. She writes three lines about the family on a Christmas card once a year."

I waved away the smoke from Isabella's cigarette.

I wanted to tell Isabella not to mess with my mother. This was a woman who was not squeamish about taking dead mice from a trap, or killing a big, blue fly with her bare hand. And for the first time since I had been away, I missed my mother. I missed her so much my eyes watered. I was lonely for her, and that made me feel closer to her than ever before.

"They are all out there," Isabella went on, lighting another cigarette.

"West. And they all suppose that Isabella has passed away, and so be it. But I'm not gone, you see?"

She inhaled deeply from her cigarette. I think Isabella saw herself as a tragic figure—very much like a misunderstood country, one that hadn't gotten its way after all. She was Viennese, yes, but she was not Austria. Because she had stayed during the occupation, you didn't wonder if she crossed the streets to Russia's side or Germany's, but how many times.

In Vermeer paintings, the women look out of windows—forever they hang looking out of windows, reaching for the jug of water, or they tune the lute, half-smiling, looking wistfully out at you, the light on their faces, the oriental rugs on the tables, the maps of Europe on the wall behind them. But those are Dutch women. The Viennese women—Klimt's women and Schiele's women—are self-obsessed, consumed by passion, headaches, sex, or maybe their very thinness. Or maybe it's something else.

I wondered then why Isabella's mouth was coming up at the corners and why *she* was bitter. She stayed. She stayed. She had no new world to conquer. She stayed with her old mother; she stayed with who and what she knew. And now she was bitter because somebody somewhere had not given her what she felt she deserved.

I had read somewhere about the malicious character of the Viennese. That the Viennese does not abuse anyone because he dislikes that person. He abuses him because it does himself good, and he even likes the person who affords him this pleasure.

Through the smoke, I could see Isabella squinting.

Instead of going to the Hofzeile on my last day in Vienna, I went to St. Stephen's. I sat in a front pew, staring at the women who mumbled to Mary. A man knelt next to me, crossed himself, sat down beside me, then reached out and put his hand on my knee. I stood up, knelt toward the crucifix in front, crossed myself, and left.

For a long time, I walked around and around the Ringstrasse, and where spectators once strolled to glimpse Franz Josef riding in his carriage, I looked at the buildings and their windows, and back at the people in cafés and those others who walked as well. I had read somewhere that to visit a city, really visit, you must look into the eyes of the people. That is the real and only way to know the city. In Vienna, the eyes of everyone—even the young—are old. In one of his monograms, my grandfather wrote that Greece was a land where only the dead lived, but he might as well have said the same about Vienna.

On the train to Grinzing, I overheard two women talking in German about how clean Magic Island was at Disney World and how impressed they were by the crowd control.

"They herd you like cattle," one woman said. "But you don't *think* you're cattle. That's the beauty."

"Yes, yes," the other woman agreed. "It's not like you ever feel you're surrounded by twenty million people."

I got off at Grinzing for the cemetery in which Rosette was buried. The daisies I had were wilted, but I put them next to her stone anyway.

The Viennese aren't as good at keeping up with their own countrymen or their homes as they are at keeping their cemeteries. Fine, I thought. At least there in the cemeteries the ghosts of my mother's past have room to take walks and breathe.

All around, the grape vines grew and grew—as though Hitler had never been there. I stood in front of my grandmother's grave for a long time then. I read the marker with her name and the dates, and the inscription: *Going Home.*

A few feet away, an old woman led a blind woman to one of the gravestones, which they both touched.

The blind woman faced me, and, in English, she said, "I could smell you were a lady. I am visiting my mother. This is my sister."

I nodded. We could have been holding drinks, standing around at a cocktail party, making the introductions. "Yes," I said, turning toward Rosette's gravestone. "This is Rosette. She's my real grandmother. The one I never knew."

"It's good that the Germans didn't get to our people," the woman went on. "This is one of the few Jewish cemeteries left."

"Jewish?" I looked at Rosette's headstone. Beside hers was a marker for my great-grandmother, Anna. Then there was Joseph, Kara, and Cosima. This was where the Engel de Bazsis were buried. Rosette must have felt that this was where she belonged in the end. Of course, I thought, but why was Rosette buried here, and not my grandfather—the real Engel de Bazsi?

At my grandfather's grave in a different cemetery up the road in Grinzing, I asked a gravedigger what kind of cemetery my grandfather was in. He spoke in rough German and he said that it was a Christian cemetery, of course.

I looked down at the mound of fresh dirt and the marker bearing my grandfather's name. "*Comporre La Sua Vita*—Composer of His Own Life"—that is what is written on my grandfather's gravestone. So. He had composed his own life and his own death. I had heard him once say that he was born with the Lord Jesus Christ in his heart and I suppose he died with the Lord Jesus Christ in his heart, too. Who was I to doubt that?

Still, still. He chose not to be buried next to his wife Rosette. But there was a space next to his grave for Isabella.

If Ezra were here, I thought, he would comment on the good, loose soil. Good enough for digging, but it would do no good to dig up my grandfather and demand that he tell me why and how he could deny his family, his heritage, his wife, and his own mother. I considered why my grandfather had been so hell-bent on forgetting about my mother—his only daughter—and me. Could she have reminded him of everything and everyone he wanted to give up?

In his last work, Plato wrote that the learners themselves do not know what they have learned until knowledge has found a place in the soul of each. I wondered what bits of history had reached my grandfather's soul—which people and events were allowed access? His knowledge of me was next to nothing—and my knowledge of him? My grandfather wrote in his memoir that when a student asked him why he wrote history, he responded with a quotation from Plato: "I want to know how it *really* was." But what is *really?*

When I think of the proximity I had, when I think of what I could have asked him; if I had known more about their circumstances in Vienna; if I had known more history, science, anything so that maybe I would understand. When I think of this, I get short of breath. I will, I think, lie awake tonight unable to sleep—just like all the other nights. Then I will pretend I am in a hospital room dying and he comes—my grandfather—because I am dying and it is what he has to do. He *must* be there. He will not miss this death scene because, he says to himself, he missed all the other important ones.

In a chair next to my bed he will take my hand and I am not too weak to begin the questions. I ask him: But how could you? How could you? He answers all my questions one by one, and I know by the way he pauses and says, "So," that he is not exaggerating or lying. He knows, after all, that I am dying. He knows that I must find peace. And only after I have imagined this scene of my grandfather telling me the truth about himself in my hospital room do I stop shaking, and finally, I am able to fall asleep.

Before I left for the train, Isabella packed me a lunch: two packages of sugar wafers with chestnut filling, two hard-boiled eggs and two sausage sandwiches—one liver, one summer sausage. She told me to buy coffee on the train. That was a fine thing, she said, to sip coffee from a paper cup while you looked out at moving countryside.

She wore long, geometric, Picasso-like earrings for my leaving and she announced that her mother would very much like to say good-bye to me for the last time, though she had never said hello. In a supreme effort, her mother rolled herself out of her room in a wheelchair, dressed in a long black dress with a high lace collar. On her dress she wore a pin with a real pink rose stuck inside. Even though she wore dark sunglasses, I could see her deepset, shrunken eyes.

Isabella stood behind me with her hands on my shoulders. Perhaps she thought I would flee. I wanted to tell her that this woman in the wheelchair did not scare me.

I spoke with Isabella's mother. I told her how much I liked Vienna and my visit with Isabella. She smiled, her sunglasses rising on her cheeks for the occasion. Then she said something quickly which I did not understand.

"She wants you to bend down," Isabella said, already pushing me to bend down. "She is telling you to stand still so she can feel your face."

I bent down and I could smell the rose on her dress. The old woman's hands were on me before I could move away. I closed my eyes. Her fingers spread out like chicken bones.

It occurred to me then that I did not even know this woman's name, nor did I care to. She was Isabella's mother, and I did not think she had any right putting her hands all over my face, blind or crippled as she was. At that moment, I felt great pity for my grandfather. He had left my mother and my father and me to live every day with this.

When Dorothy got back to her black-and-white home in Kansas, she mentally underlined what she had said in Oz: There's no place like home. But what she had rediscovered was not Auntie Em, her uncle, her room, or even the farmhands—it was herself, she had come to realize.

I wondered then what my mother would look like to me when I got back. I wondered what my father would say. I wondered what we would eat. And I wondered if Ezra would say yes.

I looked closely at the silver pin on Isabella's mother's black dress. It was the bottom half of a sterling silver knife and I recognized the pattern. The top part of the knife had been cut off, and the handle fashioned into a sort of mini-vase which held the rose in place. At the tip, on the handle-turned-bud-vase pin, I saw the Engel de Bazsi family crest.

"Come, come," Isabella said. She insisted on walking me to the gate even though she could barely move. She wanted to, she said.

I picked up my bags and the viola d'amore case. Isabella looked at the case. "You are such a strange, silly child," she said, her head shaking. "Of all the things to come away with. A guitar."

When we got to the gate, she wanted to go farther. She wanted to go down to the end of the shaded path, where the highway started. When we walked, we got along. In motion, people usually do. Maybe because the body knows it can always flee.

When we reached the bridge, she stopped. I put down my bags and the viola d'amore. I gathered she wanted to make this a meaningful good-bye. She took a bundle of letters tied with string from her purse. "They are Rosette's letters. The ones your mother did write when you were a little baby," she said.

She pressed the bundle of letters into my hand—as though they were letters smuggled out of a difficult, forgotten war and she was the trusted friend.

I did not ask Isabella why she had kept these letters addressed to a different woman—the first wife—for over thirty-five years. I did not say to her, Why didn't you get rid of all these things from your husband's past as I know I would have? Did you like living with a ghost?

On a piece of paper, Isabella wrote down her address and phone number for me even though I already had these. Her handwriting was shaky but very legible, and she kept all her numbers and letters within the lines as though to prove something.

"You're engaged," she said, giving me back my pen. She did not remember that the ring I wore was the one she had given me a long time ago—the one half of my grandmother Rosette's ring. "But why didn't you tell me this? Do you think that's very nice?"

"It's so personal," I started, realizing as soon as the words came out of my mouth that, in addition to lying, I had said the wrong thing.

"But I've been talking about the most personal thing in my life with you," she said. "Come. What is his name? Where does he live? What does he do?"

I didn't want her to have any of my life. I didn't want her to have Ezra's name, so I made up a sketchy story. I lied the way I used to be able to lie about my grandfather's past. But I might as well have told Isabella the truth because there was not much response.

We hugged. She had tears in her eyes and she told me to write. I lied again and said that I would.

"Do you know what your mother's reaction was to her father's death?" Isabella said, as though finally she was giving it to me straight. "Never did she ask how I was. All she said was: 'Is it genetic? Will Elizabeth catch it?' Can you imagine?"

And then I realized—all these years I had been ruminating over my grandfather and missing my great-grandmother, my mother had been thinking of me.

Once when I was in high school, I had read a How-To piece on raising your child in the newspaper and I clipped it and left it on my mother's bedroom bureau. "Say the right things to your child," the article said. "Say, 'You are more important than a clean house. You are special. You make my life richer.' And finally. 'I am taking very good care of you.'"

"She was worried about me." And as I said this to Isabella I knew that this was not a lie but the absolute truth—that my mother had not only been worried about me, but even as she faced her father's death, she had not thought of herself or her own sorrow and loss but of me. And though I did not know this then, I knew it now, and perhaps—just perhaps—this was the knowledge I had been after all along.

"I remember when you did write me your first letter," Isabella said. "You started it out: Dear Granmother. You left out the 'd.' What happened to that little girl? Where is she now?"

I could remember the day I loved Isabella. I could recall the feel of her soft leather glove when she held my hand and said, "Darlink Elizabeth. You must think of hoppy things."

When people go abroad to discover their family roots, they should come back with stuff they didn't want to know about—that maybe your grandfather really wasn't the kind old man you thought he was, but a man who not only denied and maybe even hated who he was, but a man who denied his family of love. Regardless, you need to find out something that is disturbing enough to make the journey worthwhile so that you can look back and point to the city on the map and think to yourself or say to your spouse, "That's where I found out everything." And you both can look at the black dot where you were and sigh and think to yourselves, Well, at least you faced the truth. You know your past. This will help you. This will help out with your present and future.

"Now you are such a grown-up girl," Isabella went on. "You look so Austrian." Then she laughed a bit mischievously. "What will Mummy think I have done to you?"

Off in the distance, the light in the tower on the Prater was white and Isabella's place was a muddy light orange and the windows were screenless and left open. The place was at its climax of neglect—its age and shabbiness charming, but one more year and it would be depressing and uncomfortable. It would not be as photogenic. It would be a slum. Isabella wanted me to feel pity for her and of course I did. I felt the pity the way she said "pity"—spitting out the "p."

"Come," she said finally, near the bridge. "Let me bless you." She made the mini-sign of the cross on my forehead between my eyes, on my chin, and on my chest between my breasts. I stood there and took it.

If I told people of this, if I said my step-grandmother blessed me near the bridge next to the Old Danube before I left her, they would smile and sigh and picture the scene and see it all wrong. They would say, "That's so nice." But they would be wrong.

She held my shoulders and looked into my eyes. I could see her eyes involuntarily twitching back and forth behind her thick, round glasses.

"You are so much more like him," she said. "More than Mummy ever was."

In the end we both cried, for different reasons.

EPILOGUE

I SHOULD KNOW MORE ABOUT WOOD. AS IT IS, I HAVE always been aware of wood—how it smelled right after it was cut and then how it smelled days later. Steam can bend straight planks into shaped bentwood chairs or a beautifully shaped musical instrument, and a length of beech can be watered and molded into a spiral as though it were not hardwood at all, but pliable copper. The oak from Bohemia is some of the world's best. Even after it has been polished with linseed oil, you can smell a whole forest in one piece. My father did not teach me any of this, though he must have known. He must have known how the virgin oak from Hungary was brought into the Linz factories, then polished and fitted together into a parquet-floor puzzle which my family and I trod upon daily when we lived at the Hofzeile in Döbling. Most hardwood floors squeak, especially in the North where it is humid, and it seems the more pieces there are in the floor, the more squeaking it is likely to do. But my father didn't care about any of this because he didn't care about wood.

I used to be able to see the straight edges of the pieces of wood fitted together. Now, I look down at the floor and the edges are fuzzy. Wavy. My view of straight lines has turned completely crooked. There are times when I feel let down by my unseeing self, but there are other times when I like that the hard dividing lines are getting blurry. No more boundaries, I tell myself. Nothing to cross.

I had measles in my eyes that went too long untreated and now that I am sixty-five, I am almost blind. It is not quite a total blackness. I can still imagine the shapes of things. I know when you or your father are in the room. I know where there is a closed door in front of me. Even though I cannot see things at all clearly, I can at least feel and know what is in front of me, behind me, and, most of the time, what is to come.

There are some things I will not miss seeing. Did you know that once a month, I get a bill in the mail to maintain my mother's grave? Isabella sends these unopened envelopes in one of her own gray envelopes without a note. Once a month. She started doing this when she married my father. She didn't think it right that the new wife pay for the old wife's grave. This is how my father explained it to me.

The most recent bill did come with a letter from Isabella. In it she wrote that she was donating all of my father's books to the library at the University of Vienna. With all of his notes and marginal markings, these books were important public documents, she wrote. They belonged to his motherland. Well, I think, *his* motherland can have them.

Even though I cannot see clearly, I do still have the memory of what was good sight. I asked Dr. Smith once, in my seeing days, why we see better when there is more light. He was patient and he drew me a picture of the eye and he told me how the retinal mosaic becomes finer as illumination increases. But, he added, actual color interferes with judgments of brightness. In my new blindness, I stare at the diminishing light in my mind and I listen.

I know a woman who is a survivor. Every Independence Day, she wears a red dress with white shoes and she rolls up her sleeve and points to the blue numbers. "See?" she says. "Red, white, and blue." I asked her once what gave her strength. She said her source was the Jewish family and I said, "Oh come on." She said, "No, no. Really. The family is what makes us survive. As long as there is one member of my family alive, I can go on." I thought about it for a minute, then I said, "What if you were the only one left?" And then she looked at me and said, "You have a daughter, Jenny. You do have a daughter."

Sometimes, when I sit alone in a room and listen for the floorboards to creak, I can't help but wonder what those first ten years of my past have to do with me. It is as though those ten years belonged to someone else and the memories are not memories at all, but figments. Illusions.

Dr. Smith tells me that illusions point to ways in which the visual system is failing to transmit visual information correctly, and these failures always tell us something about how the system must have been constructed. Apparently, we can learn a great deal from our illusions.

What is it like not to see? It is not as dark as you might think. Each day I stare out at an uninhabited, barren land to which I have no map. My father always told me, never go to a country and not know the language. The three of us were speaking our new American English after the first few months of living in Washington. Sometimes I do wish I knew how to learn the language in this new country of non-sight.

Take away sound, and you'll still hear a hum or ringing in the ears. Mystics call this the singing of the universe, the music of the spheres. What would they call the bits of light that I can see? The mosaic of the universe? The sparkle of the spheres?

The farthest point that can be seen clearly with the eye in a completely relaxed state is called the far point. The near point is the nearest point to the eye at which clear vision is possible. When the eye is at rest, we say it is focused for infinity. I often tell myself that that is where I am right now, not my eye. Defect or no defect, I am focused for infinity.

Your father poaches me eggs. He says he read that I should eat eggs for my eyes. I can smell his worry. I know that he thinks that maybe I might spend the rest of my days just sitting and listening for rain and footsteps. And what's wrong with that? I ask. I am at rest and focused on infinity. Certainly there is a degree of nobility in this waiting. I am respectful of what is to come—whatever it is. I want to be ready and attentive to its mystery and greatness.

Long before she died, your great-grandmother often sat outside in the garden of the Lisner Home. It was there during one of those quiet moments, after I had married your father, that we talked about how my life was going to be. I was living in Mississippi at the time, and we were saving up for a vacuum cleaner. I didn't even pretend to be happy then. Out of nowhere she said to me, "No matter how American you become, Genevieve, you will always have one toe in Vienna."

Isn't it true that everybody's life is mostly made up of houses and decisions? Sometimes it's up for grabs who examines and judges.

And in the end? In the end you lose everything and everybody— the houses, the furniture, the silver, the children, and the husband. Maybe even the religion you were born with; or maybe the religion you acquired. You die alone no matter how many people show up at your deathbed.

I miss the Hofzeile. I do, but it is a loss that you don't get over so much as you get used to having. I knew the Hofzeile before I knew anything else. I knew the walls and the floorboards of that yellow house before I knew my own body. It was my first home. My first ground. It was what I knew first. How can you replace that?

As I record this now, there are wars not here but far away. I do not hear those bombs; I don't even have to read about them now. You can distance yourself from calamity: that is the privilege and the danger of the wealthy and the crippled. It has taken the threat of blindness in order for me to see my past clearly. That is also the pity of old age. An Englishman once said, "There must be a threat to one's own skin to wake what is left of things remembered into things to die with." I think the sin is to forget.

I missed my mother all my life. I miss her now. When I said good-bye to my cousins in the South of France, they all cried readily. I have heard that Russians, when parting, have a moment of silence before the journey. Some sort of ceremony is helpful when good-byes are required of one. Every farewell, as the French have it, is to die a little. Recollecting my mother is in a way to die a little less. Her memory is to me a religion.

Years ago, when our parquet floors were set down, a workman explained to me that minor gaps between tiles are unavoidable. I told him, yes, I understood, but I asked him to mind the big gaps. The big gaps. How do you overcome those? Maybe it's because I never got over my mother's death. Maybe I never got over my father moving back to Vienna, our home—my home—without me.

I do try now not to think of all that I've lost but of all that I have and all that I will leave to you. It is something—is it pride? That would be the real deprivation—not to leave what you most loved behind for loved ones. I imagine that that must have hurt my mother and father and I am sorry for that.

Once I saw a house in New Orleans surrounded by a beautiful black wrought-iron fence with all its top posts shaped like corn. The man who built the house wanted to make his wife happy. She was from Iowa or some such state, and she missed it. She missed her first home. Her husband wanted to surround her with what she knew. And what she knew was corn.

That is love, I think every time I recall that house. That was a kind, tender man who understood homesickness.

In his memoirs, my father wrote about the Hofzeile: "In this house occurred—with the exception of the years of the First World War—the greatest part of my life until my Emigration."

This is the way I feel about this place I am in now. This house we moved into twelve years ago is a gift. Through the years we have collected and put into it everything that we never had or weren't able to keep. I may not know all there is to know about wood, but I have learned about beaded ceilings, exposed beams, and wide, open rooms. I know that buttermilk helps wash out the newness of brick. I know the importance of the right pea gravel so that the pitch is good and crunchy when someone comes up the drive. For me, the details are tangible. I don't want to know that there are paintbrush hairs left in the finish of my walls and I don't want those walls made of drywall—the voices in rooms will be dulled. My mother used to say that even the dumbest guest knows good food. You can say the same thing about the ambiance inside a house. I know a lot about what it takes to build a home now, and I know that no one else can ever love your house as much as you do. They say God is in the details. I say He is in this home.

My great-grandfather traipsed through the narrow streets of Döbling, followed by his gardener, in search of a house. He saw the Hofzeile, and that night the two of them unfolded their sleeping bags and slept there. After that one night, in his mind, the house was his.

Here we sleep in rooms where the new parquet floors have been left exposed and bare. Once upon a time I told the workmen I wanted to smell wood in my old age and now I do. I consider the sturdy beams which support the roof and I am thankful that we exposed them as well so that we can always know how weak or strong they really are. This house will not fall, I say to myself. It is too sound, too sturdy. And often, thinking I tempt fate, I knock three times on a floorboard or a doorpost, thinking surely someone will hear and take note. Mornings I wake up thinking we have seized possession of this house. It did not take one night, but years of nights.

My father once told me a story about a man in the Middle Ages who invented stained glass. He said that the light flowing into the church through this new glass became divine light. The church, he said, was this strange, wonderful region of the universe suspended between Heaven and Earth.

When I walk through this house, I stand in front of a window and I imagine the shiny, wet blue-gray of the slate on the church roof from my childhood in Döbling. In my semidarkness, I am that dark, cool chapel. I am that church and I am *geistliches Leben* all in one, and at these moments, light comes to and through me in thick, wavy, colored beams.

I have not come this far to die. I have been traveling all this way, all this time to this place of sounds and smells and stained-glass light. I was meant to come to this house. This has been my spiritual emigration.

There is a picture of Anna Freud with her father in 1938 on the day they left Vienna for the last time. They are in a train, of course. Anna has her arm on top of the window, which has been lowered. Her father is beside her, pointing toward something or someone in front of them on the platform. He is saying something as well, because his lips are open and curled. Anna looks tired, but she is smiling.

They are more than father and daughter here. They are traveling companions, compadres, friends. They are bound by their work, their lives together, and by blood—a predicament, I imagine, that she worked toward all along.

I suppose I could have been my father's *Lebensgefährtin*, his life's companion. I could have studied what he studied, typed up his notes and his books, done his research, and catalogued his correspondence when he died.

When Isabella called with the news of my father's death, adding that it was not his wish that I attend his funeral, I slept and then I started to pack to spite both my father and his silly, new wife. But I just sat down on the bed next to my open suitcase thinking about what

Isabella would wear, and what she would say and do to me. She would probably remind me that my father had asked me not to come. A funeral is more for the living than it is for the dead, I would have told her.

I don't know how long I sat on that bed next to my suitcase, but suddenly it was dark again and your father was there. He knelt before me and he looked so worried. "Don't go," he said. He said it as though it had just occurred to him. He said it like this is a viable option. He said it like, let's consider this, let's consider what would happen if. And when he said those two words I felt like I was letting out a sigh. It was not my final act of vengeance so much as it was a relief.

In the years that followed, I do see how it became the kind of passive point my father had made all his life. My father was not there for Mutti's death, for Grossmama's death, nor was he there for me in my later years; therefore, I would not be there at his death. He had not let me in on his life or his death. This was not at all what I thought at the time. My not going to his funeral was simply what happened. It was a way out. It was my way out. I think it is Mephistopheles in Goethe's *Faust* who claims, "In the end we all depend on creatures we ourselves have made." So. I really was my father's daughter. So.

When Dr. Smith told me, "Jenny. Your lens substance is hardening," something in me burst at the word "hardening." I don't have to go in that direction, I thought. My father went up that road. In the Bible stories he read me, people were never just mean or unjust; they were never plain wrong. No. Their hearts hardened, then whole kingdoms were lost.

There are times when I think my life does not belong to me. Hundreds of others just like me—with better names than mine—died. There was no reason I was supposed to live. I look at you and I see a miracle. You weren't even supposed to be born. When you lose everything and everyone, you'll do anything to keep what and who you eventually get back.

When you came back from Vienna and gave me that tattered black case, you were so casually curious. "Mom," you said. "A man named Henrich gave this to me to give to you. He said his mother was Inge." You said, "Now, who's Inge again?"

When I heard you say her name out loud, it was as though Inge was right there with us, in the kitchen. You opened the case to show me and I saw Uncle Rudi's warped viola d'amore with its broken strings, and I recognized the lining and the initials stitched in black on the side. It was as though my life had come full circle and I could even hear Cook's yellow voice in my mind, telling me about her dough: "There. Now it is good because it is whole." You asked me why I was crying. That was when I knew and I thought to myself, My God, you don't even know how much Inge and this instrument mean to me. And how could you know? I never told you. And that made me feel terribly, miserably alone. You brought me back something I thought I had lost a long time ago, and I knew that if you did not know about it, it would be lost again.

I plucked a few of the strings. I thought of Inge and Uncle Rudi and I thought of everything I had left to tell you. And there was still time. Sometimes it takes a lifetime to rebuild the trust in human nature that you think you lost. I decided then and there to write you a notebook of my recollections and tell you everything I could from my spotty, wavy memory before it all disappears.

My mother died without ever having told me who and what she really was. I realize the consequences of not knowing such things now. I will not do this to you. I write these memories down not for St. Ignatius. These are for your eyes, so that you may see my past and your future. You will not be left wondering who I was when I am gone. This is for you. My memories are what I want most to leave you.

———

So, now you have announced your plans to marry. The Habsburgs gained land through their marriages, and I suppose in a funny way you will acquire at least the knowledge of some lands—the man is an archeologist, after all.

I imagine you will prepare for your marriage just as you prepared for your trip to Vienna. For you, everything is a project. You will arrange for a rabbi. A woman rabbi. I will insist on a priest. We will argue, and maybe there will be both. I will say, Couldn't we skip the guitar music just this once? You'll probably want me to play the piano, but I have a better idea. How about some Vivaldi or Bach for the viola d'amore?

In between fittings for your wedding dress, we will sit close together on two moiré-covered stools in the dressing room. You will be worried, I know, but this is life, I will tell you. You've got to move on and your mother is not going to live forever. The near point exists for all eyes, but recedes with age because of presbyopia. The closer you get the less you see. What *is* the farthest point and what is the nearest point at which to view your mother or your daughter? Maybe there is a distance that is the right distance. And maybe that distance is closer than two continents and further away than two stools in a dressing room.

And in the end, after the wedding, when you leave, it will be difficult to say good-bye to the day. Something in me will die. Maybe I will feel as though you are just like all the rest—abandoning me, and even though it may take a long time for the sun to go down, it will not be long enough.

For you, for your wedding, we will bring out all the silver. I know I will look down at it spread out before us and think of all that is missing, but now I know to remind myself of what we still have. As we polish, I will tell you that once upon a time, in my lifetime, there was a spoon for everything—one just for asparagus, another for honey and berries, one for ices, and other tiny ones for loose salt and pepper. I will explain to you that now there are only two. A soup spoon and a teaspoon must do the work of a dozen ancestors. And they do.

ACKNOWLEDGMENTS

Many thanks must go to the Indiana Arts Commission and the National Endowment for the Arts; King's College in Cambridge, England; Harlaxton Manor in Grantham, England; and the University of Evansville for providing information, room and board, and research grants. I would also like to extend many thanks and much gratitude to Adrian Wanner, John Meredig, Henry Minor, and Bill Hemminger for their translations; Von Anna Corinth for her tea and comfort; Ray and Mary Gallagher, Steve Williford, and Joseph La Corte, all the Hemmingers, Bill Baer, Arthur and Poem Brown, Dan Gahan and Heidi Gregori-Gahan, Dale and Becky Edwards, Brian Ernsting and Jeana Lee, James and Jessica MacLeod, Tamara and Eric Wandel, Steve Finley and Pascale Perraudin, Wes and Susan Milner, Dave and Carrie Dwyer, Davica and Alexi Bellamy, and John Streetman for the dinners, conversations, baby-sitting, and friendship; Mike Carson and Don Richardson for their kind advice; Jim Whitehead, Bill Harrison, Donald Hays, Barry Hannah, and Phillip Lopate for teaching, reading, and helping; Heather Ross Miller for liking greenhouses; Candace Flynt for saying, "This isn't a story, it's a novel"; Beth Lordan and Margaret-Love Denman for their generous words; my mother, father, and sister, Carlette, for wanting to read; my son, James, for being born; Ed Stewart for being there; Charlie Mae Scott for letting me be with her; M. M. Lieberman for walking out of class; James Kissane for asking to read the first draft; David Gugin, Carol Abrams, and The Inklings for always asking; Rob and Tiffany Griffith and Paul Bone for bringing luck with them from Arkansas; the Reverend Sam Salter for his letters and kindnesses; Maureen Duncan for keeping me organized; Ann Adelman for her copyediting; all my students for their hope and endless curiosity; and Michael Siegal for leading me to my inspired and talented agent, Jennie Dunham, who then led me to the indefatigable editor, Sally Kim.